PASSING THROUGH

Passing Through

JOSEPHINE PLUMMER

ISBN-13: 978-1-970083-09-5

Passing Through is dedicated to the brave ones, the people who fought and lived, the people who lost the fight and passed on, the ones who watched and were alongside the survivors and the unfortunate ones who lost the battle. Know the fight is seen by many, you are brave beyond what you thought you were capable of and have come through the battle a changed person. There are no more words for your bravery only you know how it has landed.

Hazel

June 2021

I HAD BEEN TOSSING AND TURNING ALL NIGHT FOR THE PAST WEEK, EVER SINCE the file of Rayner Martin had crossed my desk. Being in the records department, I had been asked to search for any other files containing that name or information leading up to the case. Rayner Martin had been found deceased at the base of a tree on East Twenty-Third and Cherry. He had been sitting on the ground and looked like he had been taking a nap—but he didn't belong there by the look of his expensive clothing, which she was surprised had lasted anytime at all. The only difference was when he didn't respond to the gentlemen stealing his jewelry, his new Nike shoes had been stolen by the first person to come upon him at 7:00 p.m. The second person had stolen his wallet and watch; the third had removed his hat and then tried to get his necklace. That was when they ran: after they reached behind his neck to unclasp the expensive necklace, their hand came back with blood. His nape had been slit all the way down to and through the spinal cord. Inside the hat was a note stating, "You should have known what would happen."

As I opened the glass doors of the precinct that foggy Thursday morning at 7:00 a.m., it hit me. When I had been stationed in San Diego a few years prior, before retirement, there had been a case of a drug deal gone wrong in Carlsbad, right up the coast. A sailor had been on shore leave for a few days and had gotten into a fight in a Carlsbad dive bar. He had just wanted to get away for the weekend and see some new scenery, explore a new town. Someone had stolen his drink, started a fight with him, and planted what appeared to be cocaine in his jacket. The police were called, he was arrested. and I had been assigned to pick him up, as our laws dictated what happened to military personnel even off base. After retrieving him from the jail and during the scenic trip southbound on Interstate 5, he stated there was more going on than the fight and the missing drink. The fake drugs were found on him at the jail and were not something he had purchased or had any idea were there. He claimed he had been used as a distraction for something else.

The guy stole his drink and started the fight as the bartender was in the back. He had met with a guy named Ray earlier who said he would return shortly. Ray took quite a while to return—possibly hours—and when he finally did, the two men had an argument about something that was said to be missing. That was when the other guy had walked up and stolen the suspect's drink. The sailor tried to leave, but Ray hit him and said he wasn't telling anyone what was going on, that he had not seen anything today. The sailor threw a punch just as the bartender walked through the swinging metal doors carrying a tray of glasses meant for the night crowd, which was anticipated to start showing up shortly. The bartender, who hadn't witnessed the prior events, then called the sheriff, who arrested the sailor for assault and disorderly conduct. These were serious charges for a sailor who wanted to pursue a career in the Navy. He seemed genuine to me. I had a copy of the report from the sheriff; after pulling it up, I saw that the name of the victim was Ray Martin.

Shifting my thoughts back to 2020, I remembered that Ray Martin was the name of Esmerelda's uncle. She had been shot on December 23rd the previous year on her annual Christmas vacation, visiting from Bakersfield, California. There were still no credible leads in her case. Detectives had scoured the streets and the neighborhood where she had been killed, and the only clue was a single casing in the street about thirty feet from the scene of the crime.

I wondered if Ray Martin could be the Rayner Martin from Carlsbad who had disappeared before the trial of the sailor. All charges had been dropped on the caveat that he compensate the bar for the damage done there. A night in jail; a ton of worry and investigation; the cost of one barstool, a glass, and a single towel, and the sailor was free of all charges.

I did some research on Ray/Rayner Martin and found he did have connections in Bakersfield, Carlsbad, and Seattle. Esmerelda, his niece, had been used to move heroin and whatever pills he could get his hands on. Esmerelda was from Seattle and had started college two years prior at California State University, majoring in agricultural business. She had big dreams to save the world of famine; she had earned a scholarship and wanted to help communities around the world grow their own food. Her immediate plans were to travel the world and show communities how to set up gardens for sustainability. Esmerelda was lonely due to being so far from home, and Uncle Ray bought her a car so she could drive down to visit him on the weekends or shorter breaks. He was the geographically closest of her family and seeing him made her not as homesick. Little did she know that one of Uncle Ray's "friends," Robert, had a key to her car, too. Someone who knew the location of the special compartment that was capable of holding a large enough quantity of drugs that the sale of them could cover a few years of living expenses for most people.

Ray had gotten greedy on this Christmas trip. He thought it being Christmas meant all the money would be his. He had planned for years to pull this off but had never actually believed he would do it. His plan was to scam this one last load and disappear. This opportunity was ideal as long as he had restraint and could precisely follow the steps he'd made. He brought the load up in Esmerelda's car; she had made plans to fly into SeaTac Airport and had just arrived, not on the schedule he had set for the purchasers. In fact, he didn't have any drugs with him at all. Everything was stashed in a heated storage locker in Torrance, California, which was rented under his alias, Martin Rayner, thinking he was clever switching his names around. He planned to have a little vacation on his drive up the coast—take a few days off. He deserved them, he thought, as he'd never had a real vacation. He left days before he was supposed to, dropped off the drugs and other belongings that fit into the trunk of Esmerelda's car at the storage facility, and was a free man: just him, the car, and the road. He didn't have to worry if he got pulled over or anyone was watching him; he was free to do as he pleased, and the car was empty of illegal product.

Ray had only been in Seattle a few hours when Esmerelda was shot. He couldn't figure out how they'd found him or how they'd connected Esmerelda to the drugs, although many years ago he had been warned to never lose a load of product. They had to have mistaken Esmerelda for me the in the dark carport next to the car. Robert must have put a tracker on the car; this was a thought Ray had had before, but he never truly believed it would happen. Everyone involved knew and agreed that Esmerelda was not in on the drug trafficking; she was an innocent victim and after all these years he thought they trusted him. How could they have shot her? It had been agreed upon that she was just an unknowing driver. She had truly been a sweet young lady with a heart to help, and now she was dead.

Ray knew exactly who this murder was connected to, but not who did it. Probably one of the lower-level rings he had been committed to deliver to the previous night at 11:00 p.m. They had warned him to be on time, alone, and have all the product—the same story as every load. Ray knew the potential consequences but hadn't known that they were aware of where he was hiding in plain sight. As soon as he returned to California, he would sell the product for ten times more than his commission of delivery to Seattle, which was still below street value for this large a quantity. He could return, sell it all, and relocate anywhere in the world he wished. His thoughts had turned to somewhere warm. He wasn't close to his family, not even his brother in Seattle, and now he felt a bit of remorse about Esmerelda and that she had been murdered so close to Christmas. The family would never have guessed his true occupation; it was like that with many people who lived far away. They could put up a front for a few days a year and then return to their actual life. This was messing up his whole retirement, the rest of his life. The plan he had so carefully and for so long planned was now potentially gone. Did they know where he had stopped and left the drugs? Or had they just tracked his destination, thinking he would deliver once they had proved to him that they were serious? The drugs did not belong to him, not really. Throughout the years he had been delivering drugs, they had never belonged to him.

Ray spoke to the police on the night of the murder, stating he had just arrived from California and had not seen anything. He was genuinely distraught for various reasons: sad because he knew Esmerelda was a good person but also angry that his well-laid-out plan was possibly destroyed. He was rather suspicious looking, as he was in a suit and the rest of the family were in pajamas, ready to settle in and watch a movie. For every year as long as they could remember, they had the Christmas tradition of eating candy cane ice cream and watching a movie. This year's events would put new meaning on the tradition. Ray's dress clothing made him stand out to Detective Muncer, who had a feeling that there was something more to this story. He had no way to prove it, however; nothing stood out except Uncle Ray himself. Everyone's story checked out at the scene. Until the murder of Rayner Martin, whose wallet had been stolen but later found in an alley a couple blocks away with nothing but two driver's licenses in it. Rayner Martin and Martin Rayner were one in the same and both gone. Had he been hiding in Seattle since Esmerelda's death? Almost six months here—where would he have been so concealed that no one could find him? Not the law or his criminal posse. These two cases were connected, and Muncer knew immediately after attending the scene of Rayner Martin's murder.

I filled the detective in on the story from my Navy days and the suspicions I had. There would be further investigation with Muncer hoping to travel to nowhere hot and without micro rental cars. He'd had enough of that in Tempe, Arizona. He often wondered whatever had happened to Bender George, Rizzo Loman, and Ohm It Up Electronics. The two criminals were hopefully locked up for many years from their various charges.

It took me a few days to remember the name of the sailor I had escorted from the jail in Carlsbad. Douglas Smith—I wondered how many people sported that name. I contacted a few former officers and found out Douglas had been injured in a training accident and had been discharged a couple years ago. I found him living south of Seattle, in Tumwater on his family farm. I pictured him with cattle and then pumpkins; I would need to ask what they farmed. What a twist of fate that he now lived nearby. I was not sure what I needed from him or if he would even agree to meet me, but I had a set of questions to ask him. He might be the only person alive who had seen the gentleman that Ray had talked to in the bar—the one who had waited on him for all that time. He would have the best description of him, too, since he had been in the bar to watch a game and they had both been rooting for the same team.

Douglas agreed to meet me in Tacoma at Wapato Park off Seventy-Second Street. I thought it strange to be meeting him at a location far from the original meeting place but still connected to the same circumstance many years apart on a different crime.

I arrived early and was leaning against my Lincoln SUV when Douglas pulled up. It was like seeing an old friend; no one would even guess why we were there. He was a civilian now, and I processed records for the Seattle Police. Neither of us looked like we had any affiliation to the military or police. There wouldn't be any reason to suspect we were trying to solve two murders that were connected but that had taken place a few months apart. Douglas only had knowledge of the events that had taken place in the bar; he knew nothing about what had happened in Seattle. I filled him in without giving away key evidence. Douglas had brought a description and rough sketch of the man from the bar; he said he would be able to help by phone or online if a sketch artist could clean it up. He did not seem willing to travel all the way to Seattle, nor did I ask him to.

He said he would never forget what Ray, or the other guy looked like. Medium height, blond hair, younger than Ray, lots of tattoos; the two men didn't look like they belonged together. Ray was more put together while the second man looked like he had escaped from prison and was pretending to live on the outside. It seemed as if their roles should have been switched by the looks of them, as Ray was business-like and, on the run, and the other guy was worldly, like he had experienced more than most people. One thing that did stand out was the neon-yellow reflective vest the guy wore, as if he had just left a job site; he wore it like a uniform.

Douglas and I caught up on the important parts of life and said our goodbyes. I always knew things happened for a reason; I hadn't been the one who was supposed to pick Douglas up from Carlsbad that morning so long ago, but that was how it had worked out due to staffing issues. Now I saw the significance in that switch-up.

I headed north on I-5, the same highway Douglas and I had been on years prior, but now traveling in the opposite direction. I got off the highway exits before mine; my craving of fish and chips had gotten the best of me. Perhaps I was missing my home, Eastbourne. Maybe it was my career I missed or my mum, Vera Violet Skylar. It had been about sixty years since I had lived in Eastbourne. I had traveled the world during my Navy career; nowhere was home anymore. My Navy career had been finished almost thirty years ago, and my mum had been gone about eight years. Where did the time go? I found a cozy café that served chowder and fish and chips. One order eaten there and another to go for tomorrow.

I felt the need to be by the water at all times. The water was always with me, in my sight, in my mind, and in my heart; I could physical and mentally feel where it was located no matter where I was. I decided during dinner that I would schedule a trip to Eastbourne when I got home and apply for time off, something I hadn't done since working for the Seattle Police. The need or want had never been there before now. I would clear my mind and recharge in Eastbourne. Of course, I would have to stop at City Square Cemetery tomorrow and tell mum about this new happening, leave some bright flowers for these dark days, and assure her I would return.

I ate in peace, surrounded by a calmness I had not felt in many years, watching the water, the boats, and the sun set on Puget Sound. I paid, left a generous tip that was more than the cost of the ticket itself, packed up my extra meal, and headed north on 509. The interstate wound around the south end of SeaTac Airport and through an industrial area. I was in no hurry to get home as my plan solidified during the drive. When the road turned into East Marginal Way, I knew I must pack my Globe Trotter tonight and book the flight or I may never go, never see Halverson again. I turned eighty-two years old this year and may not be able to take a trip alone in the future; this needed to be a solo trip. It was decided. Muncer would be pleased with the progress of the sketch; I would relay all the information to him tomorrow and let him know of my plans to travel and see an old friend before it was too late. I could still see Halverson, who lived in the English Channel: 100 feet long, emerald-green-and-blue smile, yellow flames for eyes, and coal-black scales. Halverson was my dragon, and I must reunite with him. Muncer did not need to know my friend was a dragon. We all had secrets, after all, and this one was harmless compared to what I had seen in the records department.

I crossed Fourth Avenue, then Third, and arrived at my alley, ready to use the remote and open the big brown door. Suddenly, I remembered my mum sitting there with me. It had been her first time in Seattle, and she had been very ready to be with me and explore the new city. Mum was an adventurer, always ready to explore. I entered the concrete parking garage with my fish and chips and rode the elevator; the evening and days ahead were planned. *Halverson, I am coming home.*

I scheduled my days off for two weeks in the future. It was on the calendar, and my flight was confirmed. The Globe Trotter had been packed, and the sketch had been turned in to Muncer. No one had questioned why I needed to see my old friend. Even I was not sure why I needed to see him, but time would tell. Suddenly, my British accent was in full swing, as if I were already there and had never traveled away. It was strange how the words came out differently, as they would have if I had always existed over there.

Detective Muncer

June 2021

ANOTHER SWELTERING DAY—THIS MADE SIX IN A ROW OVER NINETY DEGREES. THE heat had arrived early towards the end of spring. I preferred the nights, but daytime seemed to be my destiny this year. Dispatch had said on the phone that I would want to attend this interview. I entered the building with steam rising both in my head from aggravation and from the sidewalks, which had not had a chance to cool overnight. I appreciated the A/C more today than ever.

I looked through the two-way glass, and there sat Pearl Swanson, a lady I had never wanted to see again. Something told me this would not be the last time. She had created scenes across the county, with murders happened under her directive, and she had been a free woman until now. Murders and chaos happened behind her on the path she'd created, and then she walked away unscathed. Pearl had been brought in by the patrol officers for loitering but refused to leave for some reason. I knew she was up to something. She said she was waiting on a puppy to be delivered from an online ad, which must have been either a code name for something or a made-up story, as nothing about her could ever be that innocent. Officers had let her go with a ticket for loitering and a promise to appear and advised her to plead innocent, guilty, or pay the citation. My first thought was that this incident had left no one dead—that we were aware of, at least—in Pearl's path.

Almost two weeks after the loitering ticket was issued, there sat Pearl again. She was in the same area as before but this time had been arrested with sixteen tablets, clearly from Ohm It. It appeared she was still connected to the group led by Bender George. Last, I had heard, he had been in a rollover accident and was headed to prison in Arizona with Rizzo Loman. They could not be out of prison that quickly. I decided to see what Pearl had to say this time. Where had she gotten the tablets, and why was she at First and Marion during both of her two previous arrests? She had to be staying around that area, or perhaps there was a storage place full of stolen goods that she was heisting from or being given product out of to sell. Her usual operation was to sell in bulk, not one product at a time. My guess was she was taking the product, stealing from the thief who had directly or indirectly stole from Ohm It. I guessed that Bender George was somewhere in the line of thievery.

As we interviewed Pearl, I saw through the interview room window that Rizzo Loman was being escorted into the next room. I was quite surprised to see Rizzo and in this condition; he had clearly been in a scuffle, as his head was wrapped up like he had recently undergone surgery and his eye was covered by a bandaged patch. I popped into that interview room, leaving Pearl to sit and create more dialogue for her bogus story.

Rizzo stated he had been walking along and someone had jumped him. He had no idea why he had been left passed out on the sidewalk; he didn't even remember being downtown. He woke up in the hospital all covered up and restrained, feeling like he had been run over. The hospital had called it in because he hadn't had any identification or wallet, and he couldn't tell them his name. Actually, it was more like he hadn't wanted to reveal his identity to them. They wanted to make sure he wasn't a missing person or a fugitive. All they did find on him was a cigarette butt in his front pants pocket, a small baggie with a few crystals of methamphetamine in the bottom hardly enough for identification. And a comb that should have been thrown away long ago. The police couldn't hold him, as he had not committed a crime. He was antsy to leave, said he had a meeting to go to and could not be late. I could only imagine who he could be meeting with. I would tail him nonetheless, as I knew this was connected to Pearl, who Rizzo had no idea was sitting in the next room.

I followed a distance behind him, and sure enough, he headed straight to a building on First and Marion Street, ducked in behind the scaffolding, and was gone, through the door behind the construction debris. A few minutes later, I heard the light tap of a horn behind me. Rizzo was on the corner across the way meeting someone, selling a tablet just like the ones Pearl had been arrested with. He had to have entered the building on the front side and exited in the alley, crossing from the side to make sure he had not been tailed. I saw him take the cash and walk away. Rizzo's name was hollered from a window up above; I looked up, and there I got a glimpse of none other than Bender George, who was suddenly in front of me, faster than I could have imagined. Bender knew who I was from our previous encounters and his last arrest, during which we had spent a great deal of time together. He asked me which way the criminal had gone. I had not seen, as I had been extremely surprised to see Bender in the upstairs window of the four-story brick building.

At that moment, I saw Rizzo across the street, coming out of the scaffolding with a box bigger than him and heading down the alley. I didn't tell Bender, instead crossing the street as quickly as I could in the heat to catch up with Rizzo. By the time I got to the alley, Rizzo was gone, had just vanished, huge box and all. He must have had a ride waiting for him to transport the crate, which was big enough to hold two hundred or more tablets. All I knew was Bender would not be happy. Rizzo had gone, possibly to meet Pearl—then I remembered Pearl was in custody. I had left her there in my haste to follow Rizzo. I radioed in for officers to hold her, but she had already been released on her own recognizance. I heard the call of a gray SUV stolen from First and Columbia Street and wondered if it had been Rizzo's people or even Pearl. Bender was off, going in the direction Rizzo had gone.

Having no idea which way Rizzo and the tablets had gone, lost in the maze of Seattle, right in the light of day, looking like any other delivery,

I headed back to the precinct. I researched the business licensing on that building, printed it, and left. I was exhausted, again realizing I was one person and could only fight as much crime as time and opportunity allowed. There I was in the Emerald City, working on solving open cases and getting probable leads to follow up on, and now those three were back on my caseload without solid crimes yet set in place.

Most people did not talk, especially in front of others, but for some reason they would call later, like they were doing a public service or would explode if they continued to withhold the information. My time on the street was never wasted. It gave me an edge, being able to see where people chose to live or hang out, how they dressed, who they associated with, and the biggest clue was body language. Did they fidget, look away, talk too much, or never answer questions? They also turned questions around on me. I didn't know the answers, but they always wanted to know how much I did know—which I never revealed. These were all clues, but some people were just too nervous or high to sit still. They didn't expect to have a meeting with me. Or they would act like we were old friends and reveal too much, sometimes exactly what I needed to hear. And others spilled too many words which had nothing to do with the case I was currently working on, trying to divert me. Or they were just nervous in my presence, guilty or not, although they were probably guilty of *something*.

My present focus was Esmerelda Martin and now Rayner Martin. Esmerelda and her family deserved justice. The only way to solve those two murders was to put all my energy into Rayner Martin's associates; I believed that would solve both cases, that they had taken out Esmerelda as a warning to Rayner and to punish him. He had known what could happen, after all. Or maybe he had been the target—not her. I had always known the two cases were connected, but I hadn't suspected anything like this. Helpful Uncle Ray had been a first-class slime ball. Esmerelda's poor family had now lost two people; all this time, they had thought Esmerelda would be safer in California with Uncle Ray and unaware of his underhanded assistance. They had never suspected he would involve Esmerelda in his scheme or that he did not have an honest career, as he had told them he was a manager in the shipping industry at the Port of San Diego.

Leave it to Hazel to have found a clue in her memory from years ago. Now with the sketch and statement, we could confirm that Rayner Martin had been in the bar in Carlsbad, had been the drug runner, and had known the connection to a large drug ring. He had to have worked his way up in the ranks after spending almost thirty years (that could be confirmed) with this smuggling operation. We were not exactly sure it was drugs that was being trafficked, but it was a high probability. Before this, Rayner had been another murder without leads; now there was a warrant for his possessions that had been left behind at Esmerelda's parents' apartment.

I did not approach them about the items prior to arriving just in case someone there was in on this; at that time, everyone was a suspect. Rayner had been hiding somewhere, as he had not wanted to stay there after Esmerelda's murder. He had sold her car, since it was in his name, to a used car lot north of the city. The family thought it was odd that he had just disappeared, but they kept the one suitcase he had brought in a hall closet along with Esmerelda's suitcase, which they couldn't bear to open or part with. Inside of Rayner's, there was a key, a one-year rental agreement to a storage locker in Torrance, California, a map of other stops, clothing, and personal effects: a trip already taken, and the return one would not be made by him.

These items were enough to send me to California. I arrived at the McClellan-Palomar Airport just shy of 7:15 a.m. The temperature pushed the thermometer past 80 degrees; I knew coming here was a horrible idea prior to my departure. I walked up Aircraft Road and arrived at the rental car location. This was nothing like SeaTac, which I was used to, and which was an enclosed airport and air-conditioned. The rental car company representative agreed to a midsized sedan; apparently, the staff saw my discomfort with the heat and had the car cooled down before bringing it around for me to inspect. As I drove off, I saw a lineup of micro vehicles that looked a bit suspicious. I refused to get in one of them; there had been enough of that in Tempe last year.

After heading to Rayner's last known address, which was close to Tamarack Surf Beach, and finding it occupied by a couple who had moved in a few months ago and who had never heard of him, I headed north out of town on I-5 and stopped for breakfast at a small café in Dana Point.

Back on I-5 through Costa Mesa and Signal Hill, all with spectacular views with the interstate changing names but not pavement nor direction. I exited I-405 at 190th Street, made a right on Normandie, and met the Torrance Police Department at the front office of the storage lockers for entry and accompaniment. They were more than willing to help. If solved, it would be as if they had solved this crime—that was what the papers and news would report. If there were drugs in the storage locker, they would not reach the streets of their town nor Seattle; instead, they would be destroyed. It felt random that I had been plopped down in Torrance, California, to tell the police that there were drugs in their city. Almost like I was an actor on the set of a Hollywood movie. All I knew was I needed to get back home and out of this heat as fast as possible.

The officers and I entered the temperature-controlled building, took the elevator to the second floor, and opened the locker, which looked like most storage spaces. It was only a five-foot-by-five-foot area but was fully packed with furniture, dishes, and other household items all the way to the ceiling—or so it appeared. We removed each item from its carefully placed position and noticed oddities about the sofa, the dresser, and almost everything stored there. They all contained well-disguised homemade compartments, each full of heroin, cocaine, and assorted pills. The officers and I carefully lifted each bag out and placed them in evidence bags for fingerprinting, hoping for more than Rayner Martin's prints. These compartments would not have been noticed had we not been aware of what might be in the locker.

This was the load of drugs Esmerelda had been killed over. All I could see was her blood and body next to the car, along with the peppermint candy cane ice cream she had recently purchased. Just lying there six months ago, over two thousand miles away—for what? Some dull-witted plan, a plan in which she had been used as a pawn. And the plan had never mattered because now Uncle Ray was dead, too. He couldn't have expected that it could go this wrong.

There we stood, with someone's drugs, which would not be returned. They had lost a vast amount of cash, were on the hook for two murders, and had no idea where their drugs were since Ray had apparently not spoken prior to his death. The murderers most likely thought the drugs had been sold or used by Ray and were likely heading back to report the loss to their superiors with two murders under their belt, probably not their first by the looks of the precision. Uncle Ray had imagined he had a well-thought-out plan—all except the tracking device on the car, which had probably always been there. That was where this all had gone wrong.

In the back of the sofa was a note from Danna Martin on one of those monogrammed pages. It stated, "See you soon." The note had not been stashed there but appeared to have been lost in the seams from people sitting on the sofa. The note was not supposed to be there, but I was grateful it was, as it was one more clue in this gigantic puzzle. Upon finding it, I knew I was not driving my rental car back to the airport that afternoon. Instead, I would be getting a hotel room in town or somewhere close to further investigate this mess of Martins. One guilty so far, one not, and now another possibly connected.

The officers found Danna Martin in Bakersfield; I chose not to call prior to my arrival. This was a helpful tactic in most cases—showing up without notice could be beneficial. Sometimes I caught people outside and they did not have time to flee, or they were just relaxing without any knowledge of the questions coming their way. I drove three hours north to Bakersfield in my newly acquired, air-conditioned car, enjoying the day as much as I could while seeing new sights.

I pulled into a neighborhood of houses built in the 1950s, one of those places where all the homes looked the same with small variants. A chimney on the left over there, a thin window next to the door on that one. Danna's house stood out from the others; it was a split-level, unlike the ranch style, and was painted cream and bright orange.

She was in the side yard, which was about as narrow as a lawnmower path, mowing grass that had long since been dead, dust flying up, her hair speckled with clumps of straw like grass. She was clearly shocked that a tall man in a suit was watching her, was trying to get her attention, and knew her name. She didn't look like she would give up any information but invited me to enter the narrow chain link gate after I revealed my business and badge.

Her interest was most likely Ray, as her mood softened at the mention of his name. She had not known he was dead, but I guessed she had known he was missing and that someone was looking for him. We went around back and sat at a table under a humongous white umbrella sporting flamingo. There were two glasses for iced tea, as if she had been expecting me—or someone else.

I asked her about Rayner, and she laughed, saying, "He was such a clown, acting all rich when he wasn't. We all knew his financial state." She said he was her cousin by marriage, so there was no blood relation on her part. Her husband, Michael, had tried to keep his distance from Ray, but it seemed Ray always wormed his way into their lives somehow. He was forever coming by to leave a box, suitcase, or duffel bag with Danna and Michael while he traveled, telling them it was his valuables. Danna said, "My husband is a long-haul trucker, drives primarily for an electronics company out of Tempe, Arizona."

I told her I had been there a couple years ago in the touristy spots and saw Ohm It Up. She asked if it was for a case, and I said, "No, just visiting an old friend." Danna looked like a smart woman, and at that exact moment, we both knew we were on parallel paths in the same story. I was on the legal end with Bender George, Pearl, and Rizzo. Danna connected from the opposite end with Michael, Ray, and Esmerelda, sitting on her piece of the pie right there in Bakersfield. She didn't have to work—only keep her mouth shut. Protecting herself and Michael was her end of the bargain.

I thanked her for her time and the iced tea and proceeded to leave out the side gate. Danna followed, standing in the front lawn, which was made up of equally dead grass. I waved, and a ray of sunshine cut through her hair, revealing a clump of weeds or dust from her mowing activity prior to my arrival. I knew she was in on this or at least knew something. This could have been a stash house, a piece in the holding pattern. She may or may not have known any players other than Ray and now Michael. Torrance and Bakersfield were a few miles apart, but Bakersfield was a straight shot up I-15 from Tempe. The story parameters were narrowing with the lines of underlying evidence that were revealed without any actual clues laid out.

The pieces from last year and the year before were now all playing out in an order only, I could see—and the people on the other team were starting to emerge. I was certain Danna was on the phone at the exact moment she heard my car door close, telling someone of Rayner's death and what she suspected I was onto. This might be a larger situation than Danna had knowledge of.

I settled in at the hotel chosen by the department and called Detective Allen from the Tempe PD. He was surprised to hear from me, as the last we had met was on the waterfront in Seattle after Bender George and Rizzo Loman were arrested on a multi-agency case involving the Feds. We had figured they were away for a long time, but now both were out, picking up right where they'd left off, and no one noticed since they were supposed to be locked up. They had to have rolled information of someone bigger to get away from their charges, especially with their prior lengthy criminal records. I informed Allen of my sightings of them both and brought him up to date on the other connected cases of Esmerelda Martin and Rayner Martin, my visit to Danna Martin, and her unspoken connection to Michael Martin, Rayner's cousin, who drove long haul for a company contracted by Ohm It Up. Now Allen realized this was a considerably larger piece of ground to cover over many jurisdictions and miles. There were electronics that were being stolen or used in the rioting industry to communicate, drugs transported and sold, weapons that were known to be in the safe last year, and electronics being stolen by the drug transporters and trickled down to the lower levels of operation in Seattle. Of course, I saw Rizzo stealing from Bender, and Pearl was possibly in on the thievery or at least the sales of the stolen product, with or without drugs attached. Allen said he had an inside connection at Ohm It Up; he knew he may need that after the last encounter with the electronics store and had made his way in with a large purchase of equipment and maintenance contract. He said he would keep his ears on the case.

He laughed before saying, "I wonder which one of us will get to the other's territory next—me north or you head south?"

We both laughed at this insane ring of thieves, knowing we would see each other soon, and hung up.

Rayner

June 2021

I had been hiding in or around Seattle, waiting to return and offload the product. My plan was to have disappeared on that kind of cash, but I had either waited too long or not long enough in a city I should have disappeared completely from on the night of December 23, 2019–the night of Esmerelda's murder. That plan could have happened if I hadn't spent all that money vacationing on the way up to Seattle; I knew it had been a bad idea to pamper myself. Why had Esmerelda gotten murdered? I had been counting on Christmas money to get back home to California, to my stash and retirement. I knew deep down what was coming for me after watching what had happened to her. I was undoubtedly more scared than I had ever been.

Most of the money had been used for that memorable, extravagant vacation on the way up, so there were not any likely hiding spots for me to take advantage of; I only had my brother's house, but that was not a safe place anymore either, and I didn't wish to put the family in any more danger—even though they had no idea it was because of me that Esmerelda had been murdered. After freeing myself of the rental truck and drugs, I had retrieved Esmerelda's car and headed to north Seattle without any worries.

As far as anyone else in the organization knew, I was planned to arrive right on time—until December 22 at 11:00 p.m., the scheduled meeting time at a vacant warehouse on Airport Way. The one with the unlit Christmas tree in the window, which stood for many holiday seasons unused.

I knew I was being paid for the delivery, not the product. That was where this had all gone upside down for me—helpful, caring Uncle Ray. I had deserved and wanted the product money, which after all those years could have been mine—but I had chosen to live an excessive lifestyle, always convincing myself I deserved more and trying to show off for others with expensive clothing, electronic gadgets, vehicles, and jewelry. If the money had been saved and I had restrained myself on even half of those insane purchases, I could have invested in product, but for thirty years, I had been just a driver, plain and simple—lowest on the roster and longest employed member of the crew. I didn't feel right being their lowest and longest; I deserved better—or, at least, more. Most others had stolen, died, or dipped into product that wasn't theirs. I had always been a trusted member—until now.

My sole mistake was not knowing of the tracker on Esmerelda's car. It had possibly been there from the beginning, and it was what had led them right to my family's location after I'd failed to show up that night, never thinking they wouldn't trust me. I had figured the car was hidden well, back under the dimly lit apartment building carport, tucked in like it belonged there. A person couldn't even see the California plates unless they drove in. Last spot on the right. They must have been watching, and when Esmerelda left for the store, they had followed her there, had seen someone next to the car, and had shot. Either it was a warning, or they had thought it was me.

My plan after the murder had been to use the newly gained money following the car's sale to a lot in north Seattle and return to Torrance, fleeing without any trackability, on a bus or train, under my alias, Martin Rayner. Then there was the cash lining my pocket. My drug habit had been controllable for thirty years or more up to that point. But now there was the paranoia, constantly watching my back. Esmerelda's death was on my conscience, over me, consuming me from every angle, a death I knew I'd been responsible for. I could not escape the truth.

I stayed in Seattle two days too long, one to obtain drugs and the other to use up my cash. The next step would be to walk to Torrance, which would have been a better plan than being dead on the side of the road.

I knew immediately that it was one of the crew I had worked with when they followed me closely through the alley and down the sidewalk. They stayed a couple feet behind, and I thought if they were simply hoodlums and I collapsed and sat by the base of a tree, they would move on. They certainly wouldn't off me in the open city block with night starting to set in. No one in their right mind was out at that time of night there, not in the alley. Just me and them. Truthfully, no one was there except us and the knife, I thought. I didn't even hear it, just felt the heat and sudden jerk of my tired body. I was almost relieved to be put out of my misery, the drug habit and guilt eating at me. I heard them asking where "it" was, but with no real answer provided, they completed their end of the deal. They should have asked a bit more, but they were inexperienced street thugs who had been hired by my organization to prove I was at fault.

The nightmare was over for me. It was all over; no one knew my last thought: *I still won. I have the product and am now escaping guilt for Esmerelda's death.* I had escaped, but it had just begun for my unsuspecting family—the one I had never had the proper intentions for, not the ones in Seattle or California. The trail had been cold until I had been found sitting on Cherry Street in Seattle. I was the clue without any leads . . . or so I'd thought.

Carl III

July 2021

I KNEW SOMETHING NEEDED TO CHANGE IN MY LIFE. ALL I COULD THINK OF WAS Ethan. Grief seemed to overwhelm me the further I got from the reality that Ethan was gone. There was a greater distance from myself due to my realization that Ethan had been my rock, my stability, my reason for being. That was the end of the story for Ethan, but not for me.

Lorena might have been the lucky one on that end of the story, although I would never envy her life or choices. That had never been the case before, me thinking of her as the fortunate one; I had always pitied her unstable lifestyle. I was the one who had been able to enjoy Ethan's company and life day by day. She had no idea that our son was not there anymore. To her, everyone was nonexistent until she needed something or just happened to come around for that reason only, acting like she cared if only for an hour a month or year. It had been quite a while since Ethan, and I had seen her—a slew of weeks was my best guess.

Ethan had given her a few months' notice on the biggest event of his life. She had been supposed to go to Ethan's graduation, but I was under the assumption that she had not cleaned up enough or had forgotten. That was a narrow window of relief for me. I hadn't known if I should tell her or avoid her—not that I would have even known how to get a hold of her in the unpredictable state she was in. Would this news put her addiction over the edge? Could she handle news like this? That was not my problem, but somehow, deep inside, I felt responsible for deciding whether or not to tell her. She was the one who had chosen to leave Ethan and me to return to her drug-addicted ways. That had been almost fifteen years ago, and I still felt I owed her something. I knew I didn't; she had chosen her lifestyle.

When she had come to visit Ethan, I had always been present. She had not had her son to herself since he'd been two years old. I was always in awe of how she could be gone for months, maybe even up to a year, and then come back and say, "You have grown." I did not keep track of her visits on a calendar; she would show up, always planned with my consent, habitually empty-handed but sitting at the dining table like she had always belonged there. Every time quiet, studying Ethan, never revealing her feelings. She had to have known she was a failure as a mother, a human, and who knew what else. I wished I didn't have those thoughts and could simply love her for being Ethan's mom, but I had always had to protect Ethan from her, and that made the resentment stronger. When she had visited, her clothing had been clean, she had been polite, she had eaten whatever was put in front of her, and she had always done the dishes after each meal, with Ethan helping and me in the other room. She had a routine: someone would drop her off and then retrieve her at a time not set by her but when her ride was ready. She had never revealed anything about herself, like where she stayed, what she had been doing, not even miniscule, daily things like if she had gotten potatoes at the food bank. Ethan and I had known nothing of her. Some knowledge about her life would have been nice for Ethan, some comfort to know what she had been up to.

Ethan had always accepted her as she was; he would sit and tell her of his day or the one before but never the whole story about why he was excited about college, had passed a class with perfect grades, or any of the challenges of his high-school days. He never spoke of his successes. Perhaps he knew his success could or would send his mom off the trail with her addiction and even further from normalcy, but I thought deep down Ethan knew she was too far gone. There would never be normalcy with his mother. He was a child aware of the world far beyond my perspective and its ways from his time at the shelter with me and Gloria. Ethan accepted people as they were, not how he wanted them to be. Nothing changed his path. Peer pressure was not a problem; he could walk away from anything except the one bullet on November 12, 2020. His kind heart had taken him to that location on that night, his last night on this earth.

Every day, I woke up expecting Ethan to be there, not saying much in his normal morning routine. Now I woke up in the condo and the sky was empty, nothing inside those walls except my noise and all of Ethan's personal items—things he had picked out, treasured, used, gifts he had been given, all still there, sitting as if waiting to be picked up to resume their purpose. Sometimes I could see my son's hands holding an item; the power of smell was shattering. I walked by Ethan's room; it was still his room and smell. There was a faint whiff of his toothpaste, and it paralyzed me. I felt I should take most of Ethan's possessions to the shelter, as there were other boys his age who would have enjoyed the treasures. Maybe at some point, I would be able to bring myself to cross the threshold of my son's room and not lie down. When I entered, I always fell on Ethan's bed and stayed for a long time, not knowing how to get back up and leave, only conscious that Ethan was no longer with me. My son.

All my body craved was to feel sleep, which was no escape, either. The vivid dreams happened when I least expected it. I woke in the middle of the night, sometimes sleeping in Ethan's bed, knowing somehow that I had seen him.

I had visited most of the tags Ethan had done in and around the city. Gloria seemed to enjoy the trail that Ethan had left all over the city; it helped to know they were where Ethan had existed and had added his rebellious artwork to the city. Graffiti had been his goal, but what had he been escaping in his rebellion? Purposely, I had not visited them all; I needed to leave a few so there were still parts of him out there, at least in my mind. Places on the map Ethan had visited but I had not.

Every day, I showed up at the Women's Shelter, just like clockwork. My grandmother, Gloria, wasn't working there anymore as of December 31, 2020. She had contributed her entire being to the city, had imparted her wisdom and kindness to every woman, child, and family that had walked through the shelter's door. I still worked at the downtown facility, so it was not a lot different for me to arrive at work daily except Gloria was missing. Gloria had left to work in the new building a while before Ethan's death; she had transferred her office to Charlene's Place. There were only occasional classes at the Women's Shelter as well as intake meetings. It was where I set up a plan for each individual family to succeed. I had ideas on how to expand services and needed to speak to the new director, Nancy. One of my ideas was to create a weekly space for teens who were headed in the wrong direction. Possibly have a connection to the Seattle Police and other governmental agencies such as King County Metro, the United States Postal Service, and the Better Business Bureau to gain access to the community in a positive way by cleaning up unplanned graffiti, repairing broken fences and other property damage, and investigating what else they were missing on their journey to adulthood. Help those teens feel as if they were a part of the community by directly involving them.

The city was a different entity since Covid. The officials wanted to rent out the space as a pop-up vaccine clinic, and we weren't sure we wanted that many people traipsing through the facility, using the bathrooms. We would have to put away items used daily so the vaccine clinic staff could come in and rearrange.

On my way in, I noticed some stores which had window displays I had previously admired were gone. Overnight, they'd disappeared, trucks rolling up and taking the beautiful merchandise off to where? The owners—how did they survive? There were jobs everywhere; most didn't want to work. What would a person put on a resume after their livelihood closed? Would they tell the prospective employer they simply couldn't keep it together, there weren't any customers, Covid happened? Would they tell of their failure? The failures were not anyone's fault, but they sure didn't look nice on a resume. I assessed this from the point of view of my current occupation at the Insulated Business Corporation. People's dreams were being shattered; life savings dwindled. They had put their all into a store or service only to be shown or told that they weren't needed any longer—their doors must remain closed. All the merchandise was sold online, services were offered from afar, people were fearful of seeing people. Humans were not created to operate like this. Dinner clubs, dance studios, theaters, restaurants, friends that met for mutual interests, libraries, utility companies—all closed and turning people away, not by their choice but under the guise of the virus. Companies set up employees at home; employees were frustrated and testy with customers, making a bad name for their corporations. Collection agencies ran rampant due to all the nonpayment of debt—due to what? The people would pay if they could open shop and accept customers; this was no fault of their own. Landlords lost their properties and sold, tenants purchased big-screen televisions and new cars, all due to the virus and rent not being a required fact. This created higher rents and rental housing shortages. Homelessness was everywhere, tents on most corners. People took a piece of the land for their own; some ended up there due to addiction, others just could not or would not find a way, living in the "oh well" world, eating what people brought them, choosing to not have a choice.

Everyone's safety was on my mind—the security of the people in the tents, security from the people in the tents, tents catching fire from installed propane heaters and people smoking inside, people dying from heat and cold exposure. *We are humans*, I believed, *and we must fight for life, but one cannot fight for everybody*. Each person who was helped must want it more than the helper; the helper couldn't be the only one to see the end vision. A person shouldn't continue to feed someone who never tried to feed themselves.

My mind was going in circles, knowing I had it all, but I had it because I tried. I grasped the rope that led up. I did not have it all; I did not have Ethan, the reason for my being. I was broken at this point. After over a year of the pandemic, it had hit me that day. Some of the buildings were still boarded up from the riots, businesses never to return, empty busses running or some full of the homeless in the downtown ride free zone, people just wanting something to do, to stay warm or dry, people not thinking of Covid. The hospitals were overfull, shortages of nurses, beds not available, surgery being postponed unless critical. Life ran at a different pace and on newly generated rules; sometimes the rules changed daily. Laws were not enforced. Jails were being emptied to protect the incarcerated from Covid, but who was protecting the general population? I felt I must think of Ethan;

he had been my rock. I wondered how Ethan would have scaled through this pandemic nonsense. Moving forward in whatever way life allowed was what needed to happen.

Ethan had been out doing all this stuff that I had no idea about, and I hadn't even been worried about him. I couldn't imagine the parents who sat at home, imagining what their child was doing—then the police called and told them. I felt I could make a difference in those young lives and in my city. I had the resources, space, and connections to bring my vision into play for my own sanity and their lives.

Insulated Business Incubator would be the umbrella over the new business, Ethan's Edge. First, I needed to contact Detective Muncer. He would know who to partner with in the juvenile system. I would talk this over with Gloria and see who she knew in the other agencies. Bob at City Square Cemetery seemed to have access to products and the skill to complete these tasks, and he might want to be involved in instructing young people on how a job was done, as I had no construction knowledge—just ideas. I could learn some new skills, too, be a white collar with some blue-collar skills. I'd never grown up with tools. Maybe some required community service could be done by helping seniors with yardwork or errands. Everyone would feel better after pitching in on others' needs.

I spent the evening putting a plan together, a spreadsheet and lists of necessities for Ethan's Edge to evolve. Maybe city and federal agencies would bring a speaker in now and then to cover the scope of property damage that was caused by vandalism and negligence, to thank the young individuals who had stepped up to the plate for the betterment of themselves and the environment they lived in. This could expand to their own homes with their newly gained skills.

I needed to call Gloria that evening; I hoped it wasn't too late. It hit me that I had not paid her a proper visit or made many phone calls to her since Ethan had passed, and she had retired, doing what, I truthfully did not know. I lived my life on autopilot, thankful I had a schedule to keep that distracted my mind from being on Ethan all day. Gloria and I had spoken, but mostly about business and the turnover of her duties at the shelter. I had been processing my unimaginable loss internally and alone. So many others had to be missing Ethan, not just me. I would bring Gloria takeout dinner tomorrow and share this plan—if she wasn't still quarantining during the endless Covid mess. I felt I was safe to meet with her since I worked alone and lived alone.

Gloria seemed happy to hear from me and agreed to meet the following day if it could be for lunch. I was happy to take the afternoon off with a forward purpose on my mind and a set meeting with my grandma. She was always an inspiration.

It amazed me that Gloria was so self-sufficient. If she weren't, she could not have survived Ethan's passing. How had she been getting groceries and other necessities, which Ethan and I had gotten for her prior to his passing? Also, what about entertainment and a daily schedule since retirement? I felt I should have been more on top of the situation. Gloria had stepped in and had helped me raise Ethan when Lorena had abandoned us. Why had I not thought of her those past few months? I had been living in a vacuum; it seemed I was always pushed to the back and not moving forward. This plan of Ethan's Edge was my first feeling of moving forward since Ethan had been gone. I imagined this had been just as hard in Gloria's world as it had been in mine, and she had handled it without pestering me. That was not her nature. She had given me space and had waited until I had come to her, ready for forward motion.

As we ate the takeout Chinese, she had requested from her favorite place with eco-green chopsticks, I showed Gloria the binder with the projections and ideas. She looked at it, didn't comment at all, went about eating, cleared the table, and presented a cake. She said she knew when Ethan's birthday was—September 2nd—and had no idea if we would be able to celebrate or if it would be too hard, so we must start now, right this minute, have a piece of cake for Ethan, Ethan's Edge, and all the other young people who would be spared unneeded troubles in their lives because of this plan. Gloria said she would do whatever it took to make this happen. Something good had to come out of this deep tragedy. The loss of Ethan had worn on her; I could see age where there hadn't been any before. The only thing she wished to change was the logo; it needed to include the colors of all the colleges Ethan had considered.

After my visit with Gloria, I called Detective Muncer and requested a meeting soon.

He said, "What about now?"

I headed down East Pine Street to Bellevue Avenue, over to Seneca Street, and turned left on Fifth Avenue, finding parking easily that late in the day. As I walked toward the building where I had picked up the map of all of Ethan's tags months ago, I saw a familiar face. One I had wished to never see again and one I felt obligated to run to, to shake out of stupor. It was Lorena, my ex-wife, Ethan's mother. She was almost nonexistent, blending in, dirty, wearing clothing that should have been trashed months ago. I hardly recognized her, but the movements and voice were hers—things that had not changed from the woman I had loved so long ago. Her face looked sixty, maybe seventy, years old—not in her forties, as my mind calculated. She did not see me; maybe she didn't see anyone. There might have not been much in her head except looking for a fix, a meal, a roof, or another need at any cost.

I turned to walk toward her, her back to me. I felt an obligation to pass on knowledge that would surely shatter her being. A strong gust of cool wind hit her coatless body, and I could see her ribcage through the sheer shirt she wore. The sight left me just as unprepared as she was, being without a coat. As I hesitated one more second, a man who surprisingly looked normal and clean approached Lorena. She followed him around the corner, disappearing, to my relief and guilt, the decision still not having to be made of delivering the tragic news. I had no idea why, but I had been saved of performing the task of crushing her spirit for a bit more, maybe forever. I hoped to never see her again due to my inability to translate the story into a reality. It was a fact to me and had been, but it would be new news for Lorena, news that could crush her, take her down, possibly bring her somewhere she could not recover from.

I entered the Seattle Police Headquarters a few minutes late. Detective Muncer walked up to me; I did not recognize him, perhaps because I had only seen him twice prior—on the night of Ethan's death and when Muncer had delivered the news of catching Ethan's killer, a boy called Ice, a.k.a. Jasper Walters. Maybe I did not recognize Muncer because I still had the previous scene in my head from moments ago. With a questioning look Muncer asked if I was doing okay, and I told the tragic story of what had just transpired outside the building. Muncer was quite shocked; he'd known Lorena was absent but had not been aware of her state. He saw cases like hers daily; it was a harsh fact of his being on the streets for his occupation. But those addicts from his past had not been people Muncer had known or had been connected to. Lorena was the one who had chosen to leave over a decade ago, leave not just me but our son, who mattered the most. She could never right that wrong. I didn't want her to change for me; it had to be her changing herself and nothing to do with me. Truthfully, I didn't want to ever see her again. I thought maybe I should put the burden of telling her of Ethan's death in someone else's hands, although I did not know anyone Lorena knew. Leaving it to chance weighed on my mind.

We walked down the hall to an empty office, me handing over the binder and relaying the vision of this new venture. Muncer said he liked the idea of Ethan's Edge and would investigate avenues to implement the plan. He asked if he could make a copy of the spreadsheet and said he needed to hit the streets, as it was getting late. He was only one in this free-for-all crime spree and was attempting to do his part. His prime territory was ready for him to explore and uncover the oddities which were reality. Most people chose to not see the other side of life but live life as they are.

I left the station, purposely looking down so as to not see Lorena if she were there at all. I drove on autopilot to my house in the sky, knowing I would box up a few of Ethan's electronic items that evening. I thought maybe they should be given to teens who completed a required number of service hours or maybe given freely to a teen who had lost it all due to someone else's choices. Some had been there before; to others, this was new. I saw the children, babies to teens, arrive with mom or dad, sometimes both, head held in shame or false confidence to cover not knowing where the road would take them. But they were there nonetheless, listening to a parent tell their version of what had brought them there, knowing for a fact the story being told was not what had happened or even the half of it. They were brought to the sign that said "Intake." Prior to this, they had been in charge of their own lives, maybe responsible for their siblings, their parents out working or just out. Someone had to feed the younger ones. They hoped for a place to sit and decompress, a meal or a bed, somewhere else since they could no longer return to whatever had brought them through the shelter's door—fear, death, violence. They pictured their treasured possessions in the room they used to sleep in and arrived at the shelter sometimes with nothing, other times with a pillow or a picture, a tablet, a backpack, knowing they could not return to their favorite teacher, school, or friends. Those times of stability were over. They knew it had truly not been stable at all, but it had been a good run at it each time. Some came out of the shelter steady, secure, and firm in their newly acquired pathway; others ran back to whatever they'd been fleeing from, returning numerous times and then never to return, the shelter staff not knowing the end of their story except that it was not pretty. All we could do was offer care, meals, and programs for stability; we couldn't do the work for them. Milestones were placed to honor each person who completed each step of their journey to self-sufficiency it was simply up to each individual how long this process would take, the tools were there if they chose to use them.

Hazel

July 2021

It was a settling feeling to be there, home in Seattle, a place I had been longer than anywhere except the seas of the world. I loved my townhouse, job, and now the new plans to cut back on work, travel, and take Halverson with me on my sales pitches of coastal towns. Whoever thought I would complete my military career, work for the police, and then travel the coasts of each continent with my dragon, Halverson?

Upon returning, Muncer informed me of the stagnant progress regarding who had been involved with the murders of Esmerelda and Rayner. He had the pertinent information from their files on a wall in an upstairs office. The second board, resembling a whiteboard, had Pearl Swanson, Rizzo Loman, and Bender George listed. Some of the pieces were from a couple years ago, and some were current. Muncer said it was only a matter of time before that case would blow apart or come together. My suspicion was that it would come together, especially with the new breakthrough of the suitcase leading to the storage locker in Torrance. Life really was connected behind the scenes, good or bad. It was just putting the pieces in place for the right or wrong connections to be made. Imagine if Bender and Rizzo had never met in prison or they had never met Pearl or Pearl had never met

Ethan and inadvertently got him murdered or Five Pin. Connections, like me and Douglas Smith so long ago, were all for a purpose. I had always paid attention to the intricate details, and that was what had kept me safe along my journey.

June

July 2021

THIS WOULD BE MY SECOND ANNIVERSARY AND THE SECOND FOURTH OF JULY without my Charles. It had been ingrained in me to celebrate our usual way, with fireworks and watermelon. This year would have made sixty-four years of marriage. It seemed like just yesterday I had met Charles at the fireworks stand. Since then, we had traveled the world, and now, I was alone in Seattle—no living relatives, without children, living in a house bigger than me and Sandy the cat needed. It was a house I might never leave because it was where Charles and I had finally settled down after decades of travel with his Air-Force-directed stationing.

I was obsessed with the view, the people, my part-time job at Blossom Up Flower Shop with Rochelle. I loved the traditions Charles and I had made that had brought stability to us and our marriage, a marriage of a million miles that had landed me there, right on Prospect Street, Seattle, Washington. I enjoyed the community interaction I experienced at my job; it was an outlet for me. I believed I should be paying them to let me work there, as it allowed me freedom of creativity with flower design, interaction with people I would never have been able to meet if I weren't working, and a great deal of community service.

Gloria and I had had lunch a few times before the pandemic became overwhelming and everything went into lockdown. We were still in contact, but in-person fundraisers were not allowed anymore, which had put a strain on the shelter and other nonprofits. The flower shop had taken a financial hit with the pandemic. Offices, weddings, funerals, and parties were limited to a small number of indoor attendances. These days, most flowers were purchased for birthdays, anniversaries, or by individuals wanting to brighten up their home with so many people working in home offices.

I took the leftover flowers to City Square Cemetery and brightened the headstones of people around Charles's grave. Last time I'd been there, I had seen Bob Barton; he was a vital asset to the community. With the loss of his wife, Charlene, who had been gone about ten years, Bob had given his time to the people who grieved at the cemetery. He had gotten to know many. He was the head of grounds maintenance but knew how to clear land and erect a building, parking garage, or roadway. He had a vast number of community connections, government and at a city level, too, and he acted like he was a farmhand doing what was required to get any task completed without a thought of his inconvenience. He used what resources he had to the best of his ability. Bob Barton was a man I was honored to have met. Going the extra mile seemed to be his forte. Most people lately were in their own world, worried about money, occupation, children doing remote schooling, but I imagined the only effect the pandemic had had on Bob was the loss of more people. This was something I knew about Bob; he always had the same temperament and was genuinely happy to see whomever he met.

It was an hour after I had sat down to write my grocery list and three hours before work, and all those thoughts had come over me. An hour had passed, and there I was with pen and paper on my lap, without a thought of my needs. The list was not written nor ordered on the app for delivery the next day—my day off the only one before my private fourth of July celebration, the only day I could receive this service and make my plan work. That sounded unusual to me since I had just started working after a long period of retirement. I had to have watermelon to celebrate our anniversary, a personal-sized one now without Charles, who could have eaten a whole watermelon by himself. Watermelon and fireworks were our traditions around the world and the reason we had bought this house with the view of the Space Needle.

The list might not happen, but the groceries still needed to be there. I ordered potato salad, burgers, baked beans, paper plates, plastic forks, cat treats for Sandy, soda, watermelon, fancy napkins, a cake from the freezer section, and buns. The feast would be a picnic on the deck, an after-dark one since my hours had changed lately. I was up half the night watching the vehicles, boats, and air traffic—another realm of life I had never paid attention to since I had been an early riser all those years. Now I ate breakfast at noon, lunch/dinner at four if I wasn't working, and snacked later in the day. With Charles gone, I'd had to recreate myself; there would not have been a way to stay on the same routines and schedules as before. I was used to living that life with Charles at a particular time or in a way that couldn't happen by myself. We had cooked together; I would be boiling something, and he would be cutting up vegetables. How could that system work with only one of us? When Charles had first passed away, I had tried to stay with who I had been before he was gone, but that hadn't worked. That was who I had been with Charles, and that system was now obsolete, taken from me without a choice. There was no way I could cook, listen to our favorite music, and expect Charles to take ahold of me and dance when he was no longer physically there next to me. My entire process of life had had to change for me to continue on with the journey of life and stay sane. I couldn't say this had been an easy process, but it had happened suddenly. I'd been down, grieving, almost not functioning at all. Then, upon the gradual awakening back to life—thanks to Sandy's help—I had created this new way of life, a system that seemed to revolve inside of the life Charles and I'd had together, an extension of us and our beautiful, active, multi-faceted life. My life now with the cat—it made sense that I was up half of the night.

I backed out of the neatly organized garage—truthfully, the vacuum, broom, dustpan, and golf clubs were all that existed in there. I headed to work in the brief rain shower, watching pollen fall from the trees. I arrived at Blossom Up just in time for a rush on red, white, and blue flowers; the shop always lifted my spirits and changed with each festivity, made me more present and aware of each moment. I loved when the shop went from Valentine's Day to St. Patrick's—one day pink and red, the next green: the year in color. I believed all holidays should be recognized—each person, too, for the celebration of their life and accomplishments—and this place was a reminder for me of how precious each day was. Charles had always said, "Pay attention to each moment. It is a gift."

The shop had a couple customers that celebrated their wife's birthday for the whole month, coming in each day for a small bouquet, and on the actual birthday, they purchased a very large arrangement. There were others who bought for themselves or a special person; the shop even had one gentleman who bought two of the same bouquets, one for his wife and the other to give to a customer the staff thought might need it that day, a customer who bought for someone else. The shop would include the special bouquet purchased by a stranger; many times, the recipient would do the same for someone else. There was beauty all around, in creation, in people, moments, structure, and weather. What else would I need in life except to be aware of all the beauty?

Gloria walked in, the first time I had seen her in person in what felt like forever. I felt the recognition in my head bring joy to me as Gloria entered. She wore a mask, so I wasn't sure if my eyes were deceiving me. Was my friend there? She came in with a tall, slender woman, a woman of confidence and a slight hint of a Southern accent. Gloria introduced her as Simone and said they were setting up a banquet fundraiser for the Women's Shelter. They wondered what they could get in the month of September, as they were just getting ideas and laying the groundwork. Simone asked if I would like to join them on this venture. I looked to Gloria, who nodded, and they both knew I was on board to help. To be safe in those Covid times, we agreed to meet at Simone's place on July 5th, which was three days from now.

I had plans other than working at the shop; this thought was overwhelming and made me giddy, first to finish my shift today, next to enjoy the anniversary dinner and fireworks celebration, and then the following day to have lunch with friends to make plans to further help the community. Gloria and Simone left, laughing like old friends. I was excited to be included in their many years of friendship. I needed to get out and see people after being isolated during the pandemic; the meeting would be good for me. Gloria had said she would text me Simone's address for our meeting.

After my grocery delivery the morning of the third, I unpacked the food, leaving the special items at the front of the refrigerator so they would be handy for the next couple days of celebration. I headed out to the garage for the bin that held my red, white, and blue scalloped banner—the one Charles and I had picked up at the BX in Germany many years ago. That banner had traveled with us all over the world. I hadn't brought it out last year, as Charles had just passed a few months prior and I had been in a fog, not up for celebration or decorating. The year had gone entirely too fast, almost like it hadn't happened, and I felt strange making new friends, having those activities, and working in the flower shop with Charles not at home for me to return to. A marriage like ours was ingrained in me since it had been from early adulthood until retirement.

The bin held the banner, a couple American flags to wave, and some patriotic cloth napkins. One red, white, and blue folding chair was still in my trunk from the Memorial Day celebration at City Square Cemetery two months prior. Thanks to Bob, it had not been lost. He always watched out for me, and I was sure he did the same for other people. I retrieved the chair from the trunk, the banner, and other items; put them all in the fold of the chair; and discovered I wanted the other chair, too—Charles's chair—to hang the banner between the chairs with only two scallops showing, representing us: me and Charles. That was what that day was about and, of course, Sandy in her new catio, which I had purchased last month for the deck facing the Space Needle and with a partial view of Lake Union. Sandy loved her new outdoor space.

I tried to nap after getting all set up. My spirit was restless and ready for nightfall. Giving up on sleep, I entered Charles's office, which was really just a place he'd liked to be. I took out the leather journal I'd purchased after his death. I started writing about the days of that month and would continue through to the last day of July. I'd done that last year, starting to read at the beginning after my writing, which started today, reading of the loss of Charles from 2020 and remembering those emotions as if they had taken place today. They were emotions that were both old and new; grief was a place to pass through and continually remember. I would not have been the same person if I had not met Charles, my husband of so many miles. Today, I saw the strength of our marriage and my current strength.

I was surprised as I looked outside to see the lights starting to twinkle on the lake and around the city. Night was falling, and it was time for my celebration. I cooked my burger outside on the barbecue Charles had bought; it had a much bigger broiler than I needed. I decided I would see if I could find a home for it, as it was only used on July 3rd. As I sat and ate my meal—the same one I would have tomorrow—I saw the fireworks pop around the water and city, each one a celebration of us, Charles, and me. I fell asleep on the deck. Way past midnight, Sandy woke me, gently telling me that it was time to go in and lock up. There was a chill in the air with the wind coming off the lake.

Gloria texted to wish me a happy Fourth of July, not knowing how important that holiday was to me. She provided Simone's address on Linden Avenue North. I had never been to that part of Seattle and carefully looked at the route. At least they were meeting in daylight hours so I would be fine driving and wouldn't feel lost in unfamiliar territory after dark.

On the morning of the fifth, I woke early, earlier than normal, especially since I had been up watching fireworks half the night. It was something I would never get enough of; my connection to Charles was in fireworks and watermelon.

I checked my map and left early to explore the area. I headed to Gas Works Park and checked out all the towers and the play barn, which I discovered, to my amazement, was full of people sleeping. As I entered, I saw blankets move all over and heard gentle snoring from the other side. I felt unsafe as a man approached, ready to enter. I crashed into him when I turned to leave; I didn't know if he was there to harm me. I had not been faced with a situation like that before. I turned toward the towers and waterfront, feeling all sense of security leave me. I had been taken by surprise back there, never expecting to have come upon a place like that. I returned to my car and realized I was not prepared like I generally would have been. I never would have approached my car without having my keys ready in hand, hidden in my pocket. I was still rattled and fiddled in my pocket for my keys, glad I hadn't brought a purse to this outing. I pushed the remote button to unlock the doors, got in, locked them, and left.

I stopped at the first public place I came across to look at the directions to Simone's, feeling stronger to have come through that scene at the park by myself. I realized the directions I had were from my house, not where I was now, so I used my GPS for the first time ever. It routed me along the water; I turned north on Stone Way, feeling confident being away from the moving blankets. The robotic voice instructed me to turn left on Thirty-Eighth Street and then said, "Turn right, and your destination is on the left." That was one of the happiest moments of my life. I wasn't sure I'd been that excited in a long time knowing I was safe. I saw Gloria pull up behind me, and Simone came out and waved. I was safe and with friends. I couldn't wait to see what today brought.

It was 11:00 a.m. We ate the crackers; chicken salad and grapes Simone had provided. I thought of her huge house and wondered who mowed her lawn. Her husband surely could, judging from all the pictures I saw around—or one of her children. Her house was decorated with an ample amount of art pieces from one artist: everything was bright and clean.

Simone caught me admiring the artwork and said her walls were not always decorated with that many paintings, but she had an upcoming show at a gallery and wanted to see how they looked hanging and how they grouped together prior to the show. She walked over to a painting, pointing, and said, "This one is where it started. I was grieving the loss of Luther in the days just after his tragic death. His wallet was returned to me by the police; there was a slip of paper in it that had a doodle I had drawn for him twenty or more years ago. I drew it again, only bigger, and colored it in. I couldn't stop, and here I am, getting ready for an art gallery to display my doodles. Each one expresses some of my grief, me in my house alone, not a wife any longer, not a mom to young ones, but an artist who does fundraising and grave upkeep, eats small meals, and has discovered herself in this recreation."

Just as she finished, her phone buzzed and lit up on the counter next to the chicken salad. She checked it; it was Thomas asking if he could call. He said he had news. Simone excused herself, saying it was her son needing to talk. She came back a few minutes later with tears streaming down her face. "Excuse me for crying. Thomas has news of a baby. Cora, his wife, will deliver a baby boy in December. His name will be Luther Thomas Washington." Simone turned to me and Gloria and said, "I am going to be a grandma," with shock still on the edge of her tones. "Luther would be so happy; he would have made a fantastic grandpa."

I never told them of my adventure at the park, only complimented Simone on her wonderful home and offered my own anytime for our meetings. We decided on aster, thistle, and sunflowers for the fundraiser, all in season for September and bright, festive, and inexpensive. After Simone made copies of the potential donor list for me and Gloria, we decided who would contact whom. We discussed a potential printer for thank-you cards and then said our goodbyes with plans to meet next week at my house. I had never been involved in fundraising, but after today, I was excited to be part of it and looked forward to future meetings and the actual online auction.

A week flew by like it had never happened. I had news of the donors from my list that had been contacted for the auction. One would donate a coffee-related gift basket, another a set of skis, then books, gift cards, flowers, and the list went on. This was truly a community-involved event. We needed a website professional to set it up; maybe Gloria or Simone knew of those things, but I didn't have any ideas. I was excited about having company and was sure the last person to visit was one of Charles's friends, Stanley, over two years ago when he had picked up Charles for a game of golf. There would be people here, my friends. I got out my list of donors and what they were donating, the lunch I had prepared, and sat with Sandy to tell her of the happenings.

Gloria and Simone arrived right on time together; they both had news of donations of clothing, gift baskets, tennis lessons, meals to-go since restaurants were not open, boat rides, bowling games. There were activities for all ages; we would need to collect the items, store them, catalog who they'd come from and where they would go once the winning bids were in. I offered whatever room I had and promised to help in any way possible. My place seemed logical since Gloria lived in a penthouse and there would be trouble toting all the items in and out, and Simone had steps up into her house. At my place, we could pull into the garage on one level and unload, creating a system right on the existing shelving unit.

After much discussion, we ate lunch, divvied up responsibilities, and agreed to meet next week at Gloria's to catch up on the progress of our plans. We had plans to type a letter to each donor thanking them and laying out our schedule of plans.

I hardly realized that I was working and making progress on the fund-raiser with the amount of time it took and the fun I was having. Using up that empty space in my life was helping me, too.

The following week, I headed out of my neighborhood on Taylor Avenue North, turning east onto Mercer Street and heading up the hill. Traffic was heavy compared to the one-mile radius I generally drove for groceries, work, and anything else. I had been up there before, bringing Charles to his appointments. I turned onto Eastlake Avenue East, arriving at Gloria's on Belmont Avenue. Spotting the parking garage, I wasn't sure if it was entered by only residents or visitors, too. Maybe I was supposed to park on the street?

I saw Simone skillfully parallel parking. I found a place and did not park as gracefully but managed to get Blue into the spot not far away, just down the hill and heading in the direction of home. Simone had been to Gloria's before, so I took her lead to be buzzed into the building. We loaded onto the sleek elevator, which was so quiet we didn't even realize we were moving. It opened to the most wonderful view of Lake Union, on the opposite side of my home. I bet if I had a powerful enough telescope, I could see my house.

It was so comforting to be accepted as part of this unspoken operation. It felt as if I had always known Gloria and Simone. I asked them how they had met since it seemed like a long, well-established relationship.

They laughed and said at the same time, "We met over dishes." Then they explained all the dishes left from Luther's funeral less than three years ago and their adventure of returning them to their rightful owners. Death had brought them all together, and they were trying to help others in the process of healing themselves.

We promptly ate lettuce-wrapped chicken salad and crackers at the table by the window. We discussed the new results on web designers for the auction, appointed days to pick up donated products, agreed on the wording and sent it to the printer for the thank-you cards to be printed, made a list of services offered that would need to be included but not picked up, created a system of how to record the winners, and decided on a space at the Women's Shelter to store everything since my garage would not be large enough for all these donations. Carl would be there daily to check on it, and we could meet there to categorize each product and photograph them for the web auction. Gloria said this would be the first year the shelter had done any fundraising this way; she had always held them in person and had hosted a dinner for the donors to see where their money was being used. We would need to put together a slide show and short video so people could understand what Ethan's Edge was about. Also, we would need permission slips for the parents to sign for any minors wishing to be in the video. This would be the first set of children to go through the program.

I asked what Gloria and Simone thought this would look like one year from now. I knew saving even one child from the wrong path would change them and society. It was funny—Charles and I had never had any children, and there I was, helping plan for the future of someone else's children,

children I had never met but deeply cared about. I looked forward to contributing my time and resources to the city. I needed to see if Rochelle would donate a couple floral arrangements to the cause. Gloria used Blossom Up for all the fundraisers, but this one had not gone public just yet. We were thinking of advertising Ethan's Edge in August to hold the auction the first week of November, deliver everything the second week, and open on November 12th, the one-year anniversary of Ethan's tragic death.

We wrapped up the meeting in record time, and Gloria asked if Simone and I would like to go for a walk. I automatically thought of the moving sleeping bags. I was not familiar with this neighborhood, but Gloria had a place in mind not far away. We arrived in no time at Tashkent Park, a lovely getaway close to Gloria's residence, less than a five-minute walk. It was as if the park were a pocket of nature tucked right into a city block. Shade was much appreciated from the towering maple tree; the tiles surrounding it soaked up warmth from the day, making me wish I could lie on them and nap. I was suddenly tired from all the extra activity and brainstorming, an appreciative sort of exhaustion. I was ready to drive down the hill with my newfound mission, curl up with Sandy, and rest until the city lights returned on my side of the lake.

We said our farewells, agreeing to meet at the Women's Shelter the following week for the rest of the plan. I agreed to bring lunch. Gloria hollered as I drove away, "Don't forget—Carl likes to eat, too." I left with Gloria laughing in the road, knowing to bring an extra meal. Simone eased out of her parking space as if she were made to drive in the city. We headed down Mercer Street, honking as we parted ways by Westlake Avenue. I pictured Simone's artwork and home, also my own home, which was very near and a place I could nap.

As I pulled Blue into the garage, I remembered the photographs I had made into slides from my and Charles's travels around the world. There were many scenic ones from all the continents, ones without Charles and me in them. I was revived from my sleepiness and went into Charles's office to retrieve the projector and a tablet and to close the blinds. I made notes as to which photos to get enlarged prints of and have framed. I would contribute to Ethan's Edge, too. This was the reason Charles and I had traveled all over the world–to help people right there in Seattle, Washington, a place that was now home to me. Now it was time for the nap. When I woke up, I would locate a photography shop to create the prints and figure out where a craft store was to purchase frames in bulk. This would be completed by next week, so I would have something to bring besides lunch for the women and Carl.

Hazel

July 2021

As soon as I landed at London Gatwick Airport, I knew I was home, on my soil. I would spend a day in London, rent a car, and head north to Bury St. Edmund to explore Abbey Gardens and Suffolk Regiment Museum. I'd always wondered if my dad had not passed and my family had stayed in Eastbourne if I would have had a career in the Royal Navy—or had I joined the US Navy as a comfort, knowing I had crossed the sea to get to America and knowing I belonged on the other side of the Atlantic, the water being my only solace in life.

I drove the rental car as closely to the sea as the highway would allow. I took the coastal roads but felt the pull to Eastbourne so strongly. My first stop was to visit my dad's grave and tell him of Mum's passing—although he probably knew.

Calvin Earl Skylar had been buried here at sea. Hazel stood on the pier, paying her respects to Dad, Mum, and her childhood—all gone, taken suddenly except from her memory. She supposed the journey was also to pay respect to the road and sea traveled behind her. Hats off to the city of Eastbourne and the city of Seattle all at the same time. Hazel could never seem to get the salt water out of her head; her lungs and heart depended on it. I was like my mum no matter where she was in the world, she could always feel which direction the salt water was.

This was when I realized why I was there. I had not even checked into my hotel nor driven by my old house, even though it was probably gone with new development built over my family's land. Maybe it hadn't even been ours back then. When I was a child, home was home no matter who owned the ground. When we left, I'd been young, and thoughts of ownership had not been mine to have. Young girls had stayed young and innocent back then.

When I'd left Eastbourne, I had been distraught by my dad's passing and leaving the only place I knew, the place with all memory of him and my childhood erased. The secrets I'd had of the days spent on the pier; the days I had been left to entertain myself. How was I supposed to pick up where that life ended? All of that had not been a thought prior to my family's day of departure until now. It had been shocking to be uprooted and placed in another country as a young teenager. I had traveled thousands of miles during my Navy days and had probably been running from thoughts and feelings I had never expressed. I was here now to revisit Halverson and bring him to all coastal towns—but first Eastbourne and then Seattle. He could be on t-shirts, on posters, in children's books, made as figurines, turned into snow globes with flames that floated when they were shaken. Also, patches, pins, and decals that said, "I saw Halverson." *Thank you, Halverson, my friend, for seeing me through this life's journey and bringing me back here to this pier, to the Bandstand, to home.*

I checked into my seaside motel, exhausted from the sixteen-hour flight days ago, the drive to Bury St. Edmund, and the arrival to my moment of knowing why I was there in that location, a place where I'd been born and pulled from, a place where I'd landed and started healing already now that I knew I was wounded. Before, I had lived to fill time. Life had been an adventure. Sometimes a person didn't know she was broken until she broke again.

I fell asleep with the window open to the sea, knowing the smell was one of safety and now hope of my future. I was not sure how long the journey would be, but I did have a return plane ticket for eleven days from now. I might stay longer or take less time. While I was there, I would make a list of what would be needed to bring Halverson around the world with me, my next adventure being to travel where me and Mum had visited.

Jin Mae

March 1992–June 1995
August 2021

I HAD BEEN BORN IN THE UNITED STATES BUT HAD CLOSE TIES TO THE KOREAN community. I loved to continue all the traditions and food preferences from when my mother would cook noodle soup so rich that I couldn't see through it—noodles to slurp and play with. I could still see my mother at the one-eye propane gas burner in the corner she'd called the kitchen, and it had by all rights been a kitchen if the place had really been a house and not just a rectangle of walls constructed by my mother, Yong. Upon returning to Korea after being in the US for only a couple of years, Yong had gathered pieces from around rural areas where throwaway items were scarce and had put together shelter for her and me, thinking it was a palace. We had lived that way until Yong's death in February 1992. I had lived there another month, not leaving the shelter and in deep grief for my only living relative. I had never met my father, who had run off when our family had been forced to return to Korea.

I had been eighteen years old and heading off to the Korean military as required—or so I thought. As I'd carefully packed what little could be brought with me and had separated what I would leave outside the tin-roofed shack, I noticed a piece of wood slightly sticking up from the floor. Carefully digging around it, I found a picture of my father and an original birth certificate from King County, Washington, of a baby born on March 17, 1974, at 2:34 p.m. at Harborview Hospital, Seattle, Washington. That was my certificate. Seattle, Harborview, and my American citizenship were not things I had heard of prior—but I had learned about them just in time to leave for America. The Korean military would have to be left behind. There was no checking out, no telling anyone, just one backpack, the money Yong had stashed from her odd jobs in a jar embedded in the dirt floor of the back closet, and my newly found passport that Yong had kept renewing upon expiration. Back to America, even though I had no memories of my first trip there.

It felt unrealistic to return to somewhere I did not know I had previously been. After a thirteen-hour flight and a significant amount of reading on the plane, thanks to a book purchased at the airport gift shop, I knew some basic facts about Seattle. I had a map and no idea what I would do or where I would go. I had entered a country just like that; a person did not move about as easily in Korea. I would check into a hotel, get a job and a place to live.

After a couple of days of seeking employment, the skill levels on the aptitude tests allowed me an entry-level position at Downtown Engineering. My responsibility would be to file papers, sort incoming mail and merchandise, and deliver parcels to the proper departments. My education had allowed me to understand the CAD programs used at the engineering firm, even though they did not know that yet. My English was satisfactory for the company. I would prove myself and work hard to move up the ladder. I was Jin Mae, an American, even though my learned mannerisms and accent did not indicate that. Yong had taught me the value of being honest and working hard.

Searching the newspaper, I found a studio apartment on Boren about a month after gaining employment. The leasing agent who showed me the apartment, which was luxurious in my mind, stated it was only 400 square feet and a had very small balcony. There was a strict no long-term guests and a no pets policy. I applied on the spot, assuring the agent no one would be there to stay with me, nor would I have pets. On Saturday morning, the application was turned in, and by Monday afternoon, I received a call that I had a roof over my head. Paying three months' rent and a security deposit at the lease signing, I did not think I would ever leave that location, which was perfect in my mind. With all the trees outside my sliding door that let the breeze in it was as if I was living in a forest, the trees with swaying branches and leaves rustling. The appliances and flooring had just been replaced. I would need to purchase a chair, a bed, and dishes. It had been so long since I had eaten Yong's noodle soup, and my heart yearned for home even though I knew this was truly where I belonged—in this concrete, fast-paced, oversized village called Seattle.

Every Saturday, I would walk from my front door up Boren to James, passing two hospitals, knowing others were born there—but they were of no interest to me. I would take a right on James and circle Harborview, coming around the back where the helicopter pad was located. From the park, I would see the most beautiful views of the city where I'd been born and had no idea I belonged. After only a few months there, I did truly feel a connection and was comfortable with life as it was, as well as my newly acquired routine. A tradition now, the weekly walk and stop at the grocery store to obtain supplies for my pot of noodle soup. On my walk, I would think of being in Korea and how close I'd been to joining the army, wondering what would have happened if I had gone that route or if they were looking for me now. I was a United States citizen, and that was where I would remain.

I had been in Seattle two years and at my apartment almost that long, enjoying the sounds of the city and festivities nearby. On Friday evenings, I always stopped at a restaurant on Second and Pine for a cheeseburger and French fries before catching the bus up First Hill to my home. This particular Friday, the first one of spring, on a warm evening, I saw the most beautiful lady. She was short and full of business; her movements were fast as she took notes from something she read. I imagined she was a student with finals coming up. We left at the same time and rode the bus towards home together. I got up the courage to talk to her as she dropped a shiny red pen, I picked it up and handed it to her. The woman said she lived in the building behind where we were standing; she seemed frustrated and mentioned she was applying for a loan to open a nail salon, as she already knew the art, had a place in mind, and had established clientele. She seemed rather surprised at the release of her story to a stranger as we stood on the corner under the large maple tree. I was amazed that we had never crossed paths before since neither of us had a vehicle. We lived on the same block, both worked downtown, and had so much more in common, like our shared last name. Her name was Ha Yoon Mae.

After meeting Ha Yoon, I had much to think about, as up until this point, I had only thought of surviving and going day to day without spending too much money. Her dream of the nail salon opened my eyes to more sizable business opportunities. I had been raised poor and did not have Ha Yoon's expanded mind. I had enough money saved to go into business on the nail salon; our combined money would open it without the bank and interest due on a loan. Somehow it felt right to talk about the subject even if it was with a total stranger. I remembered at that moment I did not know where she lived exactly, her phone number, or her schedule. If it was meant to be, it would line up and progress.

On Tuesday, I was held up at work on a project and was late leaving. I saw Ha Yoon at the bus stop headed up the hill to her home. We talked some more, and I asked if we could have a meeting strictly about business sometime soon, before she met with the bank. She laughed, then said she felt the meeting with the bank may not ever happen as she had not gotten any lunch hours during work with the salon being so busy. Her clients and the regular ones who were assigned to her were taking all her time. I assured her I was not up to anything harmful; I just wanted to learn more about the nail salon and tell her some ideas of mine. That evening, we stopped at a café on the corner of Boren and Madison with some outdoor seating and had the best noodle soup and conversation. It felt good to laugh as we sat at the wrought iron table balancing our napkins and food from city breeze. I had friends but mostly business ones—not ones like Ha Yoon, whom I could people watch with. She was open-minded to discussing the idea of having a business partner. We agreed to meet again at the First Hill Park on the corner of University and Minor on Saturday at noon, each of us bringing something to eat for lunch as well as some ideas written down for discussion.

Four days later I brought BLT sandwiches from the corner deli and chips; Ha Yoon brought ginger ale, cookies, and napkins. I had also made copies of my bank statement so she would know I was serious about this investment and business opportunity.

We discovered we were both business-minded, ethical, hard workers and ready to start this operation, her to leave her current position behind. We both signed the lease on the location Ha Yoon had been waiting for and worked hard on our time off to open the salon. Ha Yoon had other nail artists who each rented a chair, and we acquired revenue from them, too. This was the first salon we opened; we named it Nail It. In the years to come, we opened thirteen more Nail It spots all over the city in prime locations. It was a very successful endeavor on both our parts—even though it was Ha Yoon's idea in the beginning. We both worked with our skills remodeling, painting, and finding the appropriate furniture for each location.

Ha Yoon and I had been dating and planning our future for about three years, meeting nightly while opening the salons. Other nights I would meet her for dinner, or she would stop over for my noodle soup. We acquired a city bus map and went to most every park in the city. We both preferred to be alone and not visit in large crowds such as movie theaters.

In 1996, Ha Yoon and I got married at a simple ceremony with a few Korean friends and acquaintances from both our works. Until this time, we had not realized we did not have any close friends, being as busy as we were. No one stood out to be our best man or maid of honor. We soon moved into a two-bedroom apartment one floor up in my building so we could combine households and have an office.

A few years later, in 2010, I had been talking to Dae, who had attended our wedding reception, and whom I had seen at a few other gatherings since then. He was a friend of a friend; I wasn't even sure where he fit into this circle. All his associates had been investing in apartment buildings south of here in Pierce County. He stated he knew people who would loan money for these large real estate investments. I was interested in learning more but did not commit to anything, as I had an uneasy feeling about his pushiness. Dae seemed to want to meet more frequently and tried to be more convincing, almost aggressive in his tactics and forceful on the idea of apartment ownership, as if it were important to him that I invest. Deep down I knew I did not want to get involved with the type of people he knew.

I met Jim Minter at work one day, who was selling a building in an iffy neighborhood south of Seattle. Dae heard of this somehow, and he confronted me. I told him Ha Yoon and I would rather obtain financing from a legitimate source since the property was in the ghetto. What if it all did not pay off and foreclosure was the only option? I did not want to have the money mafia men after us and our successful nail salons. We had managed all these years to go one step at a time in an upward motion without any help or large loans, and now when we needed help for the largest adventure so far, it had to be the right fit—and legal.

A few months after the purchase of Pine Field Apartments, twenty-six not-so-great units, I started getting letters from Western Credit Services. I opened the first envelope; they were offering a refinance at a higher rate than I was paying. I received many more that were shredded upon arrival. I wished they would stop sending me anything since it just made more work for me. The apartments were holding their own, the purchase price had been lower than normal, crime rates had risen, and the seller wanted out of the responsibility. The building was in fair shape; the owner had recently installed windows and a roof prior to his decision to sell and had remodeled a few units that had been damaged in a fire. I was not comfortable during the purchase touring the occupied apartment, as I found it to be invasive to the resident and, I felt, a possible danger to me. I was not familiar with the neighborhood nor comfortable being in a stranger's home. The rule of never letting anyone get between me and the door could not apply if I had to tour the entire unit. Ha Yoon and I agreed to hire a service to perform the inspections after this experience.

A year after acquiring Pine Field, we purchased a home for ourselves on Twenty-Fourth Avenue in Burien. We were ready to be out of the city for relaxing evenings and weekends. As soon as we walked in, saw the calming view, and smelled the clean air coming off the Puget Sound, we knew this was our home, where we were meant to be.

Then we acquired Aspen Landing in a neighborhood not far from the SeaTac Airport and the Water's Edge, a smaller apartment community on a small lake in north Seattle, which was a bit more upscale. We owned just under eighty units and decided that was our limit.

The letters from Western Credit Services were still coming to our post office box located at Third and Union downtown. We had a system: I collected the mail and sorted through it since Ha Yoon worked later to ensure the safe closings of each nail shop for the night. For our employees' safety, we had always made sure everyone checked in once they had locked up and were in their vehicle or at the bus stop. Ha Yoon would leave her downtown office shortly after the last check-in and head home. Once a week, we would sit and discuss troubles with the business, pay bills, and talk of how the money was being distributed and how we could improve our ways and finances.

There had been a series of fires at a few of our salons and a couple apartments over the years. Hearing of other businesses being firebombed, too, we thought nothing of it and didn't consider that we'd been a specific target. There was nothing coincidental enough for us to add it all up.

When Ha Yoon got home on a hot evening early in July, we discussed insurance and the repercussions of higher premiums due to so many fires over the past few years. I had not sorted the mail yet, as I wanted to have dinner ready when she came home for us to eat on the balcony and make plans for our future purchases and budget tightening.

Ha Yoon came in, kissed me, changed her clothes, and started looking through our mail. She asked what Western Credit Services was, and I told her of the previous letters. She simply looked at me but was still curious as to their persistence. I told her I had not thought anything of it. There were probably many letters from quite a few companies she had never seen, but for some reason, she felt compelled to open this one. I heard a gasp, and Ha Yoon asked me why I would borrow money from them. I assured her I had not gotten money for any of our endeavors from anywhere except the bank, where she had been present and involved in each transaction. She knew of Dae and his scandalous ways, but we had never discussed it because it wasn't something we had pursued or even considered for financing. I was not sure she believed me. She read the letter, which demanded the six million dollars I had borrowed in an immediate payment due on or before July 17, 2021. There was a phone number with only an answering machine and an address of a post office box at a convenience store in south Seattle. I tried to call Dae at Ha Yoon's suggestion, but he did not answer. It had been years since we had spoken after his aggressive actions at our last meeting. Until that moment, I had not thought Dae to be connected to this corporation, nor had I had any dealings with him other than a few lunches years ago. I wasn't even sure if he was connected to Western Credit Services in any way now. Ha Yoon seemed convinced of his involvement and seemed to know more of his actions somehow.

Ha Yoon and I retrieved our loan documents and looked for the name Western Credit Services. It was not connected to anything we had financed, nor had our loans been sold. All our documentation was in order, with each file separate—a system I had learned at Downtown Engineering. Even though this was a horrible mess, I was grateful I could prove to my wife that I had not been a dishonest man. We would wait until tomorrow for answers, both taking the day off.

After a stop at our bank's main branch and finding no connection, we called Dae and asked if he knew of these guys. He said he didn't know about this or our connection to them. He even stated that I had said I would not deal in any underground money and asked why I had done so behind his back. He suddenly became very angry with me, so loud Ha Yoon could hear him through the phone. Western Credit Services did not return our call, nor did we receive any more mail from them. We inquired online with the Secretary of State about a physical address for the company and drove to the post office from their return address, but the address they provided was a vacant lot in south Seattle on East Marginal Way.

At the beginning of the month, the mail was always heavier. We certainly should have gotten a larger box, but that would have required notifying all our utility companies, insurance, mortgage holders, and other senders of mail we received. I had always enjoyed entering the small doors into a place of many possibilities and getting my stack of mail, the envelopes all stacked in the small box, telling of our history and future. It was a feeling of pride knowing Ha Yoon and I had created this small empire and had worked so hard to keep it running under the umbrella only we knew. Who could imagine what would be in the box?

I would have never thought it would be like this today. There wasn't anywhere nearby to park; after driving around, I found a parking spot on the street by Fifth Avenue and Union, fed the meter, and headed downhill toward the water, wishing for a cool breeze. On August 5, 2021, I entered as usual, except we were having a heat wave. I came in through the door, and the wall of cold air separated the outside furnace from the cool conditioned air hitting me. It was welcoming after having to walk so far to get there in the sweltering heat, heat I could see rising off the sidewalks. I imagined it going up people's clothing, making that summer day unbearable.

I had to stand in line for the extra mail that was too much for our small box, welcoming the air-conditioned lobby. After the half hour wait, I left, heading back to my vehicle, and hoping the meter hadn't expired. While I walked, I quickly scanned through the stack, which was rubber-banded together.

Just after crossing over Fourth Avenue, I saw a bus coming and hurried across as the crosswalk light flashed. It all happened so quickly, and I knew no one so was not able to communicate the trouble I was in. No one appeared to be looking at me; they were concentrating on getting home and out of the sweltering weather. I felt a pinch, some heat, a burning sensation on my lower back, maybe my left lung. It was shocking. I reached for my back and grabbed a thin, wire-like device, maybe a dart tip without the end—the flight, that was what it was called, I thought, remembering a night at a local pub when I learned to play darts.

I was down in seconds, barely able to grab the rusty pole that the streetlight hung on. I slid to the ground like I was made of gelatin, melting in the heat. I pictured the lime flavor—I had no idea where that thought had come from. No one seemed to notice my odd behavior. At least, it was out of the ordinary for me; of course, downtown, people did sit or sleep on the ground all over. There I was, thinking I was one of them. Was this how they'd gotten there? It was a normal occurrence to see people on the ground. As I walked by or around them, I always attempted to see if they were breathing but could never tell. I would feel guilty for not stopping, but self-preservation would come over me, as I was not a very big man, nor did I have fighting skills. So, I had never stopped. This was possibly the case for me: people just assumed I was another casualty of the sidewalk, the street sleepers, like a wind-up toy that had used all its energy, falling after the last twist had been unwound.

Some of my last thoughts were, *I am a businessman. Can't you see my mail?* I hovered over myself, pooling on the hot sidewalk, unable to move. For a moment, I was not willing to leave my body, my routine, my being, my wife. But, having no choice in the matter, I was suddenly aware of being shut off like a door being closed.

Jin Mae

August 2021

AT ABOUT 9:00 P.M., A CHURCH GROUP WALKED AROUND, GIVING OUT WATER and asking if people were doing okay on the streets with the heat. They tried to wake a man slouched down at the base of the pole, but he was gone, as was his stack of mail; his cell phone, which Ha Yoon had been calling; the comfortable slip-on shoes he had changed into before his final walk to and from the post office; his wallet, which he normally kept in his front pants pocket so it would not be stolen — Jin Mae was big on safety. His keys, his gray Nissan SUV, his briefcase, and several shirts from the dry cleaners were all missing items that no one knew existed upon finding him. He was just another John Doe at the base of a pole on a hot summer night.

By 10:00 p.m., Seattle police had started an investigation, removed his body, and made a report. All with no clues—just a person, dead on the sidewalk. Only this one was clean; this was not an uncommon discovery in Seattle or any other city.

Jin Mae had not been fingerprinted since he'd been a child when his passport had been issued. Those records from so long ago may not have been digitized—or might not exist at all. Of course, this was not his concern anymore, nor did he have any issues pending.

By midnight, Ha Yoon was worried but also skeptical. Jin Mae hadn't seemed too concerned or as concerned as she had been about the letters and their declared deadline of repayment. He had treated it as a mistake—or he was he guilty of borrowing the money and had gone along with their investigation at the bank to cover his tracks. She had never doubted his word before that moment. It was now midnight August 6th. They had eaten breakfast together a few hours prior on August 5th and had parted ways like they did every other morning, making comment of the highlights of their days and planning to meet back up at home for dinner, her bringing takeout since there would be record-breaking temperatures. Only this evening, Jin Mae did not answer his cell phone or call her. She didn't know whether to be worried or suspicious. She called the Seattle police at 1:00 a.m., trying to file a missing person report. They stated she would have to wait twenty-four hours. She told them of the letters, and they told her many counterfeit collection agencies were popping up, saying individuals owed old utility bills and loans. The man who answered the phone at the station knew nothing of the man found leaning on the pole at Fourth and Union—or if he did, a connection was not made in his mind.

The next morning, exactly twenty-four hours since Ha Yoon had seen Jin Mae, she filed a missing person report online and uploaded pictures of her beloved husband. She had notified his work and requested for all employees to be cautious and aware, asking the ones she knew if they had seen Jin Mae. She did not feel safe at home alone after waiting a full twenty-four hours for Jin Mae, so she packed a large suitcase, gathered some food, set the house alarm, and backed out of the garage, making sure no one was following her by taking random turn after turn to a hotel in Tukwila. This was where she would stay until they found her husband. She didn't imagine that this move to safety would make her look guilty, as she knew she wasn't guilty of anything. In the investigation, they would find she was the one who had pushed at the bank for answers. Could they honestly think it was her who had borrowed money from Western Credit Services? Everyone was a suspect in the case; she would not be excluded she thought.

At 2:37 a.m. on August 9th, there was a call on her bedside phone from the Seattle police, who stated they were outside her door, and she had no way out. They needed her to be aware they would be unlocking the door and she would be escorted to the station for questioning. She woke thinking it was a dream. She went to the door, preparing to open for their entry. As they walked in, they instructed her to freeze. She imagined they were there to tell her of Jin Mae's whereabouts, and that was exactly what they did. They informed her he was at Ninth and Jefferson. She knew right where that was; it was a place they had walked to many days during their time living on First Hill while dating and merging their lives so long ago. He had been almost obsessed with Harborview and his birth, the story he would not know. And now he had ended up there, dead in the morgue.

Ha Yoon was under the impression her husband had been found hurt and was in the hospital from treatment, not that he was gone from her and this earth. What would she do now without Jin Mae, her husband, best friend, business partner, and the comedian he'd been in their private time at home? He would practice dance moves from a video game and show her his silly ways. After getting dressed and thinking of their recent activity, she asked the police if she could get her coat. The officer got it for her, not trusting her to move without them. They searched the pockets, finding nothing, and handed her the coat. At that moment, she realized she was being treated as a suspect and knew she needed an attorney.

They had always used Mr. Clark, a recommendation from a business associate when they'd opened the first nail salon. That seemed so long ago, Jin Mae and she had recently met and were forming a business partnership. It had been good to have legal representation. They had never needed any advice except in business law and had never been in any legal trouble. She wondered if he did criminal law as well. Ha Yoon would answer the questions that had been made apparent in the past few days with the police's inquiries and phone calls. If cell phone records were subpoenaed, she would be truthful. There was nothing to hide.

Ha Yoon was led into a small room with a chipped-up wooden table that she did not want to touch, wondering if the chair and room had been sanitized during this Covid mess. What other types of butts had sat there?

She sat in the hard chair, not touching anything else. She stated her name and that she was voluntarily there; she would answer questions to the best of her ability.

The question was why she called her husband Jin Mae when they shared that last name, a name they had both used since birth. She told them he had introduced himself that way and said he felt like he'd made a statement by always using his first and last names. Did she know why he'd been downtown on Fourth and Union? She stated he had probably gotten off work like every weekday and had checked the mail on Third and Union, at the main post office. They asked where the mail was; would he have driven; where was his vehicle, wallet, keys, shoes; why would he sit on the ground? Did he use drugs? Ha Yoon stated she did not know the answer to any of this except he did not use drugs, only took vitamins. Possibly he'd been ill from the heat, which he did not handle well, and had collapsed. She stated she did not know why he would have been on the ground. She and her husband were in good health as far as the last medical reports showed.

They told her an autopsy would be performed at her expense. Foul play was suspected, as all his personal items had been removed from the scene, and this was unheard of behavior for him. The cameras would be checked from the time of his post office entry until the time he'd been found deceased on August 5th. They guessed from Ha Yoon's account of her husband's daily schedule that there would be around four hours of camera footage if they counted all angles from two blocks long. It had been at a time when commuters were traveling and the sidewalks were full, everyone including Jin Mae trying to get home after hours of paid labor, getting ready for the rewards of a day well worked.

They instructed Ha Yoon that she would be moving to another hotel for her safety. They would be taking her vehicle for the investigation and would help her make the transition. She had no choice in the matter, not even the choice of hotel. She hoped it would not be a place like the one where she currently stayed. They advised her to appoint someone to run the nail salons and banking so she could virtually disappear from society in case it was determined that she was in danger. Also, under no circumstances was she to leave town. Moving from her home had already created suspicion in this investigation.

At 6:00 a.m., they left police headquarters and headed south on I-5, leaving an exhausted Ha Yoon with an officer outside the hotel. They went in and packed her belongings. She pictured them with her personal items, feeling they didn't need to touch her toothbrush or under garments. She knew she was innocent.

They confiscated the keys to her car and home and asked if she would give permission to search both or if they would need to obtain a warrant. With nothing to hide, she gave permission on both counts. She asked them to please solve this case and gave them the paperwork from Western Credit Services, asking for a copy for herself. She felt it was the only clue she could provide. She told them all she had done to try to contact the company, what Jin Mae had said about the mail coming for years, and their efforts to find the actual source of the matter. She was sure Jin Mae had had nothing to do with it and turned over all bank statements, loan documents, and business agreements pertaining to how they'd received their money. She was moved to another hotel overlooking Lake Washington; the room had been booked under the Seattle Police Department's name, but Ha Yoon was paying for it. She stayed in the room many nights she was unable to sleep and the meals she could not make herself eat.

On August 10th at 5:45 a.m., Ha Yoon had breakfast delivered: dry toast, mixed fruit, and tea. It would sit on the small round table until lunch; she would stare at it like she had every other day until they took it away. She had not read the newspaper that came with it each day, but today, on the fold of the paper, she saw a picture of half of her husband's face. She opened it fully, seeing all his features. She had not packed pictures of them, so she had not seen his face since the early-morning hours of August 5th, for almost a week. They had never been apart this long, and now they would be apart forever. She wasn't even sure if she would be allowed to plan a funeral, who could attend, or who she could trust—no one at this point. And the police did not trust her. She had never been a suspect for a crime before, but now all her thoughts had a tag attached, asking why they were talking to her. There were so many questions and thoughts of days prior to this; had she missed something? The actions that had led up to Jin Mae's death—where had he been during the weeks and months before? Had he been involved in obtaining money from other sources or in something else? It didn't all seem possible: that Jin Mae was dead, gone, and his picture was on the front page of the local newspaper, a paper neither of them had ever read. He was famous for all the wrong reasons.

The article asked for the public's help regarding events occurring on the date of August 5th at approximately 4:00 p.m. Anyone who was in that crosswalk, had seen something or had heard something was encouraged to call in tips; they could remain anonymous. They had printed screenshots of the camera footage from the post office and the intersection of Fourth and Union but had no clues. There was nothing suspicious in the shots, just people. But the police thought that was whoever the murderers were are individuals who looked like everyone else. Ha Yoon looked at the group of people; most were dressed in business clothing. Of course, someone wishing to do harm would only want to blend in. There was not a face she recognized. She wished she had been warned of the police's action and their plea for help; it was rather shocking to see her Jin Mae's face nearly the size of the front page.

She counted the people crossing in the same direction as Jin Mae. There were seventeen individuals, nine women and eight men, including Jin Mae. No children. Jin Mae had been almost in the middle of the crowd, carrying his mail—*our mail*—and on the left perimeter, there were a couple people carrying briefcases. There was one florescent-blue shopping bag that could be seen from that angle. Most of the people wore only shirts and pants, carrying suit jackets and ties. A few wore shorts that did not provide a place to conceal any weapons.

This was all so new. They didn't even know if a weapon had been involved, as there were not any marks that could be associated with a bullet or stab wound. The preliminary report had stated a few small abrasions that looked like ingrown hairs or scratches from sliding down the pole or falling. All were explainable since Jin Mae worked with paperwork all day long. Ha Yoon wondered what other camera footage the detectives had and weren't sharing. She would have liked to see the front-facing views to ascertain if she recognized anyone. She wanted to do everything she could to help but felt cut off from the evidence. Could someone in that small crowd have possibly known Jin Mae, and would she even know whom he had known? They had both been familiar with separate people through business, as any married couple was. If the crime was connected in any way to Western Credit Services, would they have followed through on their threat in that way? Or would they have just destroyed something of the couples? Were the fires connected to Jin Mae's murder—if it was murder? Suddenly, the fires became a large part of this for Ha Yoon. There were many angles, and they did not even yet know if there had been foul play. She wanted to bombard the police with questions, not knowing if it would make her look mentally unstable, guilty, or if she would just appear as a grieving wife. She chose to ask when they next contacted her so as not to appear odd in any way. She knew of her innocence and did not wish to put any ideas in their minds of suspicion or guilt.

Detective Rubio

August 2021

THAT MORNING, I MET WITH DETECTIVE MUNCER OF THE SEATTLE POLICE AND picked up all copies of Jin and Ha Yoon Mae's financial and property records since we were working on the case in unison. The now-established murder had happened in the city, but Ha Yoon and Jin Mae had resided elsewhere in the county. I planned on meeting with Ha Yoon that afternoon. She had already been interviewed by the Seattle police.

I walked into the hotel, noticing the view of Lake Washington and the large fountain out front, thinking it certainly appeared like an upscale correctional facility. I took the mirrored elevator to the seventh floor and called Ha Yoon with the code word so she would know to open the door for me. We had considered meeting in a different location, but Ha Yoon might be in danger, as had been suspected earlier, and she did not currently have transportation. It was better for our investigation if she was not seen anywhere.

After the autopsy, we now had evidence that a set of lethal chemicals had entered the body through a needle-sized hole on the left side of Jin Mae's back. The concoction had to have been administered in that crosswalk.

Our goal today was to ask Ha Yoon the same questions, in depth; show her the camera footage from all angles, as she had requested; and put together a list of anyone we could identify in that crosswalk or nearby. Being as we did not think the murder had been done with a projectile device, the probability of the killer being in the crosswalk with Jin Mae was most likely. The crowd had been dense and moving at a high rate of speed that time of day; a projectile device would not have been accurate and would have likely hit the wrong individual. We thought that Jin Mae had been the assassin's target but had no leads as to why. His only crime could not have been crossing the street, this could have been a random killing.

Ha Yoon opened the door to a room in immaculate condition, not like a room she had resided in for several days. The bedspread did not have a crease on it; the vacuum lines were still in the plush gray carpet as if she had not walked around; the bar sat open, but nothing had been removed from it. Ha Yoon was in the same condition as described by the other officers and reports, perfectly put together. Her expression was deep and blank, like she had not moved from that chair for the duration of her stay. I wondered if she was up to this, but we both knew it needed to happen to solve this crime and get Ha Yoon out of that luxurious prison cell. I thought of where she would go from there, if there were someone after her, the same person who had murdered her husband. But did she know who that was? It did not seem as if she were guilty, but we would not know until further investigation. The hotel staff had been made aware of her needing protection, to not let anyone near her room, and to alert us if she exited.

Ha Yoon asked if it was fine to order a tray of tea and coffee. I stated tea would be fine. Room service arrived quickly, as if they'd been outside the door waiting for our order. They also brought ginger snap cookies that looked like they'd come from a box and were meant to be fed to a toddler.

We sat with a view of the lake; Ha Yoon said she had been watching a few water skiers and airplanes. Then, suddenly, she turned her head toward me and asked where the pictures of the people in the crosswalk were; had I brought them? She said she had been waiting for what seemed an eternity. I lay them on the table after removing the tray of tea. Suddenly, I was not able to resist a cookie and grabbed four, popping one in my mouth. I heard my loud chewing and wondered if it was disturbing Ha Yoon. There were shots from every direction, even overhead. Ha Yoon was apprehensive and hard to read as a witness or suspect–but maybe neither. Could she have been there? She studied the photos carefully for about ten minutes, shuffling them, laying them out of order. I thought she would not be of any assistance with that method. Was this all to cover something up?

She put eight of the thirteen photos in a pile, laid out the other five, said, "Here, these people are the only ones close enough to Jin Mae, and they would not have been able to harm others with a needle or dart at their angle or distance. These are the ones who saw my husband last." She pointed at them–seven to nine people, as the sidewalk had been packed.

Seeing her logic, I thanked her for her time and asked if there was anything she needed. I rose and left quietly with her silence to my question. I imagined Ha Yoon sitting in that chair day after day, not knowing who had killed her husband, wondering if she would be charged or found by the killer if she was a victim also. She had been of some assistance today. Of course, we could see what she was saying as well as her conclusion, but we wanted to know if she recognized anyone in the crowded sidewalk. She had denied knowing anyone. And the camera footage had been improved from a few years prior when everyone had looked the same in grainy still shots. These shots were clear but from a distance.

I took the long, scenic route heading north on Rainier Avenue. The lake was beautiful with the sun shining. I traveled on Rainier Avenue all the way to Jackson and met Muncer at a little restaurant by Sixth Avenue. The food was wonderful, as always.

Muncer said, "I don't get to this part of town often. It's nice to be away from my usual patrol and see an old friend."

I had known Muncer for twenty plus years; we had met on a case that could not have been planned any better as far as jurisdiction was concerned: a body half in the city of Seattle and half in White Center, both in the same county. We had both been called out on the case on a winter night. The rain had already washed most of the evidence away from Eighth and Roxbury by the time we'd arrived a few hours after the tragic event. The young man's murder had never been solved, but because of him,

Muncer and I had become and remained friends. We only had one issue between us that we did not discuss: music. I liked slow jazz, and Muncer liked hard rock that had a beat like the bass that came from my son's basement bedroom. Although that could be rap that Albatar listened to; I was not up on current music.

I parked at a pay lot around the corner on Fifth, walked the one block, thinking that was what Jin Mae had done—parked and walked one block or two. I passed the small doorway that was more of a gold curtain with red fringe than an actual door, heard Muncer call my name, and realized I had gone too far. I turned to go back with more questions than answers thinking of my last stop with Ha Yoon.

We got a booth made of old black vinyl and sat opposite of each other, knowing we needed more room to spread out the paperwork and photos. I told Muncer of my visit with Ha Yoon. I was still on the fence regarding whether or not she was guilty; she acted concerned and frantic, but that could have been from being alone with the death, guilty or not. We looked at the faces that were closest to Jin Mae in the crosswalk. Neither of us could identify anyone but agreed to take the photos back to headquarters for facial recognition.

We decided to put the work away, eat, and catch up on our current lives. Muncer was still living in Fremont, and I was still in SeaTac, a place I had chosen prior to the extra runways being added to the neighborhood. We talked of our first case so many years ago and how we'd never solved it for Robert McCreary, the victim who had been on his way home from work. It was a subject we always discussed since it was what had made us friends. The case was remarkably similar to Jin Mae's—just a different shift, neighborhood, and pay scale. Robert had been a dishwasher at a bowling alley, while Jin Mae had been an engineer. Both cases needed solving—one so long ago, this one current.

We parted ways and met up on Fifth and Cherry, both finding police parking. Muncer suggested using a room upstairs that he knew of which had large tables. He told of his filming activity during the riots from the windows on the third floor; his assignment had been to watch people destroy buildings and windows. We laid out all the property records and matched each with loan documents that lined up exactly. Then there were the few letters from Western Credit Services, all demanding cash.

We also had the arson reports on the apartment buildings and nail salons. So many leads and directions, but were there more of these types of arson involving the same method? Over the past two years, we found six more; they were aimed at small businesses as well. Rent It, a low-budget property management company, had been hit; Detail on Design, a detailing shop of upscale automobiles, had been hit twice and burned to the ground; Drive It Away had also been hit twice, a car lot with most cars having over 200,000 miles; and the last on record, See Through, a window-cleaning company that had a dud thrown through their front window, which had helped link the investigation of all these cases.

We took the camera images to Hazel in records; she was an expert in facial recognition. We agreed to meet in the morning to talk with the four businesses that had been hit by the arsonist. It felt strange to both of us to be working on a case together again, although this case appeared to be a few cases all attached to one murder. What was the strangest part was we had both agreed, after working the graveyard shift for over two decades, to meet in the morning. I hopped in my undercover cruiser and headed south. Muncer did the opposite and traveled north. As I approached I-5, I saw it was at a dead stop. I was generally not out in the daytime, so traffic did not usually affect me. This was claustrophobic, the exhaust and heat stifling. As I entered I-5, I wondered if I would ever return home and knew this day was on repeat for tomorrow.

Detectives Muncer

August 2021

WE MET THE NEXT MORNING AT A CAFÉ ON THE NORTH END OF THE CITY CORE for coffee and breakfast. Our first stop would be Rent It just off Aurora. The office needed exterior paint and looked as if it had been a used car lot in the past. A gruff-looking lady, possibly in her sixties, opened the door before we had exited our vehicle. From the look of her expression, she must have known we were police. She looked guilty, but it was hard to concentrate on her actions with the paperwork strewn all over the office, which we could see from outside on the sidewalk. There could not have been any order to her filing system. After staring us down, she finally asked what our business was. She was leery of us right from the start, and my guess was she was armed and probably needed to be with her line of work.

We introduced ourselves. She did not tell us her name, nor did we ask. She shut the door after we stated our business, and we saw her push a button as if someone were on speed dial. Then she came back out to the rickety porch, which looked as if it would collapse under her; it leaned more to the right with her weight. She stated we would be helped shortly.

In about five minutes, a gentleman in a green leisure suit who looked like he did not belong there pulled up in an older Mercedes and jumped out with his hand pointed forward, ready to shake. He introduced himself as Jenson Winters. He invited us inside. The office was clearly too small for four people, but we followed him, taking seats at the desk as potential renters would have. The lies this office had heard—of course everyone was a perfect tenant. Jenson was willing to talk—in fact, too much. When asked, he stated his business had been set on fire. He did not know exactly how and was surprised it might be connected to anything other than untargeted crime. He offered to show us pictures prior to the repairs and then, when asked if he had heard of Western Credit Services, a strange look came over his face like he had suddenly put on a mask. He went silent, and we let him think for a brief time. He responded that he did know of them and had taken out a loan to keep his business afloat due to inactivity in the rental industry during some slow times. He swore he had paid them back if that was why we were there. He did not want any trouble and ran an upstanding agency, although they were lower-budget rentals. We asked if he had owed them money at the time of the fire, and he hung his head, stating he was ashamed to be behind in any payment but insisting again that he had paid them off. He said he was not guilty of anything, then or now. He was embarrassed to have borrowed any money, and to be behind in payments was more than he could handle. We told Jenson that the fire and overdue payments may have been connected, thanked him for his time, and left our cards.

Our next stop was to Drive It Away. The man on the lot looked like he belonged at our previous stop; he stated the owner did not see anyone and we could leave a message. We did, as well as our cards, explaining we were investigating the fires from a couple of years ago. We promptly received a call from S. Marino asking of the nature of our social call and stating he was innocent. He did not set fires; he made square, solid deals on his vehicles. He said we could meet at his home on Third Avenue North.

Rubio and I arrived at the modest yellow bungalow—maybe a Craftsman; I was not good with architecture—and entered the residence, a clean, well-kept house with one large Doberman who politely sat next to us. Mr. Marino asked us to sit. For the record, we asked his name; what did the S stand for? "Sky," he stated. We asked what he preferred to be called, and he stated, "S, but Mister or Marino are fine, too—whichever you prefer."

We delivered the same story here as at Rent It, and S gave us the same storyline as Jenson—only this time, a payment had been missed and another fire had occurred. As with Jenson, S had never suspected the fires and the money owed were connected in any way.

We received the same story from Vern Marshall of See Through and Leah Thompson of Detail on Design. All were delinquent on their contractual loan payments and could not pay them as per the signed contract. None of the companies had been actively seeking a loan, but with such a great offer coming to them during Covid times, which had been hard on all of them, it was a relief to get enough funding to make it through until business picked back up. Truthfully, all the businesses were riding on the edge of cashflow downfall monthly; no one would have ever loaned money to these industrious people—not until Western Credit Services had come crawling in, offering help at a skyrocketed interest rate.

We grabbed a slice of pizza and soda from the corner gas station, now knowing if the firebombs and murder of Jin Mae were at all connected to Western Credit Services, and went to Trolley Hill Park, proposing the plans of investigation and taking notes since this was such a complex case. Our first thought and focus were to approach the business for a loan. Not knowing how the business found its customers, we would need a sinking small business set up to apply for a loan. They did not appear to have an office, phone number, or any contact information except a rented mailbox at a convenience store in south Seattle. There did not seem to be any city licensing—only the state license, which had expired twelve years ago. Theodore Blake was the sole owner of the company, or so the old records indicated. A multitude of things could have happened in twelve years, except we thought Mr. Blake was still in business due to Jin Mae's death. What we did not know was why Jin Mae would borrow from Western Credit Services at a 24 percent interest rate if he had traditional financing at a much lower one. Had he had side investments or projects Ha Yoon knew nothing about?

At this point in the investigation, I would still imagine she was either in danger or a suspect; it was hard for us to know how to proceed without a suspect being identified. We were there to protect everyone, innocent or guilty. Since no one knew of her whereabouts except the undercover officers, the paper and online communities had reported her missing after Jin Mae's murder and autopsy results had somehow gotten to them from an inside leak. The leak may have come from someone at the morgue, whoever had done the autopsy, someone in the department, someone who had overheard. The media was always hanging around places, waiting for the right words to be spoken, then printing or airing them. At that point, the word was out there, and there was no retrieval.

We decided a visit to Ha Yoon's hiding place would be the best plan of action. How would she react to our new findings of the firebombs? We arrived, me driving around the back, circling the building, and keeping watch as Muncer entered the long-carpeted hallway. After I was sure we had not been tailed, I entered myself.

Ha Yoon was not pleased to see us without a definitive answer to the suspect in this case. She demanded to see the street camera shots again; she had studied them multiple times, as had we. Most of the people in the photos had been identified and verified as commuters heading home, to a transit zone or the bus tunnel. Almost equally as many were headed west as east, north as south. She took the photos from my hand in such an agitated state that I wondered of her guilt. Was it because she had only had time to sit alone and think of her upstanding husband with no proper funeral, wondering if he'd had a secret life or if her plan had gone wrong? She did not know who to trust, and neither did we.

She suddenly pointed to photo number three, stabbing her finger almost through it, asking, "Did anyone identify the blind man?"

We had not identified him, as he'd been out of range and was blind. She pulled photo number one out of the stack; the blind man was on the left side of the crowd as they entered the crosswalk and made his way to Jin Mae, then off to the right as his white cane emerged from the side. Most people did not shift their position in a sidewalk, let alone a blind person in a heavy crowd.

We asked Ha Yoon more questions about Western Credit Services. Had she ever made direct contact with them; did she know Theodore Blake, or any other people connected to them? She stopped suddenly and remembered the time nearly two decades ago, early in their marriage, prior to their purchasing any real estate. Jin Mae had attended a meeting with Dae. He had come home unsettled and had rambled on, which was out of character for him. He had stated that Dae was almost violent in his thinking and pressured about borrowing money from some unidentified source other than a bank—underground money, Dae called it. He said he had connections and wanted Jin Mae to get the cash so he could expand quickly. Jin Mae had been unusually upset, said he felt threatened.

When asked how they knew Dae, Ha Yoon said a friend had brought him to their wedding reception, not knowing which friend, as it had been many years ago. Dae had walked around the reception alone, as far Ha Yoon could remember. She told them in depth about the investigation they—well, really, she had started when the letters had kept arriving, demanding money: six million, to be exact. She'd known in her heart Jin Mae would not borrow without her knowledge; he'd been a good and honest man.

After leaving, we realized that Ha Yoon had not divulged the information of her knowledge of Theodore Blake, if she indeed had any at all. We took notes to ask her at a later date.

Daniel

August 2021

It was a hot evening—Friday night, to be exact, although the days did not matter. But it seemed as if I should be doing something on a Friday. The only difference to me was Saturday night because the shop was not open on Sundays. I did not go anywhere except to the cemetery, grocery store, and infrequently for a walk along Lake Washington. It had been over four years since Iris had passed away, but it still felt like yesterday or today. I had not moved on from that moment; there were the before and after moments, but my mind refused to enter the after. I knew tonight I needed to go to Alki Beach. Something was drawing me there. I had avoided it since Iris's death. Before, I could not go; now, the need was vital to my being for some reason.

I headed south on I-5, thinking I would take the West Seattle Freeway exit, just as I had done many times to see Iris prior to her shift at Scoop It Frozen Creamery. I saw the bridge was closed, realizing I did not have any other ideas of how to get to Alki; this was the only way I had been. Following the detour signs at a snail's pace on a Friday night would certainly take up some time. I was happy now that I had decided to feed Alex the cat before I'd left. He visited every evening, a large, gray furball who did not want attention—only food. It had struck me by surprise when he sat next to me on the picnic table one evening, staring into my eyes like he could read my entire story, like he knew who I was deep in my soul. Since that evening a few months ago, we had eaten dinner together every night. I had left his portion on the table opposite my seat that evening. Tomorrow he would have some fish from the beach if I was brave enough to enter the road to my destination, order the food, sit at the umbrella-topped table, and bring some fish home for Alex. He might have belonged to another family, but we enjoyed our dinners together.

I took East Marginal, following the detour signs, and headed over the First Avenue Bridge, connecting to West Marginal, reaching Harbor Avenue. I was distraught, wishing this idea had transpired that morning. I proceeded on, parked at a scenic viewpoint, and watched the water, ferries, ships, and city from this angle. I looked to my left, knowing I had come this far and could not turn around. It was time. I proceeded toward Spud's Fish and Chips. Everything looked the same, but not one thing in my life was the same as the last time I'd been there with Iris.

It had been mid-April of 2017, the first day it had been warm enough for us to have a picnic. It had still been cold with the wind coming off Puget Sound; I had my old brown jacket in the trunk and offered it to Iris, but she ran off, grabbing her blue fleece blanket out of her green VW. I imagined she had her entire wardrobe in there. We huddled under her blanket, feeding fries to the seagulls and bites of chowder to each other, and splitting an order of fish. We talked in that brief time about taxes, laughter, semester finals for her, and nonsense in the hour between my closing the shop and her starting her late shift. I would leave that evening, and it would all be different forever. We never knew when that would happen, treating each day the same, not aware when there was a glitch in the system of life. Each day precious but us not realizing.

Today, I approached the stand for dinner, knowing this was happening, I was going to our picnic table. It was a hot evening. The crowd swayed on the slim sidewalk, souped-up cars lined the parking area and street in both directions, volleyball games were played in the sand, children squealed at the waves as the seaweed appeared to chase them, and there I stood with my order of fish, daring to cross the road to our table. I thought, *I can do this*. The soda was cold and froze my hand in the heat. I convinced myself to navigate toward the table because my hand would freeze off if I did not set the soda down. Knowing this was nonsense but rolling with the train of thought, I was there at the table, the one Iris and I would use whenever we were together, weather permitting. I set my soda and dinner down, not daring yet to relax enough to use the bench as a seat. Instead, I stared at it, thinking of all the others who had sat there since Iris, and I had been here. Feeling overwhelmed, sitting was my only option. I collapsed, and no one around the area seemed to know this was what was happening or was even watching my unusual behavior.

I opened the tartar sauce and ketchup, took a bite of the fish. Fish connected in my memory to Iris. I looked up, and there was a lady standing, staring at me with a plaid sundress, red and blue. I thought, with the sun shining in my eyes, *does she know my predicament? Has she been watching me?* She gently asked if she could sit at the other end of the table on my side. She wished to watch the water and stated this table was the only one that would work for her. I nodded as she sat, not sure I was capable of speaking.

She pulled out a sandwich and took a bite. Tomatoes fell out; she laughed and said, "I know that is you, Richard. You never liked tomatoes."

Suddenly I felt not as unstable, having someone to watch who had brought their imaginary friend along. We sat in silence for about an hour, neither of us moving. I was not able to rise and decided to stay seated.

She turned and said, "Thank you for letting me sit here. I'm Micky. This table is the last place I saw Richard before he headed out on that business trip, the last one. He died in a plane crash on the way to Boston. I have not had the courage to come here since his passing three years ago."

I watched her as she extended her graceful slender hand to me. I shook it and said, "Richard and Iris are together."

Micky nodded as if she understood why I was there today and left. I knew there was no conceivable way she could know why I had come there today but was comfortable with the bond we had made, even though we would never see each other again. Micky had made that part of my healing journey helpful, even if she had no idea.

Somehow, that moment set me free from guilt, sorrow, grief, responsibility of Iris's memory. Knowing Iris was with Richard and was taken care of whoever Richard was, that was comforting to me. I threw my remains of dinner in the trash, excluding the piece of fish for Alex, watching as the sun edged toward the horizon, the city lit up, the Space Needle tall, regal as ever, and my soul began to awaken. I wished the same for Micky as she traveled through life.

On that warm evening, I started up my Mercury Sable and headed toward home, thinking of Alex and his dinner alone, missing my nightly connection to him. I had been pondering the purchase of the shop next to mine. The decision was suddenly made; I was going to buy it—not sure why, but it would expand my business if I chose. Tomorrow I would stop at City Square Cemetery and put fresh flowers on Iris's grave, something bright for this lighter load. I wondered if Vernon and Cookie Mortelli, Iris's parents, still traveled yearly to visit their daughter's grave. Secretly, I was abundantly relieved that they had released me from taking that excursion with them. I came here a lot on my own; I knew it was their daughter, but I did not know them, and it was awkward sharing my life with them. We had known different versions of Iris, me only a few months of her time on this earth and them everything prior to my knowledge of her. I was sure the same could be said of their feelings. Once the case had been solved, they had gently released me.

Simone

August 2021

ON THOSE HOT SUMMER EVENINGS, I TENDED TO GRAVITATE TO CITY SQUARE Cemetery. I knew Luther was meticulous about his lawn and it should not be different now, especially when he had no control of the situation. I kept the metal bucket in the trunk during the warmer months so I could stop in and tend to the edging, weeding, and general upkeep of the headstone. I pulled up some days and saw a leaf or grass clipping on the stone and was glad I had come, even if only to remove that stray article. Luther had not been fussy about anything most days, but his grass being not attended to his way had been his largest pet peeve. I had never ventured into that territory with him; he would be in our yard out there for hours just being happy with his progress on the lawn. He would come in with the biggest smile, saying, "We have the best yard on the block, maybe in this city." I thought he was right; he'd put all he had into his precious yard. Growing up had not been stable for him except after he moved to the cottage on Aunt Marcella's property. I was sure she used a lawn service for her immaculate yard; this yard was something Luther could control.

I got a drive-through dinner at one of our favorite burger joints, took the food to the cemetery, and had dinner in the car by Luther's grave.

It looked as if they had been keeping the area clean—or someone had. There was not a piece of grass out of place, a piece of windblown rubbish anywhere in sight, or even a dead flower. With all the heat we had been having, I would have expected *something*.

I heard a rustle in the ivy climbing up the colossal fir tree. Eyes peeked out at me—a masked creature which disappeared as quickly as it had revealed itself. I looked over by Luther's grave, and there it was: the fattest raccoon I had ever seen. I shared my burger and fries with him since I was not hungry. I had purchased the food thinking of Luther and would never have bought it if I weren't coming here. I spent the better part of half an hour with my new friend, keeping my distance but enjoying the company, watching the movements of a wild yet semi-tamed animal.

I saw Daniel pull in across the way. He was a good man, responsible and polite. I always enjoyed his visits; this might have been an unusual place to meet, but we didn't know each other outside of the heavy load of grief we shared. I didn't know his Iris, and Daniel didn't know my Luther, but they were who had brought us together. Daniel got out, wearing his olive-green cargo shorts and orange tank top. I thought, *I am old enough to be his mom.*

When he looked toward me, seeing the raccoon, who scurried past him, he said, "I hope I'm not intruding on your dinner party."

I laughed, saying, "You are always invited, Daniel."

He knew I was serious but laughed anyway. He said he'd stopped in to tell Iris of his decision to purchase the building next door to his shop on Lake City Way NE. He said the owner was out of town and wanted to unload it to buy something in Mexico. It had been vacant for years. Daniel told me he had no idea what he would do with it. He had no debt but felt he should purchase it; his description of the place sounded perfect, with its garage bays and office.

I told him of my idea, which has been a reoccurring dream for six months or more. I was awakened at Luther's funeral by all the people's lives he had touched. He had been on a journey I'd never seen. He'd been humble and would never have discussed his charity work. I was raising children and making a home, and he was grabbing pieces of the day to be fully present with me. He was out there making sure the world was a safer place. I told Daniel I wanted to open a tire shop, make it a public statement that the new tires people got rid of for fancier ones would go as charity. Not to just anyone but to someone who had proved they honestly needed them. Gloria would know how to make that checklist. I told Daniel of Gloria and June, that we were planning a fundraiser to start off Ethan's Edge and also raise money for the Women's Shelter. I relayed what I knew of Ethan to Daniel. Somehow, we were all connected by this place right here; we'd been brought together at City Square Cemetery for those reason—to further the cause started by ones who had passed. The tire shop was a fact in my head already. I looked at Daniel, realizing this was all new to him; he didn't even have the building yet and had no idea five minutes ago what he would do with it.

But he nodded and said, "I would lease it to you for the exact cost of my mortgage payments, taxes, and insurance." Daniel was on board 100 percent.

Daniel looked at me kind of strangely, and I thought he had decided against his sudden decision. That was not it at all; he told me of his drive to west Seattle, the picnic table, Micky, and how Iris and he would go there and eat. Then Micky had shown up and had said Richard and her used to sit at that table, too, how Richard had died in a plane crash, how that entire experience had set him free. If he had gone even an hour earlier or later, that connection with Micky would not have been made, nor the story told. The detour had been a planned adventure even though he'd had no idea. It seemed as if life were directed on a schedule if you followed your instincts. He said he didn't know who Micky was but hoped he had helped her as much as she had helped him escape the pathway he had been on. It was like he'd been stuck in a loop for years.

Well, this was decided about the building. It would be a tire shop. I told Daniel if he needed any help with the paperwork to let me know. He said he would use the same attorney that Mr. Filbert had used, Cecil Collins. Daniel told me of how he had received the shop he currently owned and had not seen the attorney since the news of Mr. Filbert's passing had been delivered but still had all the contact information in the file box at home.

Daniel said he would spend a few minutes with Iris, then go home and call the agent involved and Collins to get this started in the morning. He gave me his see-through acetate business card; I realized that I knew nothing about Daniel except his first name until now, his last name is Mettenburg. The only other fact I know about Daniel is his connection to Iris. Now the picture had expanded, and we would work on something together. I would send a courier tomorrow with one of my paintings for Daniel's shop.

Daniel came back and asked if there was anything he can do for the fundraiser, said he had an ample amount of time on his hands, then turned and said he almost forgot to feed Alex. I watched as he ran to his truck, the one I did not see often. He waved as he drove off to his responsibility of Alex; I pictured a small child, wondering if it was a boy or girl. I thought of all the times I'd run off to feed the children, picking up something for a school project or one of the children, getting dinner on the table in time to fit into the evening . . . but now the urgency was to wait on my paint to dry or the store to open to buy more canvasses and supplies.

It came to mind that I should not send Daniel one of my paintings. This was a new adventure; I should paint a picture of the raccoon and send it to him. That would have meaning to both of us and would symbolize this day of joining forces.

Most of my paints were not the colors I would need. A trip to Blick Art Materials on Broadway was always an exciting event, but with the surprise of my dream becoming a reality and the unexpected stop, I was beyond thrilled to create something for both shops. With the image of the raccoon, trees, ivy, pond, and grass in my head, I headed into the store with a fresh vision. Daniel had not known that Micky could change his perspective, and I hadn't known that Daniel could change mine. We had both been on autopilot prior to our meetings, not present in our focus, having no idea of the way the day would turn.

Theodore Blake

August 2021

I ALWAYS STARTED MY DAY WITH ONE CUP OF DECAFFEINATED COFFEE SPICED UP with one shot of imported rum and a small bag of pretzels—my small addictive delicacies. There wasn't any more drinking of alcohol in my day; I just preferred to start my day off with a stunner, as I called it—never a nightcap or social drinking.

That morning, August 10th, I looked at the newspaper, which was always delivered with a tremendous thud on the front porch at precisely 5:26 a.m. My thoughts wandered to who had made front page this morning, a never-ending surprise. I always read the front-page top stories and the business section. The paper wasn't worth getting except I needed to see what businesses might need my help. I could tell from the going-out-of-business sales, the drastic sales, and other clues hidden in advertisements that gave away how desperate a business might be. I always had underground money from my vast settlement of a shady building collapse and could use my professional cover to "help" businesses that were sinking. Maybe even bring them back, over to prosperity, and I could develop some cash flow to continue the crooked mess I had created. I had honestly helped some people regain profitability. I preferred to think of it as helping and not gouging. Western Credit Services sounded legitimate, and it provided means other than a traditional lending opportunity, which these businesses would not have access to anyway. Most banks would not loan a sinking business anything.

I took my first sip of coffee and felt the burn. Lately it had been more rum than coffee in the cup, but no one knew. I looked at the front page and saw the picture of Jin Mae, a poor soul who had been found dead downtown a few days prior. The recognition hit, not of the face but of the name. I had loaned millions of dollars to Jin Mae over the years for venture capital, and it had always been paid back, but not the last six million dollars he had been warned about many times via letters. There was one problem; this Jin Mae must be a different person because it was not the man, I had been dealing with over the past few years. Was this a coincidence of the same name? My collections department would know; it was one collector whom I only had to use on rare occasions. I wasn't sure of his other business affiliations.

After reading the article in its entirety several times and filling my coffee cup up one more time, I went to my home office and matched up the names of the apartments and businesses, knowing for sure the wrong man was dead. This had never happened before; I didn't know what to do or how to find the real borrower, whom I had always assumed was Jin Mae, the man I'd known to be always reliable over the years. But now I had been set up by a thief, my ill-gotten money stolen.

Our company had strict policy on this matter and went over the terms at the beginning of each loan. We were fair and used the same approach with all clients, entering and exiting a contract. The only variation was if a payment was not made precisely on time. First, the white letter, then the peach-colored letter, then the red letter, then the loan officer whom I'd hired to initiate the loan paid a visit to the business and later the home of the delinquent business owner. The informant had reported that Jin Mae had ignored them, all the warnings not acknowledged, and he had stayed on his usual routine as if he'd never owed anything at all when in fact he was in debt. Except this Jin Mae, the dead one, was not the borrower. The Jin Mae I had reports on was not the man I had loaned millions to over the years. I did not know that piece of the story; I wondered how much more I didn't know. Feeling responsible for the murder but knowing I was not at all connected, I wondered what sort of collector I had hired. This was a man who had worked for me for two decades—had he gotten more aggressive as time went on?

Detective Muncer

August 2021

I HAD BEEN FEELING OFF THE PAST WEEK OR SO, HAD NOT BEEN ABLE TO PINPOINT the origin of my angst, the agitation growing stronger as the week rolled on. After leaving Renton and driving along the lake, I realized it was being awake in the daytime. The bright skies, the traffic, the larger grouping of humans had all taken their toll on my being. I was used to a dark city, open spaces, sidewalks with only a few inhabitants, always wondering if the person out walking in the middle of the night was up to no good. I was not fit for daily daytime life.

It was Saturday, a day I needed off, along with tomorrow. I would head north to Fremont and hide away in my upstairs cave, watching the traffic on the Aurora Bridge, listening to the hum of tires, smelling the diesel from the boats motoring through the Fremont Cut—all smells of home. I had lived there so long I could almost guess what kind of motor was on each boat, the hum and rumble as it propelled through the water.

Another thing that had been on my mind was I worked alone normally, had for years, gathering pieces of the stories that I called puzzles and bringing them to the others involved. This week, I had been working one on one with Rubio. He was a great detective and loyal friend, but that music—or lack of it—when we were together . . . and we could not agree on a genre. My mind worked on metal; that had been lacking this week. If I couldn't think, I was unable to write. Writing music would be my retirement; the producers were already asking for more lyrics, and deadlines were involved. I headed home, ready to relax with my headphones and my choice of music, cook some simple dinner while I banged my head to the music, rattling the past week out of my mind and soul.

It was only six o'clock, but I felt something was off before I arrived home. Mrs. Johnson, my landlady, had her door open, which was unusual. She was one for safety and at her age would have only opened her windows—even on a warm evening as this one—being alone. As I started the uphill climb to my residence above her in the duplex, which had been home for over twenty years, I saw the top of her head almost at the door but on the floor and the rest of her laid down perfectly as if she was napping. I ran to her—she had been good to me all those years—and radioed for immediate aid and fire, knowing she was gone. I realized I didn't know anything about her, not even her first name—she was Mrs. Johnson. I felt I should call her next of kin, felt almost like a violator as I entered her apartment, looking for a handbag or wallet. This was a place I had only been inside of a couple of times prior for maintenance issues. I found her ID and ran it for an emergency contact; there was none.

I found a stack of what looked like mail in a folder labeled important on the counter as if she had been paying her bills. She must have felt something had been off leaving one letter behind her stack of mail that seemed peculiar stating that in the event of her death, if I wished to buy the duplex, the documents were with her great-grandson, sole inheritor Everett Sunshine, with his address of the other duplex located in Wallingford. This was shocking news to me, as shocking as Mrs. Johnson's death. Everett Sunshine, the one I had looked for all those months, and he was right there, had maybe even come to this residence.

I was so wrapped up in the letter that I'd almost forgotten Mrs. Johnson was on the floor, and SFD medics were rolling up. This must be *the* Everett Sunshine we had been looking for in Iris Mortelli's case—even though he was no longer a suspect. I was saddened that I had not been home earlier to help Mrs. Evelyn Johnson, as I now knew her as. There was not a phone number for Everett—just an address. After my landlady was properly taken away, I locked up and returned to my vehicle, heading up Aurora to Green Lake Way, turning onto to North Forty-Sixth Street and turning the corner, knowing where Everett Sunshine was because the duplex was identical to my residence, both in style and Ice Cream paint and Evergreen trim. I knew these names because Mrs. Johnson had repeated them to me for two decades. "Never change the paint color," she had said on many occasions. It would be costly to do so, and the paint was stored under the stairs that I walked up daily. I knew her advice would stay with me.

I pulled up and saw there was street parking only. I was lucky to find a spot a few houses down. This was not just a notification call; Mrs. Johnson had been almost like family and the potential solving of a mystery to me were a combined reason to be there. It was somewhat confusing at the same time. I knocked.

A young man answered the door, looking at the floor, saying, "Why are you here? No one comes here."

I told him who I was, and he started saying he was not in trouble. I looked past him to the living room and saw my identical furniture from the 1970s that had to have been purchased by his great grandma, my landlady, the woman with many titles. I asked if I could come in. Everett did not say anything, just released the screen door. It slammed, and he sat in the floral 1970s rocker with well-worn wooden arms as if it was his usual spot. I asked again if I could come in; he nodded and looked away. I entered, feeling eerie, as this was my room but across town and this one was downstairs.

I notified him of Mrs. Johnson's death and made sure he knew he was not in trouble. I wasn't sure he could process the information at such a high rate of speed. He looked just like our suspect had been described, with dark, shaggy hair; black clothing; a slumped-over walk. The trench coat hung on a hook while we processed how to communicate with each other. I did not need to talk to him anymore but still wished to clear my head of his part in Iris's case. He kept saying he had to move; I assured him I was buying the other duplex and would investigate purchasing this one, too. I asked who lived upstairs, and he said he did not know. "The helper," he said a few times, seeming unsure if he should release that information to me.

I asked if I had permission to ask a few questions, and he left through a swinging saloon style door, making me wonder if he would return. Everett arrived in front of me with a sleeve of saltine crackers and two cold beers in green bottles, shoving a bottle toward me without asking if I would like one. He opened the crackers, offering me the sleeve first, saying under his breath that he was being polite, as if reminding himself.

I asked Everett about the green VW he had purchased, where he got it, and he immediately stated he would never drive again, ever. He had watched a video online showing how to drive a manual transmission, stated the purchase had been made in Seattle while visiting his great grandma, who had supplied him with weekly money. He never used a bank, instead lining his coat with cash, which explained the way the coat hung on him from the description when we were looking for him as a suspect a few years prior. He had been attending classes at a college in Tacoma for criminal justice. He loved to solve crimes on television. He pointed to the large flat-screened TV I had not seen behind the door. He did not remember who he'd gotten the car from. He knew it was wrong to drive without a license, so he'd sold the car for what he had paid so he would not be in trouble. He had no idea he had been the prime suspect in a murder case, just that he'd driven without a license and had been worried he would be caught. He'd been paranoid every day and stated this was a relief, for me to finally find him and confront him with his crime.

There was no need to upset him further, so I gave him my card, told him to call anytime, and stated I would be in touch.

He said, "I didn't do anything wrong except the driving. I had to leave school because I can't handle large spaces, spaces like the classroom and hallways that echo. I should have known that, as I did online high school. I can't even get out to get my new ID." He pulled his out, showing me that it had expired.

I told him I would help him renew online later in the week, knowing I would keep my promise to Everett. I was sure I would be back to hear his story and be of assistance. Being a landlord now, a landlord to Everett

Sunshine, who did not pay rent, could be a huge responsibility. Walking back to my car, I still wondered who lived upstairs. They were quiet or possibly not home while I'd been there. I wondered if they paid rent.

I took the reverse route home and pulled up to the curb at my duplex. It had never been a thought before, as Mrs. Johnson had always owned it. I would go home to Margo, my houseplant and only responsibility, until a few hours ago, and give her some water. Now there was Everett. These were the stories you could not make up, stories you had to follow through on. Everett could not deal with daily activities on his own; he needed me now that Mrs. Johnson was gone. With the past week playing out on such a different timetable than I was used to, and today's events, I was a bit overwhelmed. I liked that I paid rent, came home, and left as I pleased—had never had thoughts of a mortgage, taxes, or repairs. All the maintenance had been done by me since I'd moved in.

I headed into Mrs. Johnson's, still feeling wrong for doing so, but I needed the letter she'd left. Behind it was a copy of her will and a key to her safety deposit box. I thought, *this duplex is not my only responsibility, I have just inherited Everett Sunshine, an adult with limited capabilities, and another upstairs tenant.* Funny how he'd had beer and had been conscious that he had been sharing the crackers. That was the only time in all my police work that I had given a notification of death and been offered a beer and crackers. I was not sure why I'd agreed to drink it other than to close the case of Iris Mortelli in my head.

Monday, another day in the sunshine. My music writing was slacking due to the shift change. First on the list was the bank vault to get the original copy of the will and make any phone calls. That would take most of the day; people worked from home these days, and customer service was slacking. I didn't need a bank loan, as I had the life insurance money from my parents and siblings. I would gladly follow Mrs. Johnson's orders to the mark.

Next on my Monday list was to identify the blind man.

August 16th, I headed out early after a Sunday of relaxing with food and music. I had jotted down a few lyrics for future songs. I headed up Nickerson Street to US Bank and the vault that would give either peace of mind or a big hassle to my future. After presenting my police badge, the letter, and a copy of the will, they opened the safety deposit box for me. I took it out and saw there were only a few items inside: all the keys for both duplexes; the original will; deeds; my original lease, which was no longer needed; the contract for Micky Silversmith to supervise Everett; and a letter asking for me to purchase both duplexes and supervise Everett's wellbeing and trust. The last part was that no rent would come from the duplex Everett lived in. He was downstairs, and Micky, who lived upstairs, took care of Everett's daily living, grocery shopping, making sure he had his supply of black clothing, paying the bills out of an account that money was deposited into monthly, landscaping, and a cleaning service that was also provided to Everett. This would be a considerably greater experience than I had expected, but Micky would take on most of the load. I had not even thought of this situation forty-eight hours ago; how quickly life events changed. I had spent enough time in the vault thinking, taking everything from the box, and signaled I was done and locked it up. I inquired on how to close the box; I was sure there was a form.

I headed out to headquarters to determine who the blind man was and investigate Theodore Blake. Rubio and I would meet for a late lunch and compare notes. I entered headquarters, seeing Officer Metevior on the way to my office. I told him of the strange series of events that had led up to my meeting Everett Sunshine. For nearly four years, this had been a mystery to us but had never been spoken of since it didn't matter to the case anymore. Everett Sunshine had been our main suspect, and it was as if he had never existed. That mystery had been solved in one of the strangest ways I could imagine. I told Metevior of the last couple of days' events and how I'd met Everett. It seemed like after sitting with Everett, I had known him for a decade or more.

Metevior kept looking at me like I was not right in the head, saying, "No. Since when did we go from looking for a suspect, finding he didn't exist, declaring the case as solved, saying he was not guilty, to him surfacing in the most unusual way? And now you're involved with his entire life?"

I headed up to my office, not the one I'd been assigned but the one they'd placed me in for videotaping the riots last year. It had more table space, better lighting, and no one ever visited because it was not where my name tag hung. Everyone assumed it was vacant.

I found out Theodore Blake lived in Madison Park on Forty-Third Avenue East. For some reason, he did not look like what I'd imagined. I'd pictured a tall, slim man with dark hair, but that was not how he looked at all. He was short with thinning blonde hair going gray and a round face.

There was still no facial recognition on the mystery blind man. I would check with Hazel on the results that had come in so far on my way out to pay Mr. Theodore Blake a visit.

I headed out East Madison and met Rubio at the Arboretum to compare notes and make sure we rolled in together. We didn't know anything of Mr. Blake; there were no previous records or even traffic tickets, but we could assume he was capable of killing or hiring a hit man.

We rolled up at a modest house nestled between two large apartment buildings. It looked like it didn't belong in that location, as if the buildings next door had encroached on his land. The view was spectacular, but the house needed work. It was almost like no one had looked at the outside in years. The paint was peeling, the wooden screen door was slightly askew, the lawn was nonexistent except for several mounds of moss, and the sidewalk was uneven due to tree roots traveling underneath. There did not appear to be anyone home; the shades were drawn and there was no sign of a car or life. We rang the doorbell, and the screen door opened from the wind coming off the lake. It creaked and then so did the interior floor.

A small, familiar-looking man opened the door and asked, "How may I help you?"

We told him of our mission. From the smell permeating the porch when he opened the door, we could tell he was clearly a bit intoxicated at this early hour. He stated he was Theodore Blake and if he were to be honest, he'd known we would be arriving at some point soon. We asked if it was because of the firebombs. He looked confused and stated he did not know of any fires or bombs.

This was our killer, or he knew of the killer.

He held his face as he mumbled he had committed a terrible mistake—that Jim Mae on the front page of the paper was not the Jim Mae he knew. He could not live with his transgression any longer. He swore he hadn't killed anyone or authorized the killing; he felt he should stop loaning money after this mess. His loans had always been paid back after delivering threats via letters. He was not aware of any firebombs and would never use such tactics. He sincerely asked us: if he burned down a business that he had interest, in how would he then collect his funds? How could the client, who was already behind, recover?

This was the first time a loan had gotten this far behind, and it was the largest he had ever loaned. He had always trusted Jin Mae; there had been many loans issued to him and paid back on time over the years. The amount had increased with each one, as each new business had needed larger capital. Only one loan at a time was the number-one rule. He then broke down and said Jin Mae, whose picture was in the newspaper, was not the Jin Mae he knows he repeats in his inability to process where he had gone wrong. There was a rounder face and different haircut, for sure. He gestured like the Jin Mae he knew had side-swept bangs and a curl to his hair. Now he had no idea who he had been funding all those years under the alias of Jin Mae and had lost a tremendous amount of money. He asked if we could help him. He swore he had nothing to do with the murder of Jin Mae or the disappearance of his wife.

He agreed to come with us to be questioned. Before we cuffed him, he grabbed his coffee cup and made a gulping swallow, turned, and said, "I am not driving." We smelled the alcohol on him and emanating from the newly emptied cup sitting on the table. He kept repeating the color of the letters in order: "White, peach, red, and an in-person visit. White, peach, red and a visit."

We got out of the car not knowing where this would go; it seemed as if the daytime had a whole other set of crimes to solve. We entered through a metal side door. Hazel saw us from the records room and said she had news on the recognition that we had left her to attend to earlier. We thanked her and took the photo and information from her as we entered the questioning room, which had a small table and two chairs, plus another in the corner.

Theodore jumped up as we advised him to remain seated. He pointed with his nose since he was still cuffed, stating that the picture we had just received was of the misleading Jin Mae, the man he'd loaned the money to. This man was Dae Woods, who resided on Twelfth Avenue East.

We booked and held Mr. Blake on probable cause, unsure of what he knew or had been capable of. We sent officers to bring in Dae Woods. All of this unfolded before us—such a complex crime with many facets—and we had not even addressed the issues of the firebombs.

While we waited, we called Ha Yoon and asked what else she knew of Dae Woods and his recent activity. She said she had not spoken to him in years—not after the time he'd upset Jin Mae. We did not reveal any more information to her, as we were not sure if she was in on this complicated set of crimes.

Officers arrived at Dae Woods's elegant third-floor condo, finding no one home and his parking spot empty. Building security let them in under the pretense of urgency. Dae Woods was not there; the only thing left in the unit besides furniture and dishes was a coatrack with a blond, short, curly wig and a white cane folded up next to it. Dae had side-stepped this crime, had days ahead of us and financial resources to keep going, most likely five million dollars or more.

We issued a warrant and searched the basically empty condo. There were receipts in the two-drawer wooden file cabinet for all the purchased ingredients used in the firebombs. He had even used them as deductible expenses on his taxes. Dae was a meticulous record-keeper. He'd left notes as to why each person had been targeted, their usual schedules to the moment, home addresses, spouses' names. How he had hacked into Theodore Blake's computer system. He had posed as the enforcer of back payments and had access anytime he wanted through his computer. He also left a letter stating he would not be found and was guilty of all the crimes, stating they all had to pay so he could keep borrowing and live out his plan of leaving. If Jin Mae had just borrowed in the first place, he would have received a kickback and would Dae never have had to borrow any money himself. This was all Jin Mae's fault; he'd been too honest, and he'd had to pay for it. Dae wrote that he had set up a new identity months ago and would never be located with his well-thought-out plan and miles behind him. He was surely gone; the dresser drawers were empty, the closet held only attached steel hangers, the refrigerator was empty and clean. If it were not for the furniture, we would never have known anyone had lived there. I wasn't sure what the courts would decide, but I would say this upscale unit now belonged to Theodore Blake.

We went back to headquarters, asked Theodore Blake some questions about our new leads in the investigation, released him, and arranged a ride home for him since he was still in no shape to drive.

Then we went to see Ha Yoon. She was devastated, fearful to go back home, and said she would not return there. She wished to pack her house, put it all in storage, sell the nail salons and apartment, and relocate. She could not go on as she'd been before without her Jin Mae. The lives of innocent people had been upturned and taken for the benefit of Dae Woods.

June

September 2021

THE WEATHER WAS STILL WARM; LABOR DAY HAD PASSED, AND SCHOOL BUSSES were rolling again. I had always loved to watch the children as they ran or dragged their feet on the way to a bus stop. You had to be strong to go to the same corner five days a week and repeat the routine as a child. Not having any of my own and not living in one location for any substantial length of time, I had not had the privilege of watching any children grow up. Here, there were a few bus stops for what I assumed were all grades. They came about half an hour apart with various heights of children; the smaller had a parent trailing behind, unable to keep up with the unleashed energy. It was amazing how much a child could grow in one year; you would see them in red pants, and suddenly those pants showed the socks.

I thought of Gloria's grandchild that would arrive a few months from now. It made me happy that she had children to enjoy life with, and they were now in the process of sharing a new life. I had never seen anyone grow from birth to adult, didn't even remember the last time I'd held a baby. I would ask today if it would be all right for me to buy baby Luther a gift. Simone and Gloria would be coming for lunch, a meal during which we could sit and relax, not one at the Women's Shelter, where we had working lunches. I had never been as busy as this past spring and summer had allowed me to be all the activity had given me exercise of my mind and body, friendships, goals toward a common cause, and the opportunity to meet new people and needs that I'd never imagined existed. Looking back, six months ago, I wondered where I had been all those years, day to day, continent to continent, base to base, home to home, job to job, but all mostly conducted on military orders. Life had been an adventure until Charles's death just over eighteen months ago. My job at Blossom Up had allowed me to get out and had set me on the path to this group of wonderful, giving people. They had much more experience in this industry of helping, and I was honored to be included.

Sandy knew something was happening. No one ever came over, and I had put her toys up and the blankets away. I had cooked more food than would be needed for us, had cut up some chicken and placed it on her plate in the refrigerator for later, had brought flowers home, and had set the table outside, hoping the weather stayed warm enough for our lunch.

Gloria arrived first, finding parking with no trouble. She was confident in all her activities having lived in Seattle most of her life. Simone arrived shortly after with a huge bag of chips, saying they were her favorite. We ate outside with the view of Lake Union.

Gloria said, "I bet I could see my place with a telescope."

I told her of my same thoughts when I'd visited her. She laughed.

Simone said laughing, "No one can see my home from here."

I thought I knew them well enough now and didn't feel as naïve as I had before I'd visited Simone. I told them of my day at the park prior to our first visit. We all talked of crime, pop-up tent cities, broken-out windows, businesses leaving town, and our love of Seattle. We were not giving up on this mission. If enough people got on board with Ethan's Edge, Insulated Business Incubator, and the other businesses and services we provided, it would make a difference for generations. If the parents going through the programs knew what to do instead of how they'd done it before, they would be able to teach the next generation. It seemed as if far too many came into the system uneducated or with so much pressure on them from unmet life needs, ones they had no idea how to meet, that other small activities got swept under the rug and the family could not excel in any area. Many times, the family separated, which created another barrier with an absent parent or two, and the children were lost in the mix of survival. It was difficult to complete homework while moving from place to place, living in a tent, or couch surfing. New rules every time there was a move, prized possessions left behind, food and clothing scarce, meals sometimes missed.

Our program's steps provided the way to stability and personal responsibility, taught about the fears of failure and success, and showed how to handle things that were not in a person's control, like if you applied for a job and did not get hired, what you could learn from that experience. We also taught budgeting and promoted entertainment and relaxation. These were two things people living in survival mode did not have the skills for. Even if they were just sitting around all day, it might have come from fear or anxiety of not knowing what to do. When the needs of a stable place to sleep and a steady supply of food were provided as well as a path to make their own choices within parameters, as long as they were moving forward to self-sufficiency, progress began to happen. It was overwhelming to start this process from a car or tent, especially when children were involved. Many hid in shame and did not know there were places to help them gain employment, get free of addiction, and provide childcare. Sadly, for as many people who wanted help, there were more who did not. Deep down, they did, but the system they were working at the moment was easier to stay in than to take the steps to be free. It was a system they were used to, and they knew what to expect.

Gloria, Simone, and I ate outside until a gust of wind took our napkins away. We went in, facing the view of the lake, watching the sailboats glide by. The sails puffed out and pushed the boats forward, toward Simone's neighborhood. Sandy sat on Gloria's lap, purring.

Simone spoke of her grandson, who was about to be born. I asked about purchasing a gift and if they had a registry. Simone's face lit up at my interest. I told them of my earlier thoughts of never having watched anyone grow up and my desire to remain childless. She said she would make sure I got invited to the baby shower; it had probably been over fifty years since I had attended a baby shower.

Thinking back, it had been in Italy about 1958, when Charles and I had been newly married. We'd been new to each other and had never discussed having children but figured that was the way things happened. It did not happen for us, nor did we ever talk about it. We just kept moving. I did not have the desire to have children, but it seemed shameful to say that out loud back then, as almost everyone had a child or two. I would see them come into the stores I worked at on base all over the world; the mothers tried to get clothing that fit the children and that the children would wear. Most wanted a toy and not clothing, but their mother had to work with a budget in mind with the categories clothing, food, emergencies, entertainment. I thought life was freeing without children and never envied the parents. Facing this now and never admitting this before, back then I was secretly thankful for not having any children because I did not know if I would have the skills to cook, tend to them, purchase the needed items, or know what to do at all. Charles and I were easy for each other to live with and creating another human might have not been right for us with as quickly and frequently as we uprooted with Charles's Air Force career. Sandy had been our first pet, and she had found us right here in Seattle.

I was happy to be part of the baby shower, at least invited. I told Simone if she needed help with any planning, I was here for her.

Gloria said, "I had a boy, so I would love to help, too."

Simone called Cora's mom to find out if there was a baby shower planned; she discovered there was not. We set out a tentative plan and researched games online, talked about food and prizes, and waited for Simone to talk to Cora to see what her wishes were and how many people she would like to invite. That would depend on where it would be held. We had three houses: mine, Simone's, and Gloria's. Also, the Women's Shelter had many event rooms that could be used.

We had covered new ideas and much ground today, finalizing many points on our adventure with Ethan's Edge, having lunch, deepening friendship, planning a baby shower, and scheduling the next meeting. Gloria asked Sandy if she could get up. Simone got her bag and keys. I told them how thankful I was for their friendship and I was looking forward to our next visit, knowing it would be a lot of work to gather auction items, sort them for the online site, and organize with the web designer and photographer. This had been the perfect leisurely lunch; we had all been to one another's houses and had covered a great deal of ground.

Carl Sr.

September 2021

THE DAY WAS FINALLY HERE, THE ONE I HAD DREADED, HAVING TO FACE WHAT my body had done to itself. The symptoms I'd ignored for so long and knowing I should have sought medical help sooner. Garry and I had lived on the third floor for many years; the stairs had been my preference, initially two at a time. I called it my gym in the stairwell. Almost in one day last year, so suddenly, I could hardly pull my body up them, resting between each floor. Then I had to start taking the elevator. Now I was fortunate to get out at all, never on my own.

At the hospital, Garry pulled up at the circular patient drop-off, found a wheelchair, and pushed me to my appointments—but he was not permitted to stay due to all the new Covid regulations. Then he came back to get me when they called, as I was too exhausted and ill to use a phone.

I had asked Gloria and Carl , my only grandson, to come for a visit. I wasn't sure either knew about Garry and me, but that did not matter at this point. Neither one had been to my residence prior to this day; I wasn't even sure they knew where I lived. We'd always met in public places, the shelter or someone else's house, as they'd never had a reason to be here. Today required privacy, and I did not think I would be able to get out to meet anyone. I was mentally and physically spent, even though it was one of my better days. This meeting was scheduled in between my treatments, which happened a few days apart. This way, I would not be too sick to sit up and tell of my plans. I knew I would not be here on this Earth much longer and needed to communicate my wishes.

When Gloria and Carl arrived, I could see they had clearly taken the stairs from their heavy breathing, something I watched and envied. I was glad that Gloria was still in pristine shape; this meant she had not sat idle during the pandemic as so many had. I wondered what she did to stay in shape. I had not seen her since Ethan's funeral nearly a year ago, three seasons to be exact. I recalled her poise and scan of the crowd on that horrific day, a gathering of teenagers who should never have had to be in a cemetery, dealing with the loss of Ethan, a friend, an acquaintance, a face they recognized. I was certain many had skipped school to be there. I had undoubtedly been surprised at the number of attendees wandering as if they'd been lost, not knowing how to act, having never been in this situation before. Thinking back, I realized Ethan had never brought any friends around me, and I had not heard of any, but by the looks of his funeral, he'd been known and loved.

I had to face this day. I came back from daydreaming the nightmare of Ethan's funeral into the other dreaded situation that involved my demise and that needed to be explained now or never. Garry sat off to the side, being supportive, knowing what I had to say since he was living with it. I asked Gloria and Carl to sit. Our views all showed other buildings and nothing extravagant like either of theirs—no water out of these windows.

Gloria must have been on edge, sensing this was going to be a serious visit, because she started talking about the brick-making process involved in building the different structures across from us. I was surprised that she knew this information. She came back to us with a quick start, asking how I was as she was seated properly, relaxing in the green velvet curved chair in the corner, the chair that was for decoration and company.

I was in my recliner with a fleece blanket over my feet, clearly ill. I started by introducing Garry; Carl and Gloria nodded politely. Gloria thought, *That is the man from the park, the one Carl Sr. kissed last year, and he does not know what I saw that day.* Then I updated the two of them on my chemo schedule—which wasn't working—told them both of my finances, even though I didn't need to, as it wasn't their business. But I was making it so. Gloria had gotten our exceptional penthouse in the divorce and half of everything else; she had always been fair and had never even asked why I'd left. She knew now, although it didn't seem to be a shock to her. Maybe she had always suspected my preferences. I explained that after the divorce, I had bought a small condo; met Garry; sold the condo a couple of years later; bought the sports car; paid off Garry's modest flat, as we called it; and had invested the rest for Ethan's college fund as a surprise to my family.

Besides telling of my health, now that Ethan was not able to use this money, I wanted advice since both Carl III and Gloria worked in social services as to where to invest this college fund for the future of someone or something else. They looked at each other, smiling, and said, "Go ahead," at the same time. There wasn't any thinking about this between them; I knew they would know what to do. Both responded at the same time that they had done the exact same thing, as Gloria had had her fund for Ethan's college and so had Carl . They were almost giddy, as they had not revealed this to each other prior to this afternoon. I was glad I had invited them here and was happy to be a part of whatever ideas they had next. Relief was in the house at the moment; a weight lifted off me. I had told them of my money and health. I realized again they were my family and accepted me as I was, sick or not, living with them or not. They loved me unconditionally.

Gloria had Carl take the floor for the next hour, explaining Ethan's Edge. Pulling out his phone, he showed pictures of the logo and explained the progress they had made with donations, city officials, various agencies, and how they were planning on opening the program on November 12th. It would be a three-month program with community projects to start. The program would help with school organization and tutoring, and after graduating the program, the participants would agree to stay on another three months or more, either to help the next group coming in or to continue with what they'd been doing. It would start with a dozen teens who were willing to sacrifice at least two hours a week to better themselves and their community. There would also be an employment or trade school program set up for after graduation with some scholarship funding; this was where all our money could be invested.

I might not have been able to save Ethan, but this would rescue some of the ones heading down the wrong path, the path Ethan had stayed off but had gotten caught up in at the same time. I was suddenly overjoyed for the first time since Ethan had been gone. With all the restrictions and my cancer, I was limited in contact and had grieved almost alone. Garry was always a support to me but had not ever known Ethan. Grief was a private matter and was done differently by everyone. Knowing the past year and Ethan's life had not been for any reason, I was immediately tired and requested for Garry to help me lie down, as I could no longer sit and feel relief at the progress of this conversation.

Gloria and Carl thanked me for the invitation, said thoughts and prayers would be sent my way, and then left. I pictured them on the stairs departing from here, the first and last of their visits—I knew this deep in my heart, as I did not have a great deal of time left. They were both shocked to learn of my health today, I was sure. I had never been sick a day in my life; neither one had seen me unable to get up prior to this, needing help with anything. I was humbled by their acceptance of me, even after I'd left my marriage to Gloria as I had. Deep down I always felt I should have stayed, but it seemed Gloria had fared well. She was a survivor and had helped many people in the community get back on the right track. *This was the right decision, to ask them here*, I thought as I dozed off, looking at the comparison of bricks on all the buildings out the bedroom window, each one a different height and color. But all I could see was one small space from my window—three buildings. I wondered how much longer I had to compare them, brick upon brick, as I drifted off.

Ya Hoon

I STAYED AT THE HOTEL, FEELING I HAD BEEN SAFE SO FAR. I HIRED A MOVING company to pack my house, called all the nail salons and explained that I was selling, and asked all the head technicians if they were interested in purchasing the salon they managed. If so, I gave the name and address of our attorney to complete the contract. I knew these nail techs did not have cash outright to purchase and offered a payment plan. I also asked Mr. Clark to see to the liquidation of our home and the apartment buildings.

It had been nearly a month since I had been here and Jin Mae gone, and most items had sold, contracts signed, money transferred into our joint account, which would take months to close probate. We had a will stating if something happened to either one of us, everything would go to the living spouse. The courts were backed up, my bank account was full, and the attorney stated I needed to buy something bigger, flip on a 1031 tax exchange to not be stuck paying an enormous amount in taxes. He suggested an office building or something easy to handle from afar. I had not wanted any responsibility, just to sit somewhere warm and recover from my husband's death. I had never been interested in business as Jin Mae had been. He'd had it down to a science. I would come home, and he would speak of the next adventure like it was trading marbles, always sure of his ways and investments, very precise in his calculations and profitable.

I asked Mr. Clark how long I had before I must decide, realizing at that moment I didn't even know his first name or where his office was, as we communicated by email with his secretary relaying messages and telephone. I wondered if Jin Mae had been there in person. That had not been my job; it had been Jin Mae who had made these decisions, and I had agreed by choice, trusting him all these years. I was uncomfortable in this role, sitting in a hotel room, knowing I needed to leave but feeling unsafe to venture out even for a meal. My entire life had been taken from me in one instant. I still did not have transportation and needed to figure that out soon; the police didn't think it was safe to bring my vehicle here if Dae was on the run. I would have thought he'd be long gone with that kind of money, but I still needed to remain safe, so I needed to purchase another car. I would call Mr. Clark after looking his address up and have him sell my existing vehicle and locate something else.

Tuesday morning, Mr. Clark returned my call. I knew that every minute was being logged and charged since I had requested a call back. He got to the point without formalities as any good attorney would. He didn't want to know how I was anyway—that was not the point of his call. He said he had an idea about a car and wanted to know if I was open to a trade versus cash and a new purchase. He knew a place where when someone passed away, the family would bring their vehicle or if they did not wish to trade a vehicle in on another car, they would donate the older one. He suggested that I donate Jin Mae's SUV and my car; in return, I would receive a vehicle and a tax-deductible donation receipt. I was sure I would like to do this by the time he was finished speaking. I asked him to arrange for Jin Mae's and my vehicle to be towed to this place from the police impound lot. Two innocent people with two innocent vehicles in police custody for nearly a month. I wondered if they charged for tows and storage as a traditional towing yard would. There was only one stipulation: I wished to be there to clear out the vehicles before anyone touched them, and I wanted to have a few options of vehicles to inspect for trade. I wondered what other legal ventures Mr. Clark had been involved in since he knew of this arrangement.

I received an email from the Clark Law Firm that afternoon with the address and the name of the person to meet tomorrow at 3:00 p.m. I realized at that point I did not have transportation, something I should have thought of when I'd stated I wanted to meet there, wherever "there" was. I thought I would download the Uber app and set up an account, then realized maybe I should use a taxi and pay cash. I wasn't sure why this felt safer other than there would be no record of my travel.

I could not sleep that night, tossing and turning all night long, knowing I would be closer to Jin Mae—or at least his possessions—than I had been in nearly a month since as all his earthly goods were now in storage. My thoughts kept traveling to what he could have left in the car; I was sure not much since it had been ransacked, driven by the someone who had stolen it, and abandoned after the electric charge had been used up, prior to police impound.

I got up at 10:00 a.m., much later than usual, but was thankful for the sleep and time I would not have to wait to leave. At 2:15 p.m. I waited outside for my taxi. I had not been out in approximately three weeks. The air was hot, and the breeze felt peculiar, not conditioned as inside. I was extra aware of my surroundings and safety. My taxi pulled up, and I gave the driver the address of Charlene's Place in south Seattle. He said he had been there before, had taken a mother and her children there in the middle of the night. She'd had a bag and eye so damaged it wouldn't open. He looked at me, wondering if I was escaping something horrible. I saw his concern and told him I was donating a car, my car. He looked surprised that I was in a taxi and not driving myself. I didn't want to explain since a piece of the story would not cover the depth of reality.

He told me of his knowledge of the establishment; they did many things for the city, used to be right downtown and then had expanded here a few years ago. He was not sure of when the move had happened. "It is a right pretty place," he said.

I felt this taxi driver had been appointed to take me on the beginning of my new journey. This was day one. As I eased into my new life, I didn't notice anything on our trip. We arrived at a newly painted building with modern windows, black chain-link fencing, a circular drive for easy delivery and drop off. People were all over; I saw as we pulled in children played tag and basketball in the back. Then the taxi driver's story and this place came together: this was a women's shelter. These people were trying to return life to normalcy or betterment—not much different from my situation, just a varied storyline. Or maybe not.

I knew at that instant, before even entering the building, that I was not donating one car but two and would not take another back for myself. I could afford my own vehicle; I would take a taxi to a dealership on the way back to my hotel. The decision was made before I exited the taxi, giving the driver a big enough tip for a free ride to someone else.

I was brought back to reality as I heard my name, wondering who would know me here, but then remembering I had an appointment. I saw a tall gentleman with keys in his hand.

He said, "I'm Carl. Nancy, our director, is not available to meet with you due to an emergency. Can you please follow me to the vehicles?"

I walked beside him, along a manicured sidewalk, then I saw Jin Mae's SUV and my vehicle next to each other. I grabbed the keys from Carl. Without a word, I jumped into my familiar car. I would not have been able to speak even if I'd had to.

He asked, "Should I give you some time?"

I nodded. He handed me his card, instructing me to call or text when I was ready. I felt that he knew about this stuff—grief, they called it, the waves that came washing over me without any control on my part. One second, I was numb; the next, devastated. I was in an unfamiliar place with my well-known vehicles parked side by side for the last time, and I was paralyzed, thinking I might sleep here tonight. I didn't know how much time had passed by the time I was through with my vehicle, embarrassed by the coffee in the cup holder, and then was on to Jin Mae's. I was scared to open the door. As I did, I saw nothing—not a slip of paper, a piece of garbage, a registration, a stereo, not his red dangly gem from the rear-view mirror, nothing. What had I been expecting? I'd known the vehicle had been gone through not just by the thieves but the police. I'd been expecting a mess, trash from homeless people living in it, drugs, food wrappers, but there was nothing. I was shocked, almost disappointed. I wanted something to be mad about, but with his car fully intact and clean, I did not have that privilege.

I sat in the driver's seat, knowing this was where Jin Mae had sat repeatedly; knowing he had not been the last to be there broke me even more. It was his car still, with his name on the title. I rose and closed the door, emotions overtaking me. I leaned on the car, regaining my composure and strength.

I texted Carl and walked toward the front door. He exited almost as soon as I texted, as if he had been waiting for me. He had probably been watching since he wasn't here for any other reason only because Nancy was unavailable. He asked if I would like to look at the cars, stating they had brought a few here for me to view. I felt obligated to look; immediately, I saw one like I'd had in high school, just a newer version. It was blue, like the one I had wanted and hadn't gotten. I knew I would purchase that vehicle. I was supposed to leave two and get one, but I would make a donation to Charlene's Place and drive away with my bag of stuff from my old life in this shiny blue car.

Carl said, "Are you sure that is the one you want? We haven't even started it yet, and you haven't even opened the door."

I nodded, overwhelmed with the newness. He took me inside; the place was clean and hopping with activity. He explained the back-to-school supplies, clothing, shoes, and backpacks would be handed out tomorrow morning. I asked how many children would benefit; he said probably about two hundred or more. He was not sure, as he worked at the downtown location and didn't have as much direct contact with this location since Gloria had retired. I asked of Gloria and her position, and Carl told his story, Gloria being his grandmother. I suddenly needed to know if there was something I could do tomorrow to help with the back-to-school function. His face lit up, and he nodded. I saw there was something keeping him from talking; I waited until he spoke. He told me there were a few spots on the programs that needed help, one being tomorrow's event, and then told me all about Ethan's Edge. I didn't know the significance of that name; also, they were looking to expand into off-site living after individuals and families completed the programs. I wrote a large check, larger than needed for the car. I now owned a shiny blue Camaro; unlike anything I would have purchased as Jin Mae's wife but that is not who I am any longer.

I drove back to the hotel with new ideas and a promise of returning to Charlene's Place tomorrow at 8:00 a.m. to assist. I didn't know what I was getting myself into, but it felt like it was aligned for me. I emailed the attorney, telling him of the car trades and new purchase.

I ordered a late dinner of grilled cheese and tomato soup, took a long shower, watched the lights come on around the lake, and felt calmer than I had been all month, picturing my newly acquired car, which was just one piece of the renovated life I was creating. I didn't know if it was right to feel this way so soon after Jin Mae's death, but I could not sit in this hotel room forever being idle. I was used to seeing people every day, not just room service and the police with their scheduled updates. I had been alone except for police visits for nearly thirty days. I now owned a car older than the two I'd traded in. I sat up on the edge of the chair, and it hit me: where would I register this car to? I was currently homeless. Tomorrow, I would need to check the mail at the post office, rent another box at a place that had a street address, and start there. I had no idea where I would live. I had not pictured what life would look like after this room, and after one three-hour outing, I was forced with being on track with reality again. This was the day to be awakened. Then I realized the police had not released Jin Mae's body for burial. He could not continue to stay at the morgue, a place I would have never sent him myself, as I would have had a proper funeral for him. That was something I needed to arrange tomorrow after my event. Carl had said nine o'clock to noon; I hoped I had the right experience for this.

I woke up promptly at 6:00 a.m., thinking I was going to the nail salon before opening my eyes. I opened them and saw I was still at the hotel, but why 6:00 a.m.? That was my old life. Then I saw the shiny blue key fob and quickly remembered yesterday's events, which felt right. I had a new blue Camaro and an appointment to help with the school supplies. I showered and dressed, wondering if I was overdressed for this event. I ate a muffin and slowly sipped tea until it was time to leave. I was out the door, and, in the car, which was uncomfortably unfamiliar until the stereo popped on, playing my favorite hits from high school as I had preset my preferences last night.

I realized I had no idea where I was going since I had not paid attention yesterday in the taxi or on the way back. I researched my GPS settings, as I had never used it before, and plugged in the address of Charlene's Place. I arrived and saw many more people here than yesterday. There was no one I recognized; I always scanned crowds now for Dae or the other inhabitants of the sidewalk where Jin Mae had last walked. Feeling it was safe to exit the car, I headed toward the entrance. Inside, there was a commotion; people were sorting items from a list and assembling shoes, clothing, supplies, and backpacks. One for each child registered. They would start arriving in one hour. I watched, looking for my spot in the organized chaos.

A gray-haired lady in blue jeans approached me, saying her name was June and that Carl would be here shortly. She turned to me and said, "Would you like to help me in the shoe department?"

I nodded, having no idea what my duties would be, also wishing I had blue jeans that were not in storage. During my time at the event, I only saw Carl across the way; he waved a couple of times. From 9:00 a.m. to noon, we helped every person that had signed up. Some went back upstairs with smiles, while others went out the door to the bus or their waiting ride. At the end, we were left with a large room and many tired volunteers.

June asked if I was ready to go home or would I like to help disassemble the tables and have lunch in the meeting room. I was ready to be there full time, in a place that felt safe, with people I at least recognized after such a busy morning. We were all tired and hungry, which I had not been for so long that it was a like new feeling. I smelled lasagna and garlic bread and saw ginger ale on the table; there was also a large bowl of salad. It was all served buffet style. Food had not smelled this good since Jin Mae had been taken from me. I got in line, and Carl thanked me for showing up and my service. I filled my plate and sat at the back of the table by myself. June sat with me; she said she had not seen me before. They passed around a sign-up sheet for some events coming up, and I signed up for them all. June asked if I had heard of Ethan's Edge. I told her I had, just yesterday briefly. She explained what the program would do and invited me to the meeting with Gloria, Simone, and Carl. She gave me the address of the downtown Women's Shelter, the date, and the time.

I realized at that moment I was a part of something, something different. I had been accepted into this group of giving people. They didn't know me or what I had been through, and I realized my new life had begun. I wondered who Charlene was and why this place was named for her. As I left, after saying my goodbyes and thanking this group, I saw a plaque with Charlene Barton's name and picture by the door. I knew someone was missing her and was grateful her legacy lived on. I realized that I was in a place in my life that I could help, too. I was breathing, suddenly feeling alive.

I headed to South Center Mall and purchased a small wardrobe: jeans, t-shirts, a sweatshirt, and tennis shoes. Mine were all in storage and might stay there for a while, maybe forever. My new life felt as if it needed new items to propel forward. I missed Jin Mae more than I could explain, but there was nothing I could change. Death was maybe easier than divorce. In death, it was final, and there was no way back no matter what—no one to see, no one to have regrets with. In divorce, the tables could turn in many directions, especially with children involved. You must see the one you'd lost, the lost love that you'd rejected or who had rejected you, and there would be unstated violations laid out with each meeting. I always thought that was a harsh statement, but now that I was on the other side of Jin Mae's death, I could see how Kristen one of the nail techs who had relayed the story above after her husband had passed away could compare the two. I hated that Jin Mae, an innocent man, was dead—the man I loved—but being in this situation, with him gone from me, I could see better how she'd made that comparison after her husband had passed away and her friend had gotten a divorce.

Knowing I had never planned a funeral prior to this, I called Mr. Clark for advice. He shared his knowledge. Plots in the ground, urns to take home, internment of ashes. He said he'd set up an appointment for me at City Square Cemetery for tomorrow at 11:00 a.m. since the investigation was over. He stated that he would call the morgue today and that Jin Mae would need closure soon, reminding me he was still at the morgue. I was thinking he was at the same location as his birth. *Please, do not use the word "morgue."*

I rested that evening, knowing tomorrow would be another of the highest hurdles to conquer in this unfortunate mess I had been thrown into.

I got to the cemetery at about 10:30 a.m.; I'd wanted to make sure this was a suitable resting place for my Jin Mae. I had never been inside the gates before and had just seen the view of headstones and various seasonal decorations from the road. I drove through; it was extensive, with beautiful grounds, greenery at every turn, flowers sprinkled among the graves at random. I pictured myself bringing flowers. This felt off; I had never bought Jin Mae flowers. I drove to the lower part and saw highly decorated graves: tall ones, some with benches, others flat on the ground, another with a sign saying, "This space available"—advertisement in the cemetery . . . I would not have imagined that prior to my tour today. Some were so full of décor that I could not see the names. I got out and walked a bit, realizing I didn't know what to put on a headstone or even what kind to purchase—the variety was endless.

As I returned to my car, I saw a flock of mallard ducks fly to a pond. I drove over, got out, and watched their antics, realizing almost too late that I had a meeting to attend. One about my wishes for my murdered husband. That didn't seem correct.

I entered through the mortuary's front doors, knowing there were bodies stored in there—not my Jin Mae, not yet. I was met by Darian, who said he had been expecting me. He was an easy-going person fully fitted for this occupation. I wondered what in life had given him these skills and traits. He ushered me to a private room with five overstuffed chairs and an extremely large table, one fit for a family. I had to stretch across the table to pass the catalog back and forth. Whoever thought I would be shopping out of a catalog for a casket? I decided on a full burial, a white casket with red interior. Jin Mae had picked out a white car and had loved the color red—we had used it in all our signage. I chose a flat headstone with a vase including the words inscribed:

Jin Mae
March 17, 1974 – August 5, 2021
Loving husband, innocent man

I did not know how else for the world to see that my Jin Mae had not been guilty of anything but was dead. He was not someone who belonged here at the cemetery, but I would be forced to go home without him.

I left, explaining that a check would be sent by the attorney, Jin Mae's body would be transferred here, and there would be no funeral. My only request was I be notified of the burial, as I wished to attend. Shaking Darian's hand at the door, I heard my name. Fearful when that happened now, as I turned, I saw Carl. He was with another man who wore work clothing, like from an auto shop. I was not in the mindset to speak after the meeting I'd just exited. Carl saw I was not okay, not trying to invade my space. But he introduced me to Bob, Bob Barton. I recognized the name but wasn't sure where I'd heard it. Then Carl told me this was Charlene's husband—the Charlene that Charlene's Place had been named for. For being in a city of so many people, I kept winding up in this circle, which showed me a direction I'd had no idea of a few days ago.

Carl explained he was here to talk to Bob about Ethan's Edge, to bring flowers and visit Ethan's grave. I had not known yesterday, having just met him, that Carl was experiencing grief, but I'd known there was something. I still didn't know who Ethan was—maybe a son, brother, father, cousin, or friend.

I headed home, knowing I'd picked all the right choices in plot, casket, and headstone. Thinking of the vase and the first bouquet of flowers I would buy for my husband or were they for me as he was no longer here. The decision to not have a funeral was due to the fact that the businesspeople we associated with were the only people who knew I was alive. I did not want the event to be public but just for me.

I was glad Carl had been there and that I had met Bob. It was a visit that had taken the sting off my meeting with Darian.

I reached the hotel again. It was becoming my home; that had been fine when I'd never left, but now I came and went, and it felt off to live in a hotel. I would change that tomorrow. Maybe an apartment or an extended stay, but not here. I'd started here when Jin Mae's murder had not yet been solved and I'd possibly been a suspect with no options on my end. That was no longer the case, so I must move on.

I ate the same dinner as two nights ago, grilled cheese and tomato soup, booked a plain-looking room online for thirty days, and knew I would be leaving here in sixteen hours. I packed all my clothing, glad I'd kept the bags, as my suitcase was not large enough since my latest purchases, and lay down to watch television, falling asleep within minutes.

The next morning, I woke as usual, got breakfast, and requested a cart for check-out. I had been there for forty-two days. They asked if my stay had been pleasurable. *How do I answer that?* My husband had been murdered, the killer was on the loose, and the only people I had seen up until a couple of days ago were hotel staff and the police. I nodded as I looked over the counter into an office. A uniformed hotel employee was on the phone, urgently and loudly wishing to speak with Detective Muncer. They thought I was guilty and fleeing. I helped them out by rushing to my car, quickly loading all my bags in the trunk, and speeding off. *Let them think what they want.* They thought I was escaping police custody, but I was escaping that part of my life forever, I hoped.

I headed north on I-5, hoping the kitchenette would be sufficient for thirty days. I stopped at the grocery store, longing to cook, tired of room service. I loaded my cart with the items I'd eaten when I'd had a house, then put most of them back. I returned to the produce aisle, seeing all the colors of fresh fruit, gathering fruit and vegetables of every color, a loaf of healthy bread, cheese, butter, and cream. I wished to cook for a whole day, something I had never done before. I grabbed a log of refrigerated cookie dough, hoping there would be a place to bake them. I took the bags to the car, wondering what had come over me. Jin Mae had done most of our meal preparation and cooking, and I had been the recipient of his wonderful dishes. I had purchased food without thought or recipe. I was one to not waste, so this needed to be figured out.

The checking-in process was not the hard part. Since it was a basic hotel and not an upscale one, I did not have help or carts. They'd failed to mention my room was upstairs, in the back, without a view. I was rethinking my decision to have come here at all. I entered the office and saw a small, gray, scruffy looking dog scratching its butt on the desk.

A man who saw me staring said, "Don't mind him. I'll be right back."

A lady in a flowered snap-down robe with holes where the pockets had ripped away, her grayed underwear showing in spots, arrived and shoved a well-worn key across the counter. I told her I had decided to cancel my vacation and needed a refund. She pushed a slip of coffee-stained yellow paper across the counter and said, "Well, fill it out." Under her breath, I heard her say, "Another one too good for our fine establishment—out-of-towners."

I filled out the paper, knowing I would watch my credit card bill closely for the refund, pushed the key back across the counter, and requested a copy of the yellow form. I left knowing my groceries needed a home quickly in this heat. I found an Airbnb close to downtown at three times the price but perfect for my month-long stay. I checked in without any trouble, parked right at the door, loaded my groceries and clothes into the small apartment, sat on the blue striped sofa, and the next thing I knew, it was dark outside; I must have fallen asleep. Moving out, declining the motel, shopping, moving in, and establishing something more different than I had ever imagined must have been exhausting.

I could not call room service here. I could order in but got in the car and went through a drive-through for a burger, something I had not had in over a month and normally didn't eat. I savored the fries in the parking lot. I watched the Seattle nightlife go by in colorful clothing, people smiling, laughing, talking. I missed Jin Mae; people-watching had been our thing. These were all pieces of my former life. I did not smile, laugh, or talk anymore except about police cases or funerals. Normalcy had been taken away with Jin Mae's death. I thought about my new residence and did not even recall if there was a television.

I looked up and saw Dae across the street, talking to a lady in a familiar way. He leaned over her with his arm resting on the doorway of the closed business. I did not believe it was him; why would he be there? Thinking my eyes were playing tricks on me. I called Detective Muncer, who answered on the first ring and said he'd heard I'd moved even though that wasn't his business. I interrupted him, saying Dae was on the northeast corner of Sixth and Lenora. I gave his description: he wore a navy-blue, silk, pinstriped business suit and white dress shirt. He was talking to a short lady wearing a white dress with pink flowers and a black patent leather crossbody purse.

I made sure I got the description right. This was the only control I'd had in the case so far, and it was all on me. I assured him I was not in danger where I was, as Dae was not aware I was there or what I drove. I heard Muncer on the radio dispatching units to this location.

Suddenly, the weight of the entire nightmare hit me. The fries were too heavy, and I threw up in the bag containing my uneaten burger.

I saw police units at the end of each block; Dae was unaware, as his only focus was the unsuspecting beautiful lady. I wondered what their relationship was if there was any at all. The police came from every direction as soon as enough were in place to safely apprehend him. He was taken into custody without a fuss, the beautiful lady in tears, not believing his arrest. I watched from across the street as my husband's killer was loaded in the back of the police car, seeing the streetlight reflect off his expensive suit, wishing to get out and yell, possibly beat on the car, but I knew Dae should not be aware of my presence. I knew that my being there that evening had been appointed. I sat waiting; the car was confining with all my recent events, filling up with my thoughts and emotions. As Dae was taken away, I unfolded my body from the seat, suddenly hungry again, threw my vomit and old meal away, walked up to the window, and ordered another one, knowing I would eat this one, knowing this was the start of life out of fear and back to normalcy whatever that meant.

My phone rang, an unexpected event these days. It was Muncer, thanking me and asking why I'd been there. Typical detective questions. I told him I'd been hungry and thanked him for getting everyone in place for the arrest. He inquired about Jin Mae's funeral, saying he had signed off on the release of his body this afternoon. I told him where and when it would be, just not that it would only be the two of us. He let me know if I needed anything to please call and to hang on to his cell number. He said he was glad I was safe with Dae off the street; he would not be released with so many charges.

I returned to the apartment, parked right in front again, and felt a load lifted off me. I had just become fully aware that I was not in danger any longer and was free of my old house, businesses, marriage, free not by choice but a decision made by someone else's greed. I drifted off lying on top of the hand quilted bedspread with blocks of various types of ducks on them, me only recognizing the green headed mallard.

I woke to the sound of a ship's horn, feeling as if I were at home in my house on Puget Sound but knowing I was not there, now, nor would I ever be. The horn had echoed through crevices between brick buildings and up alleyways, around dumpsters, into my new life. I could not sleep with the knowledge of having no direction, my mind was used to order. I emailed Mr. Clark, telling him of my move and the burial, and asked what else I might need to do. Those were the only plans I had for the day, and it was 4:23 a.m., too early for a walk or even watch normal television, I did not need to be informed of the commute or crime.

I did not know what to do with myself today, a new day in a new life and a new area. I called Carl, wanting more involvement with the shelter and this multifaceted organization; that was the only thing I knew at that moment. He returned my call a couple hours later and agreed to meet after lunch if I could come downtown to the Women's Shelter. I was excited to have my recently purchased car and a place to take it. I ate a peach, a slice of bread, and a pinch of shredded cheese and headed out. It was too early to meet Carl, but I could see the city.

As I headed up Elliott Avenue and crossed the Magnolia Bridge, I ended at Discovery Park, wondering why I had been too busy all these years to have never been there. Hiking along the scenic trail, attempting to reach the West Point Lighthouse, I looked at my phone and saw it was 1:00 p.m. I was hungry with all the exertion; it seemed since my move I was consistently hungry with weeks of unrest behind me. I headed back to the car and stopped at a convenience store for some donuts and water.

I arrived at the Women's Shelter and parked on the street in front, not aware everyone entered through the back. After knocking it appeared no one was here, I called Carl, and he opened the front door, leading into an expanse of rooms and doors in every direction. The building appeared to be vacant. He said he was the only person there today since no programs were running. I suddenly felt in the way and that I was disturbing his work, even though he did not act as if this were the case. He seemed happy for the company, asking if I wished to have a tour. We went upstairs, downstairs, to the main floor, and finally his office with the placard stating "Insulated Business Incubator" on the door. I asked what he did and what upcoming projects I could help with other than the ones I'd signed up for at Charlene's Place, then also asked about Bob and Charlene. Carl was gracious in his answers, lifting up Bob and Charlene and their unending character, telling of the work both had done here and then Bob at Charlene's Place. He told me of Ethan's Edge and the people involved—Gloria, Simone, June, and himself—also that there would be a meeting in the near future to put some pieces in place. I told him that June had invited me. He said he'd planned on inviting me to attend to see if there was anything that would be a good fit for my schedule. I thought, *What schedule? I just want to help.* He did not know of my recently cleared calendar.

I asked him more about the transitional housing they were trying to develop and what stage in the process that were at. He said they wished to purchase an apartment complex with at least two hundred units and use 25 percent of the units for temporary housing once people were at a specific point in the program. It could be work or school, but they had to be able to contribute some to rent, on a sliding fee scale. Some would use the skills they'd had prior to becoming homeless to renovate apartments. There would be a childcare facility on-site for all residents, and monthly meetings would be required to stay on with the program. The goal was to finish the required fields and be on their own. They could stay where they were but would need to pay full rent or move on. The other units would all be rentable apartment like any other complex. It would be called The Pathway. They hoped to get the project in place by next year; they were looking for donors, available properties close by, and cooperating clientele. Of course, once purchased, the apartment complex would have maximum occupancy so they might need to offer incentives for some current residents to move so they could start intended their long-term goal as a steppingstone to financial stability of the residents in the program.

I asked who Ethan was, and Carl suddenly had a stone face. I knew I had overstepped my bounds. He stopped, swallowed a few times, looked back up at me, and smiled, the largest grin. He turned a picture around of a teenaged boy who was lanky and blond—a beautiful-faced boy with sunshine in his eyes. He told me of Ethan just as he'd told me the other stories, but with an extreme amount of passion. I apologized for asking, and he said, "No need, you would not have asked if you hadn't seen me with Bob and with all the talk of Ethan's Edge."

He asked why I'd been at the funeral home. I told Carl of Jin Mae, Dae, and last night's arrest. I told him I was homeless due to selling my house to keep me out of danger, why I'd wanted to donate mine and Jin Mae's cars, that I was somewhere for thirty days but that was as far as I had gotten. It had only been just over a month, Jin Mae's body had just been released, a funeral had just been planned with no one going except me and Detective Muncer. Carl knew Muncer; he had worked on Ethan's murder, too. I was surprised the two men knew each other. Somehow this day fit into the pathway of my new life.

I rose to leave, asking if Carl would walk me out. We exited through the back, and he showed me the designated parking for my next trip here. I told him of my intentions to invest in The Pathway and possibly live there as a paying resident. Carl looked shocked. With an uncontainable smile, he walked around front to my car with me. We said our goodbyes on common ground, knowing there was a substantial amount of work to be done.

Carl Sr.

October 2021

I KNEW FROM THE AMOUNT OF STRENGTH THAT HAD LEFT MY BODY THAT IT WAS time, time to be admitted somewhere, a place I knew but was not willing to voice. This plan had been in place since my diagnosis. I was entirely too much work for Garry and the nurse, Naomi, who visited a few times a week, giving Garry a bit of time to get away, out and about, with me in his head. Garry was my main caregiver, and he was not a medical person at all; he'd been a cement truck driver until his injury a few years back. I was surprised it wasn't him who was sick with all the dust he had been breathing for so many years, but I was thankful for Garry and his health. He had been my rock in this horrific illness, my driver, my meal provider when I was able to eat, the listener of my woes, someone to sit quietly with me and watch me breathe while I dozed off. He was incredibly patient with me and this situation.

Garry loaded me up in the car after our hour-long trip down the stairs, stopping halfway through each flight so I could regain my strength and breath. He drove us away from our home in silence, both of us knowing I would never be back—but that was left unspoken, for now and most likely forever. I took careful notice of the brickwork and windows of our neighboring buildings, watching the bricks all the way to admitting. It was something to focus on other than the sad reality of this—whatever it was called. I was not sure if Garry could come with me on the end of my journey. I needed him, but according to law, we were nothing to each other. We were not married, not family, just people who knew each other, and he was the person to contact in case of an emergency.

I arrived at the emergency room entrance, quickly being wheeled away due to my critical condition and Covid. Garry followed along without anyone saying his presence was not required; it was vital to me for him to be there. We took the elevator to the third floor, just like home. Garry was still by my side; neither of us risked talking about him being asked to leave. They came in one by one, blood, vitals, insurance, resources, dietary. Hours later, hospice, the final group, entered with a set regimen. They did not say that there wasn't much time left for me, but we all knew that was the case, the unspoken truth. Their decision was to leave me here at Swedish Hospital for the duration of my stay. They said many other things; I heard Covid, danger, transport.

I kept my eyes on Garry, not knowing when the last time would be that I would see his face. He caught me staring in fear of being alone; he smiled, his broad, beaming grin being brave for both of us. I did not have an ounce of courage at this moment—only negative amounts of energy. Moving my fingers seemed tiresome. I was overjoyed and genuinely happy we had met, had spent all these years together, and that I had been able to help him through his disability after his accident. Somehow, that fact helped me now, knowing Garry had given so much more to me than I could ever reciprocate.

They turned to Garry, explaining procedures, and voicing that he was not needed anymore in a polite way. But they did not know that he was required by me to be here. I was positive this was the last time I would see his face and asked for some private time with him. I told them he was my brother and family, and there was no need to push him out after all the care he'd given me. We were given one hour; then they explained that only video conferences would be permitted until the last moments of life. That was not enough for me; my heart felt as if it would be still the moment, he walked out that door. He was my support system and had been through all of this. I wished to be checked out of there, and Garry and I discussed this option. Knowing I could not climb the endless flights of stairs to our home, we thought of a motel, somewhere flat, but we both knew we would not be able to handle that. I was far too gone at this point; soon I would not be walking, and what if I fell? We were grasping straws for the inevitable. Our hour was up; it seemed like it had only been a minute. We had wasted it by talking about what we couldn't do and should have been talking of us, our life, appreciation, the future, even if by video chat. I did not even know if Garry understood how to use the computer, as I had not seen him use it before. I gave him Carl's phone number for instruction if he couldn't figure it out.

We worry through life, and at the end, we grasp whatever tidbits are available to fuss over, but if we have any options at all, we should be appreciative and tell others how we feel—something that is missed many times.

The nurse came in and said it was time for Garry to leave. He laid his hand on mine, looked at me with tears not quite falling, being brave like always, squeezed my hand, and using my last name said, "Wilson, I have it from here. Love from me to you forever." He turned and left before the tears fell, but as he made a right out of the door and looked back, I saw that his cheeks were covered in sheets of tears. He was weeping for me, for us, for him.

I was alone in this quiet place, so dehydrated that I wasn't sure I had tears. All I heard were soft shoes on the vinyl floor. My insides were turned around; my heart was broken. I wished to see out the window and watch Garry drive away, knowing that I had no idea where he was parked or would depart from. I envisioned his route home, to his house (no longer ours), his last visit to this hospital with me if they did not catch my final moments in time.

I was fearful of dying in my sleep, knowing I would not have family or Garry here. Carl Jr was still in Florida, and I was not sure anyone knew I was here. How would they get notified? I located my phone and saw Garry had packed my charger. I sent a text to everyone I thought should know of my location and status, being weak I copied and pasted repeatedly.

The nurse entered, wanting more blood, and explained the rules like I was unable to do anything on my own. There was an alarm on my bed to monitor if I got up. She pointed out the view of downtown, asking if I would like anything to read or eat. I was incapable of talking with Garry having just left and my reality having just suddenly changed. I was on my own.

It reminded me of when my friend George had called many years ago, asking for my help loading his German Shepherd up. He had said, "It is time, and the dog is unable to walk." We'd loaded the dog up in the back of his station wagon, placing it carefully on a blanket, then had driven ever so carefully to the vet for George's dog to be put down. I'd been there for George that day, a sad day indeed. George had loved that dog. After that had happened, George would always look behind him as if to make sure the dog was there, a habit he had picked up after acquiring the dog. Now it was me, only they wouldn't just give me a shot—they would allow my body to be taken over by this horrible disease and give out one small step at a time. I did not understand death or how this disease worked, but that was exactly what was happening. I would be here until I was not. I wondered who would keep in communication with me, my voice too soft for the traditional phone. Texting was best.

My phone brought me back from the dark space my thoughts had carried me to. It was Carl , then Carl Jr. my only son and Gloria. All let me know they were there for me in any way possible, said they would set up video chats. All asked me to call or text anytime, day or night. I knew those three were all I had besides Garry, and out of those four people here on this earth, no one could save me. I was grateful for their support and love; I just regretted my actions of not getting medical treatment earlier, ignoring all the warning signs, thinking I could control this, that it was nothing. I was not handling this well at all. It was out of my control and out of the doctor's control; my body had rejected all the treatments. I would die right here, overlooking the city of Seattle, the place I had lived forever but not long enough. As I drifted off, my thoughts wandered to places they shouldn't: how long would I be here in this state, deteriorating? Would I wake up from my first nap here? Did I want to, or was I done? The question was, was my body done?

Gloria

October 2021

It had been three months since Carl had been over with the proposal of Ethan's Edge opening and almost a year since my sweet Ethan had passed into eternity. For some reason, when I thought of Ethan, the vision of him lying on the concrete parking space downtown came to mind. I erased it; this was not the image I would like. He had always tried to help, and some troubled girl had gotten him killed. Pearl had been on the train when it had happened and hadn't even known, but if she had just left Ethan out of her escape route, he would still be with us. After his death, we found out he'd been considering a college on the East Coast, but he would still be here on this earth instead of at City Square Cemetery along with Charlene and my dearest friend, Rachelle. If it had not been for Rachelle's passing on and that hot August evening that had led me to her grave, I would never have met Bob, who worked at the cemetery, or found out the mystery of his lovely wife, Charlene, who had disappeared suddenly from our organization. Bob had been a blessing to the Women's Shelter and now Charlene's Place, even though I had not overseen either organization in ten months I still felt connected.

I could not believe that 2021 was coming to a close. The days were shorter, and the leaves were exceptionally beautiful this year, more than ever—or possibly I was paying closer attention. Maybe I'd had time to relax and enjoy the scenery that Seattle provided since my retirement. I took my daily walks to Tashkent Park as often as the weather allowed. I enjoyed reading the plaques on the statues and seeing the painted tiles, even though I had read them at least one hundred times now as if I knew them as friends. It was a comfort to be able to get out and not be in a gathering. A freeing sensation, a place to go think and watch people, which were amazing, without a thought to their movements, walking along, swinging their arms so quickly I thought they would come out of their sockets, feet turned in, others out. It made me want to try all their antics. Secretly I did in the park, and they had already passed on the sidewalk. They never knew I was imitating them. I saw my friend the red-headed woodpecker; he was a loyal creature. I always gave him kind words to pass onto someone else.

I thought of Carl Sr. and all our years together. I wished to see him again after our last meeting where he told us of his illness. I needed to set up a Zoom call before it was too late. It hit me finally that he was in the hospital and not doing well, no longer able to go home. I was not his wife any longer and had not been for years, so they didn't tell me anything. Carl Jr., his next of kin, was far away in Florida, living his warm life; he informed me with phone calls. Carl wasn't even allowed in to see him. Covid had made it a strict no-visitor policy, especially with critically ill and vulnerable individuals. That would be my priority today: to call and see about setting up a video conference after my walk to the park.

I returned home faster than usual, still wearing my summer wardrobe and now knowing this would be the day to switch my clothing to warmer attire. The cold wind whipped up the hill, bringing an assortment of dancing leaves along its route. I had not even been able to eat my lunch at the park today with the wind blowing the last of the brown leaves off the branches of the stately oak tree I loved so much. I enjoyed my midday experiences there, wrapping my sandwich in wax paper, seeing the dogs who knew me and now expected treats; it was like I had friends, only they were canine.

I also enjoyed ordering groceries online and having them delivered, even the dog treats.

When I returned home, I called Swedish Hospital and asked for the charge nurse in the CCU where Carl Sr. was. After an unusually long hold time, she informed me that Zoom calls were only on Tuesdays between 10:00 a.m. and noon, with the patient's permission, unless it was an end-of-life situation. It was a speech that had been prepared and given many times a day, I was sure, so impersonal. It was Monday, so I set up a time for tomorrow at 10:45 a.m. She added that there was a strict time limit of ten minutes for each conference, ten minutes for the last time I might talk to him. It felt wrong and being force into this method chosen by someone else.

Carl and I video-chatted about the final steps of opening Ethan's Edge. The plan was to open next month, on the anniversary of Ethan's death. Detective Muncer, Bob Barton, Kimber a resident at the shelter long ago, and many of the shelter donors would be in attendance. We also hoped for teens who wished to participate in this new adventure to attend. The goal was to have teens go through a year or more of the program, starting at three months and then coming alongside the next group to help them participate and become a solid piece of the community. We had already gotten some national attention and planned to duplicate this program as it grew. The city was in need of these valuable teens to clean up graffiti, mow lawns, run errands, provide friendship and respect to those in need. In turn, they would gain self-respect, city recognition, work experience, community service requirements for high school and college scholarships. I never thought I would say this in my eleven months of grieving, but this was something good and lasting that could come out of Ethan's murder.

My thoughts were deep this evening while making Carl Sr.'s favorite pumpkin pancakes for dinner in honor of him, something I had not done since he'd suddenly moved many years ago. I made a list of what to say during our ten minutes of video we would have tomorrow, knowing we might not speak of anything on that list. My heart wanted to make sure he knew I wished him peace in all the time that was left for him. I had no idea of how long that would be, moments or years, I just realized no one had told me how dire this situation was, and I had not asked. Isolation from this pandemic had given me much reflection on myself and my life, not others, as my focus had been before. Also, the year of grief and retirement was almost overwhelming to the ninety-two years I had been granted so far to enjoy life on this earth. If it weren't for Carl Sr., there would not have been the rest of the Carls that I'd had the pleasure and responsibility of raising and enjoying all these years. Ethan would not have come into existence in my life, either.

I knew that no matter what had happened with me and Carl Sr., he needed to know I was truly thankful for his part in our family. There would be no talk of anything else—just gratitude for a well-blessed life and family. In my former profession at the Women's Shelter, I'd seen too many go astray and not be able to find their way back to family. So many things left unsaid, undone. If we could figure out when the exact moment was that life went off course, it would be easier. Being able to offer Ethan's Edge as one of the various programs the shelter could use to possibly catch young people and show them their value before they went off-kilter and carried too big of a load to come back from.

I thought of Lorena, Ethan's mom. She'd had it all but had to go back to her ways. Something wasn't healed. There were too many court dates and fines. Hearing how unacceptable they were not being able to keep up with it all had become overwhelming and looked as if it was impossible to return from. I had not heard of her in over a year; I wondered if she was still around, alive for that matter. She'd had such shame in showing her face to us last, I'd seen, although we had never showed her anything except love. The shame came from within her. We had never judged her actions, had only protected Ethan. If she were high or with her drug crowd, she wasn't allowed to visit. If not, she'd had all the visitation she wanted. I knew Carl would take them all to dinner at fun locations on the waterfront not too long after she'd left. She would meet them there, and then as her drug habits took over more of her being, she wouldn't show up, so Carl stopped asking and told her if she wished to see Ethan, she could let him know. Carl and Ethan adjusted the sails of life to her antics but still moved forward, Ethan always proud to have both his parents at school performances and science shows— "Just like a real family," he would say. He always gave her plenty of notice to clean up for any events. I often wondered if she had attended his graduation; she had been invited, but we'd had no way to contact her after Ethan's death, and as far as I knew, she had not been seen since, nor did she know of Ethan's passing. A mother should know . . . maybe she, deep down, did know by intuition.

I was on edge and didn't sleep well through the night. The city had its established noises, which were normally background sounds for me, but that night, I heard each one, separated them, added them all back together, and wondered if they each happened every night.

The next morning, I carefully dressed in something I knew Carl Sr. would like, my US flag shirt that I seldom wore but knew it pleased him, as he was always patriotic. I was online early so as not to miss this important meeting. It was time to see Carl Sr.; the nurse came on and said he was not doing well but wished to speak to me in private. He was sitting up, more like propped up between puffy white pillows that reminded me of marshmallows. He wore a gown. It had been many years since I had seen him in bed or this relaxed; it was probably due to the pain medicine. He had always walked around with his slight tilt to the right, almost like he was starting to bend into a "C." I pictured him putting on his tan safari hat, as he had called it, going on adventure, getting out of his new sports car, but this was not how he was now, not at this moment or maybe ever again. No possessions would matter. Right now, our conversation was what mattered.

He could barely speak for lack of air; he said choice words and wanted me to tell the story. The stories of our life, of buying our condo, of bringing Carl Jr. home from the hospital when he'd been born. Stories that made us a family. Stories of the trip we'd taken to the ocean before we'd had a child and the Coast Guard had caught us in a spot we'd thought was secluded, the blanket disappearing into the sand from our frolicking. These were the things Carl Sr. required in his possible last visit with me. Our lives had been delicately woven and intertwined for many decades. He said the word "love" so low I could barely hear, but I knew he was telling me he loved me. I responded with a genuine feeling of love, words I had not told him in many years.

My last words to him, with tears escaping my eyes, were, "I love you, Carl Sr. Thank you."

Our time was cut off by the hospital's automatic system, the conversation so precisely set in motion. I was grateful we hadn't been in midsentence, that I had gotten it all out.

At 11:01 a.m. on October 22nd, just over twenty-four hours since our conversation, Carl Jr. called and informed me that his dad was gone, passed away. It felt strange that he had been alone, and we could not be there to help usher him to the other side. Carl Jr. said he would fly in tomorrow to make arrangements. I told him the arrangements had been made years ago—unless Carl Sr. had changed them. I also told Carl Jr who the man was that should be notified; I wished to be the one to make that call to Garry. I was saddened by this news but knew in my heart I had made peace with him, a peace that had always been portrayed at past events but had never been spoken of, so neither of us had known the other's actual thoughts and feelings. There would have to be a celebration of Carl Sr.'s life. Of course, Bonsai Baked Beans would be on the menu.

Bob at City Square Cemetery would be extremely saddened by this call. As head of the grounds and functional events, he preferred to dig the graves of anyone he knew himself. Carl Sr. had been special to Bob due to all the dealings of the shelter and the annex of Charlene's Place. That was another call I would make not out of obligation but to a friend. These calls were becoming frequent lately; it seemed as if I had just made the calls of Ethan, and now this, Carl Sr.

Detective Muncer

October 2021

THE WEATHER WAS CHANGING, A SURE SIGN OF WINTER BEING AROUND THE CORNER. Autumn was a time of blowing out the heat and dust left behind by summer. The department made me wear this dress clothing; wind whipped through and up the legs like I was not wearing anything at all. The nights were worse—or so I thought, until I was called in at 9:00 a.m. again for a heist that had happened overnight. It had been very similar to Pearl's mode of operation. I could see the stink rising from this mess before I even set foot onsite on East Terrace Street. The empty, running delivery truck was at the scene, no driver in sight. Keys were in the ignition, there was a lock on the roller door, the lift was down, and it was blocking traffic. The city had put up detour signs.

The bomb squad was on the way; I had beat them here. All buildings in close proximity had been evacuated prior to my summons for investigation. The bomb squad checked the truck, which looked as if it would take off downhill. They were under it, using a drone to look on top. They checked the lock on the roll-down door, had no way of knowing if a detonation device would be triggered when they opened a door or turned off the ignition. They cut the lock on the back, slowly raised the door, and found the cargo space empty. There was cardboard and plastic packaging present, but nothing else. Relief was heard across the radio and from anyone close enough to observe the scene as held in breath was released. They used a pole-type tool to open the driver's door, which did not trigger an explosion, and turned the vehicle off, all without the event of an explosion. The truck had simply been left in the road, abandoned with the motor on.

After running the plate found under the front seat up in the springs, we discovered they did not belong to this box truck at all but were registered to a Ford F-250. I ran the VIN and found the truck was registered out of Bakersfield, California, to a corporation called Transport West. The plate belonged to Rizzo Loman.

I got back to the station with only one clue—that this abandoned truck was possibly connected to Pearl Swanson, Bender George, Esmerelda Martin, and Rayner Martin—and I already knew it had direct associations to Rizzo Loman. Why would it be abandoned in the road between eight or ten multi-storied apartment buildings with so many eyes to watch the transaction? Was it Rizzo who had left it there?

I returned to the site to watch the vicinity, seeing many trucks staging for loading and unloading to various local businesses. This would have been observed as a normal occurrence in the area, but after seeing where the truck had been abandoned, I knew there was a second truck that the load had been transferred to. It had been backed right up to this one, the gates had been lifted at the same height, and all merchandise had been transferred, hours ahead of the real possessor of this load and us. Whoever had taken the merchandise had not cared about the truck or who was attached to it—only the product being taken.

After my last outing and investigation, I ran the name of Transport West. The truck might have been licensed out of Bakersfield, but the business was out of Tempe, Arizona, and belonged to Danna Martin. I pictured her lying face; it was the lady I had just visited in June who owned this business and a truck—not a semi, like she had stated her husband, Michael, drove, but a box truck. I'd known at the time of my visit there had to be more to her story but had had no proof. Now I wondered how many trucks they had that they could afford to just leave one in the middle of the road in Seattle. This had been laid in my path to solve the murders of Esmerelda Martin and Rayner Martin, to figure out who the drugs stashed by Rayner in Torrance belonged to, to investigate if Ohm It Up had been supplying an underground racket or if they were an actual victim of theft from an inside source. They could have also just been selling a high volume of product at an extreme discount to someone either connected to the riots or being forced into it by people higher up in the crime ring. In addition to that investigation, I needed to figure out how Bender George, Rizzo Loman, and Pearl Swanson were connected to this multi-faceted ring of profit for so many. I would suspect thieves were thieving thieves and turning product into cash and drugs, all done under a cover of a legal business, right out in the open, like I'd seen on First and Marion not long ago.

Searching the cameras in the neighborhood where the abandoned truck had been located, I saw that at 4:16 a.m., an unmarked white box truck—considerably smaller than the abandoned one—had headed down Boren Avenue, turning west on Yesler Way, north on First Avenue, and stopping at Marion, right where I had spotted Rizzo and where Bender had confronted me last summer. Not one sighting, arrest, or complaint for the three suspects for nearly four months, and now one of them had slipped up and left a truck with a license plate connecting them to no crime at all. Their only error was the plate from the F-250 installed on the abandoned vehicle belonging to Rizzo Loman, who did not even own any vehicles or possess a driver's license, at least not in the nine western states that I had checked.

I went through the proper channels and waited on information, telling no one except the judge of my suspicions so as not to tip them off. With a case as sizable as this, I didn't know who might be working which angle and who would benefit from a small lead. I wanted to get into that third-story office space before anyone else had a chance to investigate. I had been on this group of individuals for years now. I suspected finding all three of my suspects sleeping with their stolen goods at this early hour. The warrant came through quicker than I'd expected due to the colossal aspect of the case as well as the manpower and cost it had taken for the city of Seattle and various other places across the western United States.

I gathered a trusted team, and we surrounded the building, entering from the rear, having undercover in front in the event that Rizzo, Pearl, or Bender were looking out of the top-right corner office onto the street below. With the restoration complete on the exterior front and scaffolding down, the cover was not there as it had been at the beginning of summer. It was a walk up, mostly offices that were not open at 7:00 a.m. No one saw us as we took the staircases as quietly as a group of well-armed and heavily geared men could. At the last red ornate carpeted flight of stairs, we turned to see the door, the portal to our arrest and knocked once, announcing our surprise arrival. There was not an answer, nor did I expect anyone to open the door and invite us in. We heard the hundred-year-old wood crack and saw the lock disable as we breached the door that had never asked for this treatment. Instantaneously, the door behind us opened to reveal an elderly man who said he was glad that they were gone, that he just wanted to sleep, had lived here more than seventy years, been the only resident of this building. He'd been grandfathered in and was not leaving; he asked us to not break his door down.

We knew that Rizzo, Pearl, and Bender had moved on, but we entered anyway. We saw the same cardboard and plastic wrap as had been left in the abandoned truck; sour candy wrappers; a see through makeup bag, probably belonging to Pearl; and garbage, just garbage all over like no one ever took it out—a pizza box here, a paper plate there. They were one step ahead of us. Of course, they'd had the wee hours of the night to load their new truck, gather their belongings from this office, and clear out of town. A heist setup just like Pearl had done in the past. Knowing every detail, she had experience regarding where to intervene and who to play. Someone else did the actual crime; she then swooped in like a vulture and stole from them. They felt foolish to have been double-crossed by their leader, someone who had so meticulously taught them the art of burglary and whom they had trusted.

I wondered how much danger the individuals who'd been driving the now-abandoned truck were in now. Had they let them go? Highly unlikely. Killed them? That was unlikely, too; Pearl did not do her own killing—she just got people killed in her aftermath. They had either been kidnapped or were on the loose and paid off, never speaking of this incident and not directly tied to it. Pearl liked to use people who were not experienced to do her dirty work then turned on them. They thought they were moving up in the ranks of criminal activity, but they were out of the scheme either by death or fear once she was done with them. She was heartless in her crimes, which did not look as if she was involved since the person, she ripped off was the actual burglar and would not talk unless they had reason to. Conscience would not be on their list of traits.

Daniel

October 2021

THE LEAVES HAD TURNED ON THE MAPLE TREE OUT FRONT, SOON TO FALL, AND gave me exercise via my ridding my parking lot of them. I had bought the building next door, had talked to Simone about my purchase, and had made promise to her of a rental space. She was making flyers, applying for licensing, and putting the word out about needing safe, new, and used tires. This was a determined project for her to open the new tire shop in Luther's legacy.

I was on the same schedule, just owned a bigger piece of real estate and had a vision to help. The building had been cleaned, painted, and inspected prior to my purchase; even the underground tanks had been dug up at the owner's expense. It was a rectangular space with four large bays, an office, and a restroom. It would need furniture, but that was probably not up to me since Simone would be the shop owner.

I walked over to look in the window of my building, not believing I owned it; owning either place was not something I would have imagined ten years ago, when I'd been just trying to keep a roof over my head and a meal in front of me. I decided I must celebrate, go for lunch somewhere. I locked up and headed away from the city center, not knowing exactly where I was going. I spotted the small deli on the right that I had eaten at before. I entered; got my usual American club sandwich, chips, and an iced tea; returned to the car, as there were only three small tables available, and I wasn't comfortable in a space that confined; and decided to eat back at the shop.

As I started to back out, I saw her, Micky. She was with a guy dressed in black, unlike her, with her flowered outfit and flowing knee-length sweater. I stayed where I was and watched; in record speed, she ran in and out with two large sandwiches, juggling the drinks. The gentleman sitting in the car didn't help at all as she set the drinks on top, opened the door, and climbed in, flinging the sandwiches in the back seat as if in a hurry. He didn't even lift his head or hand to help; he appeared to be focusing on a game or a phone, like he was not even there. She got everything set like she hasn't been expecting his help, put the car in gear, and started off. I decided to stay where I was and not approach. I did not wish her any trouble. She would have to drive by me to exit the parking lot; if she saw me and wished to say hello, she would.

She started to head out, looked at me, and backed up. "Daniel," she said. She was as shocked to see me as I'd been to see her. I was pleased that she had remembered my name and used it. She was late for an appointment for Everett she says but ripped a piece of the sandwich bag off and wrote down her number. She said, "I've been thinking of you." Then she was gone.

Now I had a decision to make: to call or not. I knew I would but wasn't sure when. Micky must have felt this would be okay with Richard, so it must be fine with Iris, too.

At 2:37 a.m., I was sitting up prior to coming to a realization about Everett. Somewhere deep inside my subconscious, I'd known. Everett was Everett Sunshine, who had been connected to Iris's murder back when I'd been a suspect, too. I dug out Muncer's phone number and called to leave a message. He answered—something I had not been expecting, I was not even sure of what to say, ask, or accuse. Even though it was not his fault, I needed somewhere to vent this discovery. I'd been planning on leaving a message for him to return my call.

I came back to reality, knowing it was not the time to call anyone as he asked, "Daniel, are you okay? How can I help you?"

I told him of Micky and Everett, knowing by the description this had to be him, asking if they had ever contacted Everett since looking for him. He reminded me that Everett didn't have anything to do with the murder and was not a suspect, then proceeded to tell me he did not know where Everett Sunshine was unit a few weeks ago. His knowledge of Everett had just happened recently and was quite unexpectant he also stated that Micky was an upstanding lady whom he had not met yet but knew of.

I was shocked that I was on the phone with the investigating detective at nearly 3:00 a.m. I thanked him for his time, hung up, and knew sleep would be elusive the rest of the night now that I had knowledge of Everett long after actually needing it. And to have seen him, feet away, after years of looking for him—now I wondered why he was so important to me. Just as I was not a suspect any longer, neither was Everett Sunshine.

Detective Muncer

October 2021

I FELT I HAD BEEN IN DENIAL AND SLACKING ON MY DUTIES TO MRS. JOHNSON AND her wishes. The reasoning I gave was it is taking a while for the will to go through probate. Truthfully, I had not returned to the second duplex, made sure Everett was fine, or found out who Micky was. Also, I needed to figure out how the bills were paid and where the money transferred from to ensure Everett would be okay. I thought of our beer and crackers, remembering how I'd promised to help him with his ID card. I called, asking when a good time for him would be. He said anytime, as he did his best to not go anywhere. I asked if Micky could attend our meeting, and a text arrived on my phone.

Everett said, "I sent you, her number. She wouldn't mind since she gave it to a boy, she met at the sandwich shop."

I got off the phone with Everett, amused by his speech patterns, observances, and the secret he had shared—and now I wondered who the boy was. I was growing fond of him even if I had only seen him once. He had been a small part of my life for four years now, one being as a suspect in a murder, two and a half just wondering where he'd disappeared to, and now I was his guardian.

I called Micky, explaining who I was.

She said, "Oh yeah, beer and crackers, as Everett refers to you." The things we were known for. She also said, "Everett does not share his beer or saltines with anyone. You must be really special."

I'd been the person to deliver the news of his grandmother's passing, and we now had a bond. She had probably told him stories of me since I had lived in her apartment since about the time Everett had been born. Everett had avoided me at all costs since he had driven without a license that one time.

I made plans to meet with Micky and Everett the following day, offering to bring lunch. After I asked what they would like, Micky said, "Everett likes anything with a cheeseburger." I knew I was taking on an adult who needed care but was thankful I could help and for Micky, who seemed flexible and understood Everett well.

I arrived at noon on the dot parking right in front. Micky ran out to my cruiser, unaware that I was with the police department; she thought possibly something was wrong. I informed her I was just here to have lunch and talk to them. She helped me carry in the drinks; I'd gotten three different kinds, all that I liked so it would be okay whichever I ended up with. Everett picked the orange soda first, Micky the lemon lime, and I was left with the cola, which was my favorite. Everett got right into eating. His old ID lay on the table. He said he was prepared for my visit, pointing at the ID and saying quietly that he could follow directions. He was overjoyed that I had come back to see him, as he did not get visitors.

We got through lunch, and Micky explained what her role was in Everett's life. Everett nodded in agreement, and I realized I was just a glorified financial manager for them and the person of contact if there was something they could not handle. We agreed to meet monthly to start with and at any other time as needed. They were both a pleasure to meet with and appeared to have a system set in place that worked for them.

I accessed the state licensing site on my personal tablet, set Everett up with an account, and explained that he would probably need to go in person on the next renewal.

He started yelling, "Micky and you can take me!"

Everett was relieved he could stay home today and for five more years on this task. I rose to leave, and Everett shook my hand, saying, "Thank you for helping me. Not everyone can."

After my job and all the insane mess that humans created, I was suddenly overwhelmed with gratitude at my part in helping Everett and his recognition of my menial help. I was grateful for meeting Micky. I pulled away from the duplicate duplex feeling peaceful and more settled than I had felt in years. This was my pseudo family; I already cared for them.

Daniel

❧

November 2021

THE WIND WHIPPED THROUGH THE TREES. THIS WAS THE FIRST YEAR I HAD OWNED the building next door. My shop was on level ground, but there was an embankment with tall maple trees over the new tire shop. The further I got into life with more property and business affiliation, the more there was to think about. The trees were on someone else's land. I would make contact and find out what their plan was, if any, so their trees did not fall on my new building and the leaves quit filling up my parking lot. The slippery leaves were a liability to me as a business owner.

Simone was still setting up shop and hoped to be moved in by January. She would call it Luther's Tire and Wheel. She had delivered artwork yesterday: two identical paintings of a raccoon, one for my shop and one for hers. There was a note attached to the back of each one about our meeting over the death of a loved one and how this had come about with the raccoon eating her fries.

I had been pondering the idea of calling Micky, if for nothing else but to find out who Everett was. I know that was Everett Sunshine; would I meet him and hear the rest of the story or was it simply to heal? So far, my meeting with Micky at Alki Beach had released me from Iris enough to even think of making this call. A couple months ago, I would have never called. Truthfully, I probably would not now if it weren't for my curiosity of Everett. The slip of torn sandwich bag had sat in the old wooden bowl with my keys since I'd received it a couple weeks back. She undoubtedly thought I would not be calling.

My cell phone, which almost never got used, was in my pocket. I knew if I did not call now, I never would, and I felt it was important to me and everyone involved for this meeting to take place. The call was supposed to lead to meeting up with Micky for coffee or lunch. I hoped Everett would not be there; I wasn't sure why I thought he would. Maybe it was the way their relationship had appeared. I texted, told her who I was, and asked when a good time would be to call. She responded promptly and said in about an hour. It was now 2:00 p.m. on Saturday. The shop would close at three o'clock, so I would call when I got home. This seemed drawn out; maybe I should have just called instead of using my "polite" stall tactic.

I was setting the alarm and walking out the door when my phone rang; it was Micky. She said her plans had suddenly changed and she only had a few minutes; she was basically on call most days, as I had suspected. She wanted to check in, maybe set a time to meet if that worked for me. We agreed to meet at the sandwich shop tomorrow at noon. I did not ask about Everett, thinking her plans had changed due to him and she would tell me if she felt it was my business.

I was antsy all evening, not sure if this was the right move—to have a sandwich with a lady. I rationalized with myself that we had already had a meal together at the picnic table—what was so different about this one? It was different because it was chosen. I had decided to eat a meal with another lady besides Iris. It had been over four years since Iris had passed away. I still had the graduation ticket for Iris on the mantle in the wooden bowl she'd given me. I had been stuck in this loop: work; home; dinner with Alex the cat, who had decided to live inside now. I sure hoped he did not belong to anyone. There had not been any response from the flyers I'd hung around the neighborhood while he followed like he knew his way around. Now he sat in one recliner and I in the other. I imagined this was how Mr. and Mrs. Filbert had sat before their deaths in these two chairs. I thought of Micky sitting next to me and wondered if she would like Alex. How did Everett fit into her life? He surely was not her boyfriend, or she would not have given me her phone number in front of him.

I woke up early on Sunday. Too anxious to eat, I mowed the lawn even though it did not need it, checked the fluids in the vehicles, and showered, feeling strange, wondering if what I planned to wear would be okay for this meeting. I was still unable to call it a date; I would call it what it was: lunch. I chose clean blue jeans and a white t-shirt that had never been worn.

When I pulled in, there was Micky by the door, looking at her phone and wearing a white lace shirt and blue jeans so unlike her usual brightly colored outfits that I had seen before. I knew this would be okay. It was only a sandwich and some small talk. Feeling comfortable, I approached her, gently saying her name.

She looked up, smiled, and said, "Daniel."

I held the door and we entered; she said she had never eaten inside since Everett didn't like small spaces but loved the Giganto Roast Beef Deluxe. She said she would get her own since Everett was buying hers. We both ordered, two for her and one for me. She ordered extra tomatoes, asking if I remembered our last meal together where the tomatoes had all come out of her sandwich. It was like we had history, at least history of one meal and now this one. We picked a seat which I envisioned as our booth. I knew we would be back here; this felt normal and easy.

As we ate, I asked of Everett since she had mentioned him first. She told me she was his caretaker and Jeffrey took care of the financial end. She told me about Mrs. Johnson's passing and that they had lived in the same duplex.

I asked if she was ready for a story, feeling I should be upfront from the beginning. I told her of Iris, the car, and Everett Sunshine, who I was sure from the description I'd been given was the Everett from the case. Explained that he was no longer a suspect; as a matter of fact, I'd been a suspect at the same time as him. They'd never found him but had found the killer, Julian Hunter, a.k.a. Five Pin.

I was worried by Micky's silence. She was just sitting there, not moving. Her poker face was perfect. She had stopped eating and was watching me.

She finally opened her mouth and said, "Would you like to bring rolls, cranberries, and a pie to Thanksgiving dinner?" She looked confident, then asked if I had a family meal to go to, saying she didn't have family and neither did Everett since Mrs. Johnson's passing. Maybe I would like to meet him?

Needing time to think about this, I agreed to meet her here next Sunday if she was free for a duplicate lunch with an answer.

We left, me smiling, feeling uncomfortable with a handshake but knowing a hug would be too much. I nodded and went to open her car door.

Holding Everett's Giganto Roast Beef Deluxe as she fastened her seat belt, she looked me in the eye, smiled the most beautiful smile, and said, "Daniel, until next week."

My Sunday, full of chores, seemed pointless now. I was awakening from my four-and-a-half-year nap of emotion. Faced with joining Everett in the most important meal of the year, Thanksgiving, I was sobered but grateful to have a place to go since I had not gone anywhere on Thanksgiving for many years and to have an ending to who Everett Sunshine was. I gave Alex some chicken from my leftover sandwich on his special little plate. I had not finished the sandwich with the confessions of my soul over lunch. It was good that it was out in the open and had not fazed Micky at all. She still had not told me anything about herself. I already knew I would be having turkey for dinner this Thanksgiving—turkey that would not come from a frozen box, the first home-cooked one in many years.

The week flew by with Simone having racks installed for the tires, painting the office, bringing in furniture, and installing an alarm system, the same as mine. She used Luther's birthdate as the code: 1220. She knew he was with her in this journey; there had been too many things that she'd had no idea how to do, and they had come together, or someone had come along to assist with what she did not know. Tomorrow, Thursday, the tires would be delivered as well as the office supplies and the rest of the furniture for the waiting room and office. This was happening now, not just an idea agreed upon in a cemetery. The spoken word was coming into fruition.

Simone talked of Thanksgiving, her children, and told me of Thomas and Cora, who would be having baby Luther next month. She looked at me and said she didn't know if I had family for this upcoming holiday. She extended an invitation if I chose. I assured her I had somewhere to go and told her of Iris, Everett, and Micky, that I would meet Everett on that day. I saw from her expression that she wondered if I was truly fine with that. I told her of my comfort with the situation, of Micky and her easygoing kindness. Simone already knew of my meeting Micky but not of the lunch last week or that I had planned to agree to attend the dinner.

Simone said, "Daniel, always go with your gut feeling. It will lead the way to peace." She touched my shoulder and left after saying her children would come with her tomorrow to see the place.

I spent the evening sleeping in my recliner, feeling the tension of the past few years unwind. I woke about midnight, and Alex was curled up on my footrest, closer than he had ever been.

Friday was my busiest day. People wished to get their windshield installed for the weekend. Needing to leave the windows down a bit on the first days to let the adhesive dry, most preferred to have this done on a day they could leave their vehicle in the garage at home and not in a work parking lot. Between all the windshields and Simone's deliveries and meeting her children, Thomas and Lucille, the day flew by, and Saturday went by equally as fast. Saturday was always filled with phone calls of questions about new windshields and maintenance of the newly installed ones. Everyone wanted to wash their vehicle as soon as it was installed which would void the warranty. Maybe the new windshield made the rest of the car look dirty.

Sunday, I showed up at the sandwich shop earlier than Micky. Of course, I was second-guessing myself as to why I had not texted to confirm during the week. She pulled in, clearly on the phone, but ended the call quickly. We ate and talked as before, but this time about ourselves. We were both from Seattle and about the same age; I was almost a year older, this being my twenty-fifth year and Micky having just passed her twenty-fourth birthday last month. I learned she'd had her car for six years and her last name was Silversmith. Also, she now knew that I would be attending Thanksgiving dinner on Thursday, November 25th, arriving at 1:00 p.m. Micky gave me her address and said she would be inviting Jeffrey but did not know if he would attend. She stated she had just met him recently, when Mrs. Johnson had passed, and he was a bit older, maybe forty, but Everett liked him. I told her I looked forward to this dinner; inside, I was more excited than I had been in years.

We left, and I opened the car door for her. She gave me a gentle hug and got in her Mitsubishi Lancer with Everett's sandwich on the passenger seat.

She smiled and said, "Daniel, see you Thursday."

I said, "Indeed you will, Micky."

Detective Muncer

November 2021

Micky had invited me for Thanksgiving dinner; this would be the first one I'd had with people in over twenty years. I always made the same meal Mom made for us while growing up even if it was just for me. I'd found her recipe book in the kitchen cupboard while cleaning out the family home after a year after their disappearance. I hadn't been aware that Mom had all her recipes in ink for us children. There were notes for me and my vanished twin siblings, Joshua, and Jill. Dad's favorites were noted as well. Thinking back, I was not sure what Mom had liked the best—maybe it was the family she had created and brought together with each meal. Mom had known what our favorite food consisted of and had wanted to make sure we knew how to make it. Her book was in a treasured place, and I had made photocopies of my favorite recipes, including the pages that were titled, "Thanksgiving and Christmas." These were the remains of my family all I had left besides memories.

It had been one of my first years working for Seattle PD, and I had volunteered to work Christmas since my family was taking a vacation to Mexico for the twins' graduation. I often wondered if I'd been there, could I have saved them? Or would I have been a missing statistic also? I was the only one of five left here. I'd cleaned up the loose ends of their disappearance, had sold the house, and had waited for answers, honestly knowing what the families I investigated for felt like, working every holiday so fellow officers could be with the family they had.

When Micky had called to invite me, my first instinct had been to decline the offer and say I was working. She did not know what I did only that I was with the department, nor had she asked; I would tell her at dinner. I had offered to bring loaded potato casserole, soda pop, napkins, boxed stuffing, and whipped cream. She said dinner would be at 1:00 p.m. Everett and Daniel would be there; I figured Daniel was a friend or family member of hers. I asked if I could show up at noon to visit and put the casserole in the oven and make the whipped cream. She was happy for this event to be more than just dinner.

I shopped with purpose this week. Generally, it was just for nourishment for me, preparation so as not to eat out daily. This shopping trip was different. Even though I made a Thanksgiving dinner sometimes more than once a year, as some months I was overly thankful to be alive after what I saw on the streets, this time shopping had brought on new meaning. I picked out individual potatoes to be sure they were not rotten; went with organic produce; and bought a few slices of deli bacon for the topping, real butter, brand-name cheese, napkins with fancy foil embossed leaves on them, cornbread stuffing in a box, whipped cream, and a new container of cinnamon to add to the pie topping.

The department had been surprised when I'd asked for the morning and afternoon off. I could return to work Thanksgiving night if needed. Being on call for twenty-seven years, I was used to the lifestyle.

I was happier than I had allowed myself to be in two decades. I had not been unhappy before, other than the normal feelings that followed my entire family disappearing, but that made me a better detective. I knew people wanted answers to their loved one's murder or disappearance.

Once home from the grocery store, I thought of moving downstairs; it would sure make grocery shopping easier. After unloading the groceries, I entered Mrs. Johnson's place. I knew it was mine, but it still felt strange. It was exactly as it had been when she lived there. I wondered if Everett or

Micky would like anything of hers. I would ask before boxing it up.

Finding paper and pen on the kitchen counter right where Mrs. Johnson had left it, I made a diagram of the place, thinking of a remodel and what could be done for my needs and music. The soundproofing and studio could be upstairs; all these years, I had used my headphones so as to not disturb Mrs. Johnson, but now I would like to spend more time writing music, as I was behind on it. It was a calming hobby that helped relieve the stress of my daily work. It used to be nightly work, but somehow that had gotten all switched up. I missed the deep beats and bass; the rhythm and storyline of the streets brought perspective into my music. People knew it was real right from the curb into their ears, through their heart, and out their mouths, into the next person, and the beat continued on. People had no idea I wrote the lyrics to the music they rolled down the road with, went into their basement to get lost from society, headed to work listening to. I was not sure where it all came from, but when I had been with the Green Pyramids and later had become a patrol officer in Pioneer Square, the beat had never left me. My sounds were natural and calming to my spirit, letting the stresses of life roll out in music that I heard sometimes as I drove around town. Detective Jeffrey Muncer, a.k.a. #MunDetJ and #DJMuncer. My secret and retirement fund were building; the music was selling. I was just on a vacation from my words for a few months. They would return; they were in my head. I was a detective but also a rap lyricist.

It was Thursday morning, Thanksgiving morning, a new start in life for me. I prepared the loaded potato casserole and gathered all the goods and tools into a box, not knowing if Micky would have a mixer or whatever else I would need. This was exciting to be attending a family dinner. I made a copy of the recipe for the potatoes and whipped cream to leave there in case Micky or Everett would like to make it later; it was like passing on a part of my family to my newly acquired one. It was 11:45 a.m. I knew it was time to go.

I was suddenly sad my family was gone; I could still see them at the table, and it was hard to break the wall I had built over two decades. This almost felt like betrayal to them. I put the box in the passenger seat and pulled away from the curb, knowing I would not be the same when I returned—I would be part of them and they of me. I had been on my own for so long that this was an odd feeling but was relaxing, a connection. I was happy to have people to eat with and someone to laugh with, knowing that I had a second chance to protect someone.

I pulled up and brought my box of food in. We would be eating downstairs at Everett's, as he did not want to venture out, not even upstairs to Micky's. I was glad I'd brought what I needed for my fixings, as Everett had limited kitchen supplies. I placed the potatoes in the oven and whipped the cream. Everett watched football and didn't sound happy about the plays; suddenly, he laughed, a hearty roar coming from his belly. Micky was drinking a beer at the table, laughing as well. These were wonderful sounds to me—true laughter. Their bond of family was evident; they were people who felt comfortable with each other.

At 12:45 p.m., there was a knock-on Everett's door. I was still in the kitchen.

Everett hollered, "It's open!"

Micky answered the door, and there was another voice. I could not see the person from my viewpoint in the kitchen. I had taken over cooking the dinner, which was fine since I loved to cook, and Micky probably needed a break from supplying food for Everett every day, who appeared to have a hearty appetite. I thought I recognized the male voice coming from the living room, but I wasn't sure where I knew it from. In my line of work, I needed to make sure all was well, and I wasn't in a house with someone who would be angry by my presence. I popped my head around the corner.

Daniel and I said each other's names, equally shocked to see each other at Everett Sunshine's house for this holiday feast. Daniel rose and shook my hand, then hugged me, which was a surprise. Neither of us told Micky or Everett how we'd met. That could happen later; right now, we were here. We were all living life solo, and today we were family. After we ate, we would be the Fuller family.

While waiting for dinner, I looked at Everett's bookshelf and watched football with him. Daniel asked if he could look at the GED preparation book, saying he only had a couple more credits to finish high school. He then told the story of quitting school due to aging out of the foster system. He told of his few days on the street and Mr. Filbert and how he'd gotten where he was now. By the end of dinner, Daniel had made the decision to take a couple online courses to get his diploma from Seattle Public Schools since that was where he'd attended before his sudden departure from high school.

He said, "You know, I feel awake, not just gliding through the day."

We all nodded, knowing what he meant.

Micky had not revealed much of herself but had had a smile on her face. She told the story of how she and Daniel had met at the picnic table shared by the story of Iris and Richard. Now it was my turn to tell Micky how I fit into all this. She had a look of relief on her face; she cared for Everett and his wellbeing. She said she'd been concerned at first that I would not want the responsibility of them and would hire someone whom Everett was not used to. She was relieved I was a detective and felt confident we could all play our roles to keep Everett safe.

Everett said he felt comfortable with all of us. He loved having his new friend, Daniel.

Daniel smiled at that statement; I had not seen him smile a true, heartfelt grin before, as our meetings had always had a somber undertone mostly to due to investigation of Iris's murder.

This had been a great dinner; the variety of pies and cinnamon whipped cream topped me off too full. We truly were a group of lost souls that needed connection. We all cleaned up and left Everett's place looking just like it had before—except he wanted a plate of leftovers and pie. I thanked Micky for the invite and Everett for allowing me into his home for this holiday meal and then left with Daniel.

He stopped me outside and asked if I would share about what I knew about Everett and Iris. We arranged to meet tomorrow at his house for the story. I told him there wasn't much to add but didn't want to talk here as I might miss something, and he might have questions.

We drove off smiling. I heard music coming from Daniel's car, a top-forty hit, one I'd written the lyrics to a few years back. I grinned bigger, was suddenly tired, and headed east toward home, knowing this had been the best day ever.

I slept better that night than I had in at least a decade. People would say it was the turkey, but I knew it was the connection I'd made with other people.

The day shift was starting to feel right to me, but I knew that as suddenly as I'd been needed on this shift, I would be needed at night again. The city was just quiet now—well, maybe not quiet, but there wasn't much the police could do since our hands were tied when it came to most crimes. The jails were letting most individuals out due to Covid for their protection, not the public's protection. Police vehicles were getting rammed by stolen cars, and we could not chase. Was the car not being used as a weapon?

Friday morning, I arrived at Daniel's. He answered the door as if he'd been standing behind it, saying he had never had any company. The place and the furniture were not what I would have expected of his residence. He said it was exactly as it had been when it had all been given to him—even the remote sat in the same location. He told me of Mr. Filbert and the attorney who had given him the news of his new house.

We entered the kitchen with new stainless-steel appliances; Daniel offered me coffee or water. Sitting at the wooden farm-style table, I felt something rub my leg and looked; it was a cat that had jumped into my lap.

"Alex," Daniel announced and scolded at the same time, informing me the cat was not licensed. He was not even sure it was his; one day it had just been here wanting dinner, then sharing dinner with him nightly.

I told Daniel my story of Everett and how I'd come into the picture, saying I'd been quite surprised to see him attending yesterday's dinner. He informed me of Micky, the meeting at Alki Beach, then later the sandwich shop, and now yesterday's dinner. How it all had lined up for him answered many questions for me. We quickly realized there were no more questions of each other; we knew fate had mastered this plan of lining up the loose ends. If it had not been for Everett's part in Iris's murder—even though he hadn't been guilty of anything—Daniel would not have had such a meaningful meeting with Micky, and I would not have had a connection that felt like family.

Daniel came up with one question: "Does Micky get a day off?"

That was something I did not know; all I did know was that Everett did not need twenty-four-hour supervision.

He told me of his recent purchase of the neighboring building to his shop and Simone opening Luther's Tire and Wheel. I asked if he knew Simone; it seemed like everyone was connected in this small town, big city. "That is a negative," I said as I left, thanking Daniel for this visit, knowing we would meet again somewhere sometime and betting it would have to do with Everett.

Don

November 2021

I called Donny on the morning of November 7th; he stated he was not well and would need a few days to start the jobs we had lined up. He didn't sound like a few days would be enough from the tone of his voice with barely any air pushing his words, but I had to roll with it. He sounded worse than I had ever heard him before, and there wasn't another choice, as he had all the equipment and power, he always had the final say on all our side work. We had obligations, and I needed the transportation and money from the secret plans we had. There was always something that we thought would be the next big break for us, but no one took us seriously, instead seeing our ideas as insignificant and sketchy, to say the least. There was always an underlying motive related to the help we would offer. Extra charges, jobs not completed, items tacked onto the bill but not approved, material returned to the hardware store prior to giving the receipts to whomever had hired us. We knew we were worth more but never were paid enough; we had to take the money our own way.

On November 8th through the 12th, I called Donny daily. On the eleventh, there was no answer. On the twelfth, no answer again. I had to go there and check to make sure he was all right. I found him on the ground, on the braided rug he had scored on one of our dump runs. His pulse was there barely, only if I pressed hard. It was thready, to say the least. He was not on this side of life, I was sure, and I regretted not coming here yesterday.

We had a system: all money and drugs were controlled and stored at Donny's, which was a more "secure" option. I knew it wasn't more secure—just that he did not trust me.

I felt bad that he was lying in such filth and had been there for days. This put some form of reality in me. Was this how I would die, alone and in filth? My place was not any better; the items inside had all been retrieved as someone else's handoffs. They were trash to others; I had settled for the castoffs. My decision was made I could not call an ambulance, as they should not know of this residence, which was so well hidden behind the garage that was ready to fall, leaning to the right as you walked up, not suitable for a human. If it did collapse, it would take this broken-down room with it. I wondered at this moment why Donny and I had settled for such filth. Where were our priorities; why did we live like this? All the collected and coveted equipment sat in the garage, lined up in order as Donny's OCD had planned out. There were items from his former life, from before the drugs had taken over and the hope of a big break that we both knew would never happen due to our lack of ambition and underlying drug habits. It was just a hope to drag us into life day by day. I knew it was too late for him but not for me.

Before I got my friend Donny to the hospital to live or die with dignity, I would empty the old woodchipper, which was so tattered the brand name had worn off. I found the keys on Donny; they went to our secret door, which led from his room to the interior of the garage. Locating the five pounds of meth we had just made, I realized I needed a larger coat to conceal it on our exit. I also found the two thousand dollars in cash that was our stash, used to make more and purchase the supplies. It was the perfect hiding spot, a broken-down shredder chute on a machine so old no one would have any interest in it, but it was a piece of equipment and Donny never parted with what he thought was valuable. I had ridden my bicycle over most of the way, stashing it in the bushes a block away to enter the property where most likely someone was more alert than not, knowing what I was walking into would not be any good at all showing up alone and unannounced or invited.

Now the purpose of the woodchipper was to act as our bank, the holding spot, since neither one of us was able to get a real bank account with our previous irresponsible financial methods. Currently neither of us made money in a way that should be recorded. We were outlaws of the system, did not conform or fold to society, did not pay taxes. We existed under the radar of the government and still stimulated the economy with our self-made system. Only the two of us knew when we made our product and where we did so. We were never out, so there were no clues as to when the actual cooking took place. We found that 7:00 a.m. was a good time to start the process; partiers were asleep, and workers were on their way to work or focused on their day. We did our own job; we were cooks and salesmen. We had more money than we would have if we had worked a conforming job. This was our occupation.

I knew I could not keep this operation going without my dear friend and business partner Donny, so I had to run with all we had and try to figure out something that would sustain me. I knew deep inside myself from previous experience that I was no good at this; my past and current financial situations were precarious, to say the least. Once this product and the money were gone, I would be destitute, begging for food again, hungry. I would have smoked away the money that should have sustained me, lying to myself every step of the way. I always ended up at that spot no matter how much money I had, or opportunity given. I was my own worst enemy, sabotaging my lofty dreams that I did not take the steps to follow, a bit of cash in my pocket, handed less than what I deserved but humbly taken anyway.

I would order a pizza, thinking I was entitled to a life I could not sustain the money to maintain, knowing the price of that pizza could feed me for the entire week. I ate it in one sitting, knowing I would regret that decision the next day. Most of my days were spent in disappointment of my actions or convincing myself that others were wrong. I never accepted the blame or consequences of my actions if I did, I would not have kept returning to the same place every time.

This was my decision tonight. I pocketed the keys to Donny's truck, the quiet one. No one could know I was here. I placed the drugs and cash behind the seat and went back to the room where my friend Donny lay on the carpet, which appeared to smell worse now that I had returned after being in the fresh night air. I coaxed him into a sitting position, or maybe it was me making him be upright, and positioned him up on the fold-out chair, never realizing that he was this much larger than me. I had not had to carry him prior to this, as he had always been the strong one. He made some noises; I listened carefully and could make out a few words about the stash, his vehicles, equipment, and money—it all went to Little Mel. I was shocked that none of it would be mine. I had been joking for a year or more that one of his trucks belonged to me. I'd thought we were closer than this, that I meant something to him. I was glad at that exact moment I had taken the steps to secure my future before waking Donny fully.

He was sort of capable of standing and dragging one leg along behind himself. He had his arm around my shoulder; as a friend, I did what was necessary to support him. All the while, I felt like dropping him and fleeing, but I knew I had to take him out of here and to the hospital so I could get the truck, money and drugs stashed. There would not be another reason for me to have come here and taken the truck. There was no way I would feel comfortable leaving him here, not giving him a chance at medical care if there were a way he could live. He had to live! Donny was my friend, the one who understood me, the one I worked with or so I thought prior to this.

I dropped him off at the hospital. They wouldn't let me past the emergency room—not with Covid happening, not without a vaccine card. Also, I was not related to him. I was worried about the truck sitting in the parking garage with my whole future in it. I recalled seeing an article online about vehicles being stolen from that garage. As soon as they hooked Donny up to the monitors, he was quickly whisked away to another part of the hospital. I watched as people ran with him. More and more joined; I heard "STAT" and "ICU." I was free to leave, touching him on the forehead and praying for healing before they whisked him away, not wanting to leave, feeling I would not see him again. There was nothing further I could do for my friend. I was kicking myself for not going yesterday to check on him. I left through the automatic sliding doors. The night was cold; no one knew what anyone out here was going through. People passed without making eye contact, which helped me navigate the garage, hoping I remembered where I'd parked.

By 11:00 p.m., I was back to Donny's truck and on my way, carefully driving home so as to not be stopped with a load like this. Jail would be too cruel of an outcome at that moment; there would be no explaining this away. I finally had my own big break. My thoughts were all over the place. If he lived, I had the stash to return to him and show I was a good friend. If he passed on to eternity, I would be very sad but would have the stash that I needed to hide. I figured I should probably hide it now before anyone knew of Donny's outcome. As of this moment, it was only me who knew of Donny's dire situation.

I looked at the clock, having no idea what time it was due to such traumatic events occurring over the last couple of hours. I saw it was 12:37 a.m. It would be November 13th.

I hated the idea of Donny being there by himself, but I did not know how to get a hold of any of his family. He had his phone and of course would not be able to answer, not in his grave condition. I went outside and found a jack and some blocks to brace my trailer up while I removed a tire. I dug a hole on the side by the shed, the side that the one neighboring house could not see; the other neighboring house had the garage bordering this angle. The only way they could see me is if someone upstairs woke up and looked out. I was not even sure the house was occupied since Donny's friends had moved a few months ago. It was the side the sun and wind hit; the paint had worn off, and the green was showing through after an inadequate paint job. I dug a hole precisely under where the tire would sit when I returned it to its original location. I entered my residence and wrapped the product and most of the cash up in separate, secure bundles. I had turned off all my lights prior to digging the hole. I looked out my windows, all of them, paranoid as I was even though no one knew what had happened so far. I tucked the packages under my coat and walked out as if to smoke. I deposited the goods into the hole, filled it back up with the dirt I had carefully removed and placed into a bucket, returned the tire to its hub, secured the lug nuts, and looked for signs that I had been there. I knew at that moment I needed to rake around the trailer—quietly, so as to not alarm anyone. I was just keeping the place clean and free of leaves with the large oak tree over my trailer. Everyone knew I kept a schedule that was not normal due to my frequent drug use, so this would not alert anyone. I also filled the back of Donny's truck with stuff I didn't need to make the area behind my trailer look more open. I could make a dump run in the morning; the truck would be in my possession hopefully forever.

The next morning, having not been able to sleep, I got Stephanie to call Harborview and ask about Donny's condition. They said he was not there; I needed to know more without giving away what I knew. I loaded up my laundry and went to Little Mel's to use his machines, as I did not have quarters and wished to see what they were aware of.

I didn't expect there would be seven people there. They ask why I had Donny's truck. I must have been ready to talk because I spilled out the hospital story. I said I think it all happened around midnight; in case anyone had cameras there, that would be when they would start looking, not an hour earlier, when I had stolen the drugs. My dirty laundry was still outside in the bed of the truck; I knew I would not be bringing it in, would not be leaving with the truck or possibly my clothing. Trying to imagine juggling my clothes in the black lawn bag for such a long walk—maybe a mile or more—back to the trailer where the drugs were buried, I no longer felt safe there since everyone seemed on edge now that they knew Donny was in the hospital. They asked where he was, what I had done to him, why I hadn't alerted anyone of my presence on the property. I told them he had said not to wake anyone, that he had felt silly going to the emergency room and would tell them when he returned. Thinking back, I had never arrived alone at Little Mel's—always with Donny, except last night. Maybe this group of people were to be feared. Or was guilt written on my face, even though I had only taken Donny to the hospital as far as they knew? I had never been good with words. That fact made me look guilty to begin with, as I stammered when asked simple questions. Of course, when the truth came out, as a rule, I was guilty—maybe not of what they imagined, but possibly worse. Usually something terrible. I had a continuous secret life in every area that I had not even admitted to myself, one that I kept returning to, then covering up. To confess this secret would be too traumatic for me.

Little Mel said he knew of Donny's heart trouble and had been confided in a few weeks prior to this event. He stated Donny had been scheduled to have open heart surgery in the near future; he was sure that was what was going on. He did not know how to contact any family. At that moment, I looked around the room and realized that was probably true for everyone sitting there. We had all done whatever it was—drugs, to be precise, our number-one choice—and family had had no choice but to give up with our sporadic visits only wanting something. But truly, we just wanted something that would allow the drugs to be number one in our lives. We all justified our actions, twisted the truth, took more than we contributed, overstepped our boundaries, but we did not see it that way. We saw that we were being cast out for no reason, that others were unfair. We never considered the children we had emotionally messed up, the ones we had not provided for, instead buying drugs. Someone had fed and clothed those children all those years, years during which I, personally, had left the area to follow drugs on more than one occasion, returning to jump right back into the same scene. The children were old enough to not need me anymore. I still saw them as babies as I did not participate in those years. At that moment, I realized this and took it to heart that it was my fault I had lost what had been given to me as a gift.

I had to flee from this room; it would make me look guilty of something having to do with Donny, but I could not remain here. I had no way to depart from my physical being and conscience wishing to leave myself behind with the seven others, nor could I escape the turmoil in my head. Reality was not a place I returned to often; it was easier to live in denial.

Little Mel said the truck would stay with him. I pulled the keys from my pocket with all hopes of the truck being mine gone. I knew that, as Donny had told me where everything would sit in the event of his death. No one offered me a ride; they all just sat there, contemplating what would be in it for them. Donny was the main operation of this side circus with his instructions and equipment, and the property belonged to Little Mel.

I walked through the gate attached to the six-foot cyclone fence. Time flew without answers of Donny. Didn't anyone care? Did they all believe Little Mel? Of course, this news was brand new to them, having only heard it minutes ago. I had been living with it for almost a day. Twenty-four hours had passed quickly. Now, my laundry was out of the bed of Donny's truck in the bag that was ripping. I could see my red sock poking through the stench coming with it. I left my junk that I had loaded during my clean up. No one knew when it had gotten there. The laundry was not heavier than the load in my heart. I found my bicycle in the bushes a block away where I'd stashed it last night and wheeled my laundry home. It sat propped up by the door of my trailer while I thought I should have left it in the truck, knowing I would never wash it.

I knew in my heart Donny was gone, dead, gone from me now, gone from them later. I had felt it at 2:00 a.m. while filling the hole back in under the tire, but they could all believe the open-heart story if they wished. Their whole life was on a surface level. The truth was never revealed so they would not have to face all the facts of their deficiencies personally and as a group. They would not move to any action until Little Mel said for them to get what they wanted. Then they would scramble, taking everything, they could for their own survival. I wondered who would remain and how this circus would continue to operate with no brains or skill. All were a bunch of pawns on the chess/meth board of Little Mel. I admitted that I was one of them, too, and had not realized until tonight how pitiful I had become in the aftermath of Donny. I was distraught over the loss of him, the kindhearted man who revealed nothing, his genuine happiness and kind ways. It made me wonder how Donny had ended up at Little Mel's. There were not many for-sure things in life; at least, this looked that way.

At approximately midnight on November 15th, I received a call from Raven one of the seven from Little Mel's posse. She wanted the truck back as well as Donny's wallet and phone. I told her where I had left the truck and when; she did not believe me. I stated I had nothing of his, that I would not steal anything from my friend. Again, she stated she wanted his wallet and phone. I told her he had had them at the hospital. She also told me the news that Donny had passed. I already knew her firsthand news—not from her, but from my sense of people. I had to act shocked and saddened, which wasn't hard. The hard part was acting like it was immediate and hadn't happened more than twenty-four hours ago. She had not been there when we had arrived at the hospital. She had not seen the final moments that I'd seen, moments of Donny barely reaching and trying to grip life and me. She had not felt his forehead as I had; she didn't know what I knew of the friendship I had imagined with Donny. But now, I knew it was different; his loyalty to Little Mel was rooted deeper that I would have imagined. This explained the days that had gone by without a return call or text. Would it have changed if life had gone on? Was I disposable—just a tool to tag along? Were we friends at all or only in the sense of the first layer that just drug addicts acknowledged? Was I only good for this friendship when I had a lead or contribution? I knew I loved him as a true friend and was truly sad at the confirmation of his passing into eternity. My life had not been the same since I'd met Donny a few years prior, nor would it be the same after his passing. Everything was different, on a new level. I was now a thief and could not admit this even to myself even though there had been many other occasions I had taken items from others under the name of survival. It was a finality now. Everyone knew Donny was gone forever.

Then it hit me that I could be in danger if anyone knew of our operation and the product. I needed to sell it fast and stash the money in different locations in case it had been marked in some way by them, whoever the other involved party may be. My mind raced, as I only had one location, and that was here. I tried to relax and make a plan. There was one person I always involved when I was in over my head: Stephanie the ex-wife I always ran back to when times were rocky. Although she hadn't been helping me as much lately, maybe she would rent a hotel room for me on Aurora, where I had hung out before and found trouble. My mistake in asking her was knowing the name of the place and describing what I would do while there, like laundry when all she heard was, I was going to use her name and be up to no good. Her experiences with me in the past had brought her to the decision of saying no more times than not. She didn't need to know I had previous experience in the drug strip. I could sell all the product in one night but wouldn't want anyone to know how much I had. Better to sell in smaller quantities.

I texted Stephanie and asked if she would get me a room. She refused, probably knowing I was up to no good. She did not want any connection to this, and I did not want her involved—had called basically out of habit. Now I was not sure I wanted this link either but had to go from where I was. This was the path I had chosen when I'd taken the stash.

I checked the bus schedules to see how close I could come to retrieving the product and leaving. I waited another day in case someone was watching. In the wee hours of the morning, again I did the reverse actions and retrieved the two packages, put them in a duffel bag of stinky wet laundry, and headed for the bus north with the other commuters who surely, were not carrying a load like I was. They stayed a considerable distance from me and made no eye contact, figuring I was homeless from the stench of my load and the looks of me. I was disgusted by the aroma radiating from the duffel bag. I got off downtown on Fourth Avenue, running to catch the northbound #5 bus at 4:18 a.m. on Third and Pine.

Suddenly, my lungs were not working properly. I was in the city amongst commuters, people who worked. I had five pounds of stolen drugs on me, cash that wasn't mine. My laundry brought attention to me as well, but I had a plan even if Stephanie wouldn't help. I always helped her, I thought, then realized that was not true at all. I was honest with myself at least for a moment, then quickly dismissed the thought.

I ran for the bus and caught it just in time. No one was following me; there weren't many people on this route at this early hour. I only had a few more stops until I would get to the motel of possibility. I saw the outlined red letters, still lit up from the night, as it was not even dawn yet. I realized it was cold and I did not have a coat. I shivered from the freezing air and adrenaline; glad I was not too high. I would buy a coat on my way home tomorrow.

The cost for the seedy box of a room was one hundred dollars a night. Without a credit card, it was double that. Cigarette-smelling furniture and walls the color of nicotine; the bedspread was from the seventies, with so many burn holes I couldn't recognize the pattern on the fabric. There were no cups or a shower cap. This was a motel of the lost, the underground, the stragglers, the trick-turners, the up-all-night crowd, the place you heard of on the local news. It did not look too bad in the dark from the outside.

It had been a while, a few months since I had been here. I used to come regularly and bring ladies back to my construction jobs to stay for free, but that had ended recently since I had no wheels and relationships had been severed. My funding had been short—or my habits had grown in ratio to income. There were hopes to see someone I might know, someone who could help me unload this product, someone who didn't let news travel fast. In this crowd, people did not talk frequently. I needed someone I could trust. I laughed at that last statement since in this world, no one was credible.

By 6:00 a.m., I saw Daniella, whom I'd met last year. She was with a respectable-looking gentleman in a suit, entering a room across the way from me. I would watch until he left and approach her with some free product in return for her help in the unloading system. I only wanted to be here one night. I also needed to leave town for good, but not too soon as to not look guilty. Daniella did not come out, but the gentleman did. He looked leery being in this seedy parking lot but familiar at the same time. His addiction was taking over his morning. I thought he was lucky his fancy car was still there and all in one piece. I doubted he would think twice before returning, though. This was his habit. Everyone had a habit whether they wished to admit it or not.

Daniella seemed to remember me from before. I never knew who would remember what, which brain cells had been destroyed, or if someone was just being selective with their memory. I had always been a giver so was known not to cause trouble, although my giving was always with a purpose of benefit to me. She let me in and right away asked what I wanted so as not to waste her prime money-making time. What I really wanted was to take her from here and run, but I needed to save *me* this time and get out of this mess that I had created not—anyone else. I told her I had an ounce and would be willing to share and give her a discounted rate to help me unload it, that I could possibly get more delivered later. I thought after this we would see how it went and if I should produce more. It was all divided in different increments for ease of sale. There was no way I could leave my room alone anymore now that Daniella knew I had product. I did not know if I could trust her or whom she might talk to. I left a bit with her. Even if she ripped me off, it wouldn't be much compared to the load I carried.

She knocked on the hollow door to my room a couple of hours later, saying she needed triple the amount. She had a car that I had not seen before and said she would be leaving the area but would be back in a couple more hours. I had to trust her even though my instinct said not to. I knew she could move product and this was easier for her than her usual occupation. So could I, but only to the people that couldn't know I had it. I needed her help this time.

Daniella returned on foot, as promised, and handed me money. I handed over more product. We had a system. It might be slower than I had hoped but with a couple big deals, Daniella would be in a better position financially, and I would be set to go sit and act natural in the trailer I would happily leave behind.

Three days in, and it was gone. I would sleep until tomorrow morning in the comfortable bed I had grown fond of, with the headlights shining in the front window from the up-all-night traffic at this seedy establishment. I could smell the gas leak from the wall heater but did not care. I would be leaving at 11:00 a.m. with money in my pocket, a clean set of clothing, a coat, and no peace of mind. I was more agitated now than before I'd arrived.

When I went to sleep, I felt something was not right, maybe it was my paranoia. It was 1:36 a.m. on November 20th; one of my quirks was always knowing the date and time. I looked up, and someone I had seen once at Little Mel's was standing over me.

He whispered in my ear so quietly I was not sure he was physically there: "Where is the product?"

He hadn't mentioned money, so I told him I didn't have it, that I'd had to get away to grieve Donny's death, I couldn't do that alone at my place. Here, there were people and friends to console me. I was not aware there were more than just the one person in my motel room surrounding my bed, but in the next second, I was being picked up by all four limbs, gagged, tied up, and carried out the door, leaving my new coat and the money so well stashed that housekeeping wouldn't find it—if they had that service here being such a seedy establishment. They loaded me into a large sedan of sorts. I heard all four doors close. I was blindfolded but tried to route the way in my mind.

I believed we arrived at Little Mel's place by the sound of the gate opening and gravel. It smelled like the garage. Sure enough, when they untied the band around my eyes, that was who was in front of me. He asked for the product one final time. There were six of us here. I sat in a 1950s chair that was missing the stuffing; the vinyl ripped into my arms, which were still tied behind me.

Little Mel said, "You don't think I know of everything that happens here? The cooking, sales, how much is on hand? Where is my product?"

At that point, I knew I was in a losing battle, outnumbered and guilty without proof. I told him the same story I'd told at the motel. They knew it was a lie since Daniella had sold a large quantity to a mutual acquaintance. She'd had no idea there would be trouble since she had not known the product was not mine. They did not believe me; this was the end for me but possibly not for Daniella. She could retrieve the money if she was smart and start over. My last thought was of Donny, then about me—how now everyone would know I had ripped him off, that I was a thief and their every suspicion up to this point was true.

Someone who was behind me fired the shot. One shot, and I was gone—but maybe not. It was a warning, but I wish they had completed the task. I might still be alive since they knew I was the only one who knew of the product's location. Don and Donny, both out of this world, I imagined. People who should be missed, but I was thinking no one would know, as we had distanced ourselves from mainstream society and our families. I was still alive but wished I was not, as all my choices had led me to this messed-up scene where I would be controlled until I talked, or they were done asking me.

I was untied. The duct tape was taken off, the blindfold hung around my neck. As I suspected, all seven people were in attendance, most likely so they would know what would happen to them if they ever got any ideas like I had. This was a say-what-you-mean-and-mean-what-you-say group. No going behind anyone's back, you did what you were told, and you would have a place to stay, food to eat when available, drug rations, and a sense of security.

I was instructed to stand. I was surrounded by the group of seven, who smelled like the products we used, a bit like cleaning additives that we mixed in, a different kind this time. As I fully stood, my legs wobbled from lack of circulation and fear. I was instructed to walk in the middle of this group of people I knew but wished I had never been associated with. I wondered where the line had been where I had gone down this final path. I asked myself why I'd chosen drugs over the job that had come with an apartment. I knew I would have been good at that but had convinced myself I was not going to work and have the government track me. I kept going backwards in my mind. That had been the most recent wrong turn; before that, it had been taking off to California for an experience and drugs. Before that, it had been getting all hooked up on methadone and buying it on the streets. I could keep reminiscing my life in backward fashion and see all the wrong turns that had been taken, but now I was here, being instructed to walk into the house I'd left a few days prior, a place I would stay until I talked.

My mind and soul wanted out of this predicament, but I did not know how. I did not have the product, the only thing they'd asked for. They knew I'd sold it due to Daniella. If I gave them the cash, all my hard work would be for nothing and I would be without a plan. The cash was worth much more than the product had originally been worth.

We got inside, and Little Mel poked me with something on the back side of my ribs, possibly a fireplace poker. He yelled, wanting to know what I'd added to the product this time. There were many people who were dead due to a bad batch, and it could not be traced back here. The police could not know of the operations here as the cash from the drug sustained the crew as he called them. He stated I would be the one liable; they would put me where Donny was and lock me in under guard until this had blown over. I knew it was Donny who had added the different long-action substance, but he was not going to pay the price. I would be the fall guy.

They took me into Donny's room, all seven people following like an army. I could still picture him lying on the braided rug. There was a sandwich that looked freshly made on the table. I was unsure if I should eat, but it truly did not matter at this point if the sandwich killed me or not because my only hope was to escape from this place. They locked me in alone; the best part was no one was here.

I was mentally preparing to get away and retrieve my cash. I was positive Donny had had no secrets from Little Mel, so he most likely knew of the door from this sad room to the garage. I was hoping the building would stay standing as long as I was left here. I looked for cameras and did not see any, but that did not mean they were not present.

I stayed for two days in the chair I had propped Donny up in and mourned the loss of my friend. The braided rug had the impression of the length of his body. It troubled me, causing me to rethink my actions. But I still had hope of getting out of this. On the second day, I knocked on the inside of the exterior door to see if anyone was there so I could ask for water. It was opened immediately; there were two of the seven, as I'd suspected. They were most likely present around the clock. They brought me two bottles of water with a warning to never knock again, as they did not wish to see me.

On the third day, I listened closely. They appeared to work in eight-hour shifts. I tracked when the guards switched, writing it down and hiding the paper under the rug.

I was ready for escape on the seventh day. I knew at 3:00 a.m., they would switch people. At 2:55 a.m., I was ready to leave through the secret door from Donny's room to the garage and out the window that did not latch, closing them both as silently as possible. As the one set headed into the house and the other moved to stand guard at my door, I went outside and watched, looking at the ground for sticks, walking on the grass to be as silent as possible. I made it to the fence, hopped over it, and was gone into a lot of bushes neighboring this property. I was going to take the same route to north Seattle as I had before.

Happy I had pocketed the shallow dish of change Donny had left behind, I caught the bus at 4:00 a.m., headed toward downtown and then north onto Aurora to get my cash, hoping they would allow me to enter the room I'd occupied a week ago. I was allowed in at 5:25 a.m. under the pretense of losing my grandfather's ring. I was relieved to find it was all still there under the edge of the nightstand. I realized I did not have any way to carry this amount of cash. I stole the stained, pink, flowered pillowcases and returned the key to the front desk, asking if he would not mention my presence. I slid two hundred dollars across the worn Formica counter where so many people had signed in agreement to mess up their life.

I disappeared, knowing I had a head start. They never checked on me until 11:00 a.m. when they brought food, which had been quite good. I was free to go any direction except south, where I had just escaped from. Oklahoma sounded like a wise choice. I headed north to Everett, bought a train ticket to Chicago, and would see where this led me, knowing I would not be on the train when it arrived at its final destination. In case they were looking for me and needed a place to look, Chicago sounded good at this time of year. I did not think this ring of swindlers was any bigger than the small complex and seven people I had left behind, but they would not be happy when they saw I was gone. There wasn't even a clue as to how I'd disappeared. I had sealed my exits well, knowing they were secret all along. The two guards would be blamed for my disappearance, which I felt remorse for. I was free for now, had purchased the ticket under Donny's name heading east at 10:10 a.m. I would pull out of the station fifty minutes before they would discover my absence at the compound. I picked up some clothing, a duffel bag, and a few western and sci-fi books at a thrift store on Broadway in Everett. I stopped at a convenience store for snacks to supplement my daily meal on the train, if I wished to stay with this mode of transportation past whatever stop I chose to get off the train.

My arrival at the depot made me feel suspicious. I waited back next to the luggage cart as they announced the arrival of my ride out of here. It only took minutes of waiting in line for passengers to arrive and me to be allowed on and into a seat of my choosing. I kept the duffel bag under my feet to protect the cash, and we rolled out of the station without incident. The slow sway of the train on the rails and the reader board at the front of my car said we were doing eighty miles per hour. I knew this was the right method to leave by, as busses did not travel that fast.

The conductor asked for my ticket, which I had ready in my pocket. He punched it and said, "All the way to Chicago?"

I nodded, knowing I would get off before then, but said, "Yes, to see my brother."

He smiled, content with my answer, and walked away to the next person. I napped, staying in tune to the motion, knowing no one could get on the train while it was moving, and I had a couple of hours of peace. No cell phone, nothing to track me, all my earthly goods at the trailer I would never return to.

I slept most of the ride through the Midwest. I felt a stir inside of me when the conductor announced Aitkin, Minnesota. It started with an "A", and I was starting over, fresh. I got off the train, the conductor warning me of the five-minute stop and the train's departure. I hid around the corner, looked in the phone book for the bus depot, and slowly made my way there.

Three days later, I was on a bus headed south with a ticket that would take me to Fort Worth or anywhere in between. Passing through Iowa, Kansas, and into Oklahoma was comforting, knowing I was miles ahead of them, the seven.

The bus crossed a bridge over a small lake, and I saw Cash fishing, he was an enemy from back in my construction days one of the ties I had broken. I was sure my eyes had deceived me in my paranoia. This made me more uneasy than I had been since leaving Seattle. Had they been there every step of my way, or had he just run from our crowd to here and I'd found him? I would never approach to find out. Our last dealings had not been pleasant. I had not even gone to retrieve my television or phone from his place. He looked up as if in recognition, but I was sure the windows only showed a reflection of the lake from his angle. All the peacefulness which had begun to feel normal was gone, replaced by my feelings of reality or it delusional. I was not sure where to get off the bus, but it would not be Fort Worth, the final destination of my ticket.

I got off in Ardmore, Oklahoma. There was a stop for a meal, a stern warning from the driver that he would leave with or without everyone and to be back on the bus by 5:45 p.m. The entire list of passengers loaded into the diner. I was one of the first to order, looking normal except for my duffel bag of cash. I watched my back at the same time. My order arrived in record time. I went behind the building and ate on a curb in the parking area. So, this was home; this was it. I found a low-budget motel for the night and rested, hoping to never be found.

Cash was still on my mind. Our last encounter had had to do with Paul, the homeowner of where we had been remodeling a home. Cash had convinced him I was pilfering from the supplies and getting the money back from the receipts. That was the truth, but both of us were doing that; Cash just wanted the entire job to himself now that it was almost done. I heard him one night when the walls were not installed yet. He was talking to Honey, a gal he had picked up somewhere. He told her he was leaving town as soon as this house was finished. I knew then he was looking for all the money he could get so he could go to his next destination and not return to the cockroach-infested four-plex a few miles away. That apartment had never been his, even though he swore it was. It had belonged to an unfortunate person named Laud. I was not sure where they had met or if Laud was his first or last name, but he had taken some severe abuse from Cash and would just sit there on the sofa, bleeding, and nodding, never leaving, never fighting back—just existing. I believe now Cash had Laud hooked on meth, or the other way around, but when Cash would get his hands on any drugs, he would become crazy. His personality would change from happy to angry in a second's time. He said he had killed people prior to my meeting him and had spent over twenty years in a Texas prison. I knew he had also been held in Washington since I had seen some paperwork but had never asked any questions for my safety. When he wasn't crazy or violent, Cash was a nice guy. We worked well together; it was during the drug-infused nights in the house that was being remodeled that I was leery of him.

Looking back, I hoped the new walls of that house were not covered in any chemicals that should not be there and that the family who had moved in were happy and safe. We had put a lot of work into that house.

Ardmore, Oklahoma, was a small town and possibly too small for hiding out. I was not sure who I was hiding from but knew Cash was too close for my comfort. I rested a couple nights in the local motel. I could not reserve a room at the nice ones with a pool due to having no credit card, but that was probably best. I did not leave my duffel bag alone anywhere.

I checked out of my room, which was not much of an upgrade from the Seattle one and walked a bit. I bought a new duffel bag ready to be rid of this one that had Donny's name on it, some clothing, and a small backpack. At the laundromat, I changed and did a load of clothes. I got rid of the clothing I had worn for so many days I could not count and got a corndog, fries, and a few sodas from across the parking lot. With the rest of my change, I got crackers and candy bars from the vending machine for my bus ride into Shreveport, Louisiana. My mind knew I had money, more than I had ever had, but I knew it would not last long unless I lived like I had prior to obtaining it. I was going to give myself a new start in life in a new town with a mindset patterned after Donny's. He had always been good with money and had known how to keep it together. Maybe I would become Donny. No one knew me here, so I could be anyone I wished to be.

The bus would be leaving at 4:00 p.m., heading east. My new wardrobe would be dry by then and packed in the backpack with the vended food. As I boarded the bus, I suddenly missed my children, my friends at Little Mel's, my pets, my old life, my trailer, the people on the property where it was parked, my old broken pickup truck, basically everything about my old life since I could never return. It all flashed before me—even Stephanie, who always somehow held it together with my interference. I put both feet on the steps and passed through the aisle to my seat, carefully holding my duffel bag of cash and becoming a new person. Donny it was.

I rolled into town a day later, clean, with money and a good presentation. All that work on Granny and Papa's farm had given me the lingo and know-how to hide in the country and get paid for it. I applied for a farmhand position. Included was a one-room cabin, which was the main attraction, not the work. I needed a secure place to store my money while I worked. The farm had an extended growing season of broccoli, cauliflower, and Brussels sprouts. The manager said there would be a bonus and use of the cabin over the winter if I stayed to the end of the season.

I was set, I was Donny, and I was hidden.

Gloria

November 2021

IT BARELY SEEMED POSSIBLE THAT ETHAN HAD BEEN GONE A YEAR, ALL THE TIME spent grieving, which was an event that did not end, just ebbed and flowed like the tide. Another thing that amazed me was the hard work me, Simone, June, Carl , Ha Yoon, and many nameless people had put into the fundraiser for Ethan's Edge.

We'd had created a system for fundraisers; it had gone just like clockwork year after year. Then Covid had hit, and no dinners or events had been allowed last year. Our regular donors still provided their planned giving, but donations were down by at least 50 percent and needs were up three times that amount.

Domestic violence had risen as people had been cooped up at home, getting on each other's nerves, and money was tight as businesses closed and jobs were scarce. Families, men, women, and children crossed our threshold looking for shelter, food, relief, counselling, whatever we were able to help with or refer them to. The needs were great, greater than I had ever seen prior to this. I only saw from a distance, as I had retired. Our insurance costs rose due to the area we were located, and we decided to cut the overnight stay insurance on the original shelter downtown, as no one slept there anymore. At 6:00 p.m., everyone was out. With funding tight, we couldn't just reinstate that insurance, hire staff to supervise, and provide everything for an entire other group of people, even though that was what our community needed. We had 120 rooms at Charlene's Place and were full to capacity, with people calling daily or just showing up.

Even though I was retired, I still looked at the budget to see where we could cut some costs. Restaurants were not open so were not donating any food, which had been a tremendous help to us. Stores were closed or had limited sales, so they were not donating either. Many offices had their workers at home so did not order extra office supplies for us as they had before. Donations at every level were down, getting creative with this online fundraiser had been a challenge.

Two more days, and the online auction would be live for three days. Product had been brought in, organized, photographed, and put online for viewing. Each donor had put a suggested retail price on their item, and thank-you cards were delivered as Simone, June, and I retrieved each donated item to save on postage but to also let them know we appreciated their generosity. We spent days in this loop of pick-up, bring-in, and photograph. June was the best; she knew about lighting and angles. Simone was the strong one, moving all the items from the vehicle to the photography station. I was the one to number the items and catalog who they had come from, putting a sticker on the back with the suggested price and eventually recording who it would be purchased by and where to deliver. Someone had made us a handy spreadsheet for our inventory.

Our web designer, Olivia, had been a recipient of this shelter when it had been our only place. She had donated her time to revamp the website and add all the items for the fundraiser. She came on the last day once all the other prep work was completed. I watched as each item was added to the site, reading to her the descriptions as she typed them in, wanting them to be described exactly as the donor had passed along, adding the starting bids. At the end of the day, there were ninety-four items and services people could bid on, a way to pay, and track who purchased each item. Olivia had even left a required spot for the donor to instruct how they would like to receive their item.

We were all about to leave when there was a knock at the door. I knew it was Carl , as he was the only one with that knocking pattern. He stood, smiling, with Ha Yoon. They had brought us a dinner of salads, macaroni and cheese, fried chicken, and a tall multi-tiered white cake for celebration. In honor of Ethan and the mission of this new adventure, the white cake symbolized a clean slate to start from.

Ha Yoon told of her need to purchase an apartment building at the advice of her attorney, Mr. Clark, and shared that she wished to help further the plan of the Women's Shelter with transitional housing. This had all been a quick transition for her. She told of her rented space, her husband's murder, her selling everything they'd owned, the new blue Camaro she now drove, the new person she was and how she would love to live at the new property as a paying resident while being involved in the workings of this shelter, Charlene's Place, and The Pathway. She would have to work behind the scenes at the apartment, as she would not want anyone to know she owned the property; she wished to just be a resident.

I asked her about Mr. Clark, saying one of our program's former graduates had a father who was an attorney, Michael Clark from Clark Law Group. He took on most of our business contracts pro bono. His daughter, Kimber, was our caterer; she was on a hard path to come back from when she'd arrived here but had since gotten things right for herself as she saw fit. This entire program relied on each participating individual to want to move forward at their own speed but not stay stagnant or return to whatever unfortunate events had brought them here. Kimber was a perfect example of that. She had started writing her dad through Charlene's pen pal exchange after she had completed rehab and had made the decision to open a catering company. The Insulated Business Incubator and Carl had helped her come up with the commercial kitchen space, advertising, a website, a menu, equipment from closeout sales. Her dad had negotiated the lease. It all had come together one step at a time, as each step taken had been thought out and acted upon.

The morning of the 12th at 9:00 a.m., the auction went live. Carl , Ha Yoon, June, Simone, Kimber, and I were here at the Women's Shelter. Our system was in place. Bidding would begin now and would end on Sunday the 14th at 5:00 p.m. We watched as the bids came in, on edge, knowing this was a weekend to just watch. The real work would start on Monday with delivery and pickup; we would use the van from Charlene's Place to load and follow the route for delivery of items. Carl would stay behind to distribute any items being picked up.

Ethan's Edge was almost up and running. I could feel Ethan here with us, knowing this needed to be done to help others. But I still could not bypass the finality of the feeling of Ethan being gone. After a year, it seemed as if I would have had that cemented in my soul, but it was not. I turned to look for him sometimes, seeing his beautiful, tall, teenaged self always smiling, but he was not there. Ethan had been special, like a bonus child to me, one I'd had the privilege of raising. He had become mine. I'd been older when he'd come into the picture and Lorena had left him behind. I hated that for him. His mother was gone, but he came to work with us and grew into a school-age child at the shelter while Carl and I worked. Then, when he started school, he never minded coming here to do his homework or help out. Ethan would always be part of this building.

The bidding had shut down. None of us had come in yesterday, agreeing to meet on Monday at 8:00 a.m. to see the results. Everything had sold! Kimber emailed the gift certificates, as we read them off to her. Then on to the delivery list—there were no deliveries. Everyone wished to pick up their items today and tomorrow. Kimber had used the kitchen to make chili and cornbread with all the fixings for our long day.

It was comfortable here for me. I had spent over twenty years under this roof, watching families who had fallen apart in one way, or another mend and others tragically go back to what had brought them here in the first place. I had learned early on that I couldn't want their success more than they did. For some reason, there were people who were prone to choosing the worst option. It was hard to watch, especially when they tried again and again. There were children involved, seeing the "so what" attitude when a parent failed and did not continue forward. We had years invested in helping some families, and then they were almost done with school or ready for an apartment and they would flee, possibly scared of success more than failure. It was heartbreaking for me, but I could not even imagine what they would feel if they were honest with themselves doing all that work for success and running from it. The cycle started: failure, then a return to drugs or homelessness when maybe only one step would have taken them over the threshold to freedom from those dark places. It was not up to me to know the answers, just to provide secure services with stipulations to protect them and us. The ways back into the program were many, but generally, once someone left, it was a while before they returned, if at all. Upon return, it was harder to gain reentry—not on our end, but for them, mentally, since they had already done part of the program and knew where their personal hurdle of defeat lay. It was almost like they had convinced themselves they could not go further. I was not sure what brought people to that point, but I always tried to give extra help before they reached their breaking point, helping them over the hurdles to success.

Carl III

November 2021

I WAS ON DOOR DUTY FOR THE DAY, HANDING OUT THE AUCTION ITEMS TO THE winning bidders. I verified that the right person received what they had bid on. It was late in the day; we stayed open much later than usual, giving people time to pick up their item after work.

I was retrieving a basket of what looked like jellies, crackers, and such. I turned, not prepared for this moment, and there was Lorena, looking twenty years older than she should. But she didn't appear to be in a drugged-out state.

She said she knew of Ethan's death, tears running down her cheeks onto her rust-colored suede jacket, making stains. I thought of the stains her drug life had made on Ethan and me. As I came back to reality, I saw her standing there, staring at me, forlorn, in a state of obvious grief. I had no idea when she'd found out about our son's death. I was having trouble with it and had had a year to process, whatever that meant. Lorena just stared. I felt awkward, and compassion overtook me as she walked to a chair across the room. I followed, knowing she was not my problem, had caused many days of trouble for Ethan and me, but this was her son too.

She looked at me and pointed to her phone. In broken words, she said, "I found out three days ago. I was never fair to you and certainly not through this. A year you have walked with this knowledge." She'd gone to rehab in July, and now this.

I remembered when I'd seen her last, downtown. I asked if a gentleman, giving a description of the man I'd seen, had taken her to rehab. She looked at me, asking with her eyes how I knew. Lorena said if she had known of Ethan's death, she never would have gone through rehab. This news threatened to take her back to her usual lifestyle. She'd had a steady support system and a ride waiting from rehab so she would not sway back to her old ways.

She said, "I hope it's okay that I'm here. This was another step I had to take. I will keep in touch if you wish."

I could not answer that statement and only nodded, feeling the load of grief now dispersed a bit more with only thoughts of goodwill toward Lorena. Gloria walked out of the back room and saw Lorena, looking my way for approval to enter or leave. I nodded again. Gloria hugged Lorena, and then Lorena walked out with her cellophane-wrapped jelly basket as if it had been too much to revisit her old life, a life of regrets over a decade old.

My thoughts were scattered. My feelings were well past bitterness; I had forgiven Lorena many years ago. Otherwise, it would have been impossible to raise Ethan and would have eaten me alive.

After the door closed, Gloria saw I needed a moment and left as I sat at the table Lorena had just risen from. Her card was there; she worked for the city in the utility department. That information was more than I needed to know, but maybe she had wanted me to see she was trying to keep it together.

My grandfather was gone, just over a week now. Covid was making everything hard, harder than I would have imagined a year or two ago. Restrictions were not lifted for funerals. This time of year, outside gatherings were not guaranteed. We planned around the weather forecast and made appointments with the funeral home. He already had a plot purchased that was side by side with Gloria's. Last year, she had given hers to Ethan. I was in charge of this and felt that since his wishes were to be cremated, we should not use the large plot but purchase another smaller one. Darian informed me it was called an internment of ashes. We could bury him here at City Square Cemetery, where he had originally intended to be buried, or somewhere else, whatever the family decided.

After speaking with Gloria and Garry, I discovered Garry and Carl Sr. had purchased a niche a few years prior, right after Garry's accident, thinking of their age and current events, as Garry had almost been killed in his work accident. Garry attended the meeting with me and Darian. The paperwork stated he and Carl Sr. had the rights to be put in the niche after the prepaid cremation was performed. Their urns had been picked out as well as a niche marker with their names but missing the dates. It was all taken care of except the actual placing of the urn. Garry wished to be the one to place the urn in the niche. He wished to handle everything, saying they had talked about this event on many occasions due to how injured he had been and Carl Sr. being ill for so long. He was prepared, and he wanted to make sure he got this exactly correct for Carl Sr.

The urn was made of wood and highly polished. Carl Sr had chosen this urn, Garry said, because he would be one with nature once in the cemetery. Together, we chose a day, no matter the weather. We chose November 16th for the internment since this process was moving slowly. We planned a celebration of life at the Women's Shelter immediately following the brief outdoor service, each of us speaking if we wished. There would only be Bob, Carl Jr., myself, Garry, Gloria, and a couple others Garry said wished to attend. We had gotten Kimber's new catering company to make cheeseburgers, fries, Bonsai Baked Beans—Carl Sr.'s go-to recipe, chocolate milkshakes, and chocolate cake. A meal in memory of Carl Sr. He had requested peach and blue carnations; some would be left at the graveside and others brought to decorate the table. Music from the jazz era would be played quietly in the background. I was picturing this meal as a celebration, but we did not all know one another, and with such a small gathering, I felt this would be awkward. That was only my opinion; Gloria always felt comfortable wherever she was, masking her emotions, attending like a trooper with Garry by her side. I was amazed by her resilience and the comfort she offered Garry. Maybe this was due to her loss of Carl Sr many years ago.

On November 16th, we gathered at the site. Bob brought the urn from the mortuary and handed it to Garry. We stood but did not speak; how could we say anything with such grief? Garry placed the urn in the niche, saying something we could not hear, nor did we wish to, as they were private words. Instead of speaking publicly, we all did the same, each of us in succession spilling our final thoughts to Carl Sr.

I would not be here if it weren't for him. My name was his name, I walked like him, my hair was like his had been, my index finger was exactly like his had been, my thoughts on business had come from his and Gloria's ideas. I had taken what he had freely given me and had made what I could of my life. I turned and looked at the others standing there, realizing I had spent more time speaking to the urn than anyone else. But I knew I had been true to Carl Sr., my grandfather, and myself with my thoughts and quiet words. I missed Ethan more than ever, picturing him standing here, but he was not. He was buried over there. I felt paralyzed but needed to move on for the next person. From that point forward, there would be a marble wall separating the pristine urn and myself. I reached in and touched it once more, thanking him for all he had freely given.

Bob called in the positioners of the stone, who had to have been waiting around the corner, as quickly as they arrived. They sealed the niche. We turned in unison, me with a salute, Gloria with a low wave and nod. We returned to our vehicles and drove off, leaving one of us behind—Carl Sr.—not by choice but out of necessity.

None of us were hungry, but we arrived together, having traveled the same roads. Garry sat in the back seat, looking forlorn, riding with his two friends, Ethel and Brett. Gloria, Carl Jr., and I had arrived in one car, and Bob had come alone. I had the feeling Bob was always alone and was okay with that. Since Charlene was gone, he was able to help whenever needed without obligations.

We entered as a group, in the unity of grievers, all for the sake of Carl Sr. We'd each had a different relationship with him and at different times in his life. The table was set elegantly; flower arrangements were low so we could see the people across from us and spanned the length of the table. Out came the milkshakes first. This felt more like a high school gathering than a remembrance lunch with this menu. Suddenly, with the aroma of lunch, I was famished. The burger and fries may have been the best I had ever had. I was proud of Kimber for making a go of her natural talent after residing here a few years back; she had stayed on track.

The music played in the background, reminding me of a prom, but this was far from that. There was not hope here of new love but memories of old love, stories never spoken prior to this. We had each known him on other levels. Gloria first, Ethel and Brett last, the rest of us in between. All filling in humor and stories of the Bonsai Baked Beans, get-togethers with Carl Sr., who had been the life of each party. He had attended everything he'd been invited to, showing up with a smile and leaving the party, making sure everyone was well. I learned some things about my grandfather that day, even though that was not what I had called him, as he had preferred Carl Sr. We were a team us Carls. I could not imagine this city without his presence in it, but I would have to and take what he had taught me and Ethan and pay that forward to the participants of Ethan's Edge.

Thinking about the ones who had attended that function just four days prior to this event, I knew there was much wisdom to impart. New openings, chances for recovery and to make the pathways straight again, hope reignited after arrests and seniors having the worry of yardwork taken off their shoulders, so many projects that were being called in to help resolve these issues. There was hope in this room and would continue to be from that moment on. I was satisfied with the program, this day, my meal, and needed rest.

It had only been one year and four days since Ethan had left this earth, and I was still recovering from that. I felt my son in all of this; he'd grown up in this building as Gloria and I had worked, had run his toy cars down the railings. I could still see him as a young boy. He had gained his spirit of giving from this room where unfortunate stories unfolded, and families came through the door. He had watched the programs reshape people's lives. He had loved people, and that was how he had died, helping. I was proud of my son, Ethan, and right now I needed to leave this event, go home, and sleep.

Tomorrow would be a day to set up appointments; today was a day of rest. I told everyone goodbye and hugged them with deep meaning, knowing Carl Jr. would take Gloria home and be by to visit later today or tomorrow before he returned home to Florida. I looked at him, knowing he was the eldest Carl now, aware we resided on separate coasts, not knowing each other as we had in the past. I mentally planned a trip to visit soon, needing to secure this bond of father and son. He was broken now with his father recently departed and me with my son passing—we were the two in the middle and still had time left for a relationship to develop and continue. That was most important right at that moment.

I took a taxi home, leaving my SUV with Carl Jr. so he could drive Gloria home. After walking in, I booked a flight to Florida for May 2022 and slept the rest of the day.

I woke at 3:00 a.m., seeing the ships on the sound returning to port and knew I would be fine. I wasn't sure of how that would happen, likely one step at a time. I knew I should stay living right where I was even though I had thought of moving. I entered Ethan's room with a bowl of cereal, sat on the bed, and turned on the television to see what channel he had been watching last, not having dared to take this action before. Cartoons came to life, vivid colors. The key word here was *life*. A smile crossed my face, a genuine one, probably the first unforced smile since Muncer had showed up that night to tell me of Ethan's passing, my boy dead in the parking lot, his blood spilled on concrete. I had learned later that Pearl had ridden away on the outbound train. This was where grief has led me: to his bed, eating cereal, watching a cartoon, and smiling at 3:00 a.m.

"Ethan, I love you forever. Enjoy your time with your great grandpa."

I could see them running, Ethan faster, of course, but they both laughed as suddenly I was too, with milk sloshing from the bowl onto a towel on the floor, milk running down my chin. I couldn't stop a year of laughter that had been pent up for this moment, setting down the bowl, knowing I was incapable of holding it any longer.

"Thank you, Ethan, for everything. For being you."

Detective Rubio

November 2021

I ROLLED UP TO HIGHLINE MEDICAL CENTER ON THE NIGHT OF NOVEMBER 22ND. It was almost midnight, but the day had just begun for me. Being a detective for King County Sheriff's Office had been rewarding and outright dangerous. The hospital had reported the twelfth death in forty-eight hours. All individuals had tested positive for methamphetamines; not one had admitted it if they had been able to talk upon arrival. They all had an unusual chemical smell to them, like a cleaning product—another bad batch on the streets. These drugs were toxic enough without the additives people used to stretch them. Everyone had a new recipe, thinking it would bring more money or a better high, advertising their ideas. I had never understood how someone could imagine that it was acceptable to give the public a dose of this or that. These drugs were cooked up and distributed throughout the city in small amounts for the most profit, a vast expanse of usage with a cheap price, possibly death.

After returning to the station at the end of my shift, I saw the reports of the deaths from methamphetamines in Seattle, Lynwood, and Everett. This must have been a large batch that had been distributed quickly. Whoever had manufactured it was most likely out of the area by now or cooking up some more; they might not even know what their product had caused. We saw this frequently: batches hit the streets and were spread county to county, city to city. None of the drugs were good, but some killed due to batches gone wrong or cooks without chemical knowledge adding what they thought would work. Someone who should have never witnessed making this product would see an experienced cook and go out on their own, sometimes blowing up buildings, catching garages or other residences on fire, maiming or killing innocent people. If it wasn't destroyed in an explosion, frequently it was dumped down the drain. The lithium exploded when it hit water; this could endanger the water source as well as neighborhoods. The vapors could seep up through the pipes into homes that weren't even involved in the manufacturing, people unaware of the danger. Homes sold, cabinets soaked in chemicals, and individuals suddenly having symptoms of irregular heartbeats after moving in. This was a drug used by choice and forced upon many in ways they were not even aware of.

The common source was in north Seattle; leads were coming in of a motel on Aurora with a red sign, a lady with a green foreign car, a cash-paying man who had left suddenly in the night, not to be heard from again. I called Muncer; informed him of my findings down here; and obtained a warrant for the check-in/check-out ledger, two rooms, and the green car.

The ledger stated Daniella Harper was in room 16; Don, with a slash mark for a last name, was in room 24—directly across from each other. The desk clerk stated he had seen Don but had not checked him in. Daniella lived there full time; she worked from home, she said, bookkeeping. We showed him the warrant. We did not locate the car but retrieved the keys for rooms 16 and 24 and entered both, which were spotless and without any personal effects in either room that we could see from the door.

In room 24, we carefully took the burned bedspread off with gloved hands and made a pile on the floor of blankets and sheets. The mattress had a hole in the center with the stuffing cut out; there were fragments of ripped cash in the coils as if someone had been in a hurry. The bottom of the nightstand fell off from our movements. We found a duffel bag of reeking, dirty clothing in the shower as well as empty gallon-sized bags and plastic wrap. The same dirt was on the clothing as the duffel bag, as if someone had been digging or working outside. I checked the nightstand's drawer and tipped over the single chair, finding no clues. There was nothing under the nightstand. I found a receipt for a single steak dinner purchased in south Seattle four days prior and a bus transfer that had expired at 6:00 a.m. on the same day. The coat hanging on the back of the door still had tags on it. A newly purchased pair of blue jeans, a pack of colored underwear, one of men's socks, and two identical t shirts were folded on the counter next to a plastic bag without a store name, a bag that said "Thank You" on it. Inside the duffel, I saw some writing. "Donny" was clearly written but had faded.

Room 16 had no evidence of anyone currently staying there, even though Daniella had allegedly been living there for quite a while. That room was clean, not a hair on the counter. It had a brand-new bedspread and pillow, dishes on the counter next to a microwave that had not been provided by the motel, a propped-up dish drainer, a box fan by the window, and a fancy towel behind the bathroom door. The drawers contained soaps, makeup, toothpaste, and drawer liners, but it was clearly all discarded product. I suspected Daniella and Don were both long gone with the cash. This was not retirement money but was enough to get out of this establishment.

We returned the keys, instructed the desk clerk to not rent the rooms until further notification, and left, knowing something but not much. The green car had not been located, no cameras were installed at this place, and Don and Daniella were both missing—together or not.

Detective Muncer

November 2021

I RECEIVED A CALL AT ABOUT 10:00 P.M., NOT WISHING TO LOOK AT MY CELL phone, as it always brought a circus and more work, but sometimes it would bring me a step closer to the actual crime that had been committed.

It was Harborview. I answered, "Detective Muncer." It was Naomi, the redheaded nurse from a few nights or months ago—this year all faded into one category. She said someone was there to talk with me, but he would not give his name. He had come in to be treated for an infection in his hand that had almost turned deadly; hospital staff had been able to catch it just in time. I asked for a description, but the one she gave fit half of the people in their twenties in Seattle: tattooed, brown hair, around six feet tall.

I made a U-turn on First Avenue after checking the building Pearl, Bender, and Rizzo had escaped from. I knew they were not there but drove by anyway, out of habit. I headed up Marion Street to Sixth Avenue, crossing I-5 at James, and parked in my designated "Police Vehicles Only" spot. I entered through the emergency entrance. A guard taking temperatures and surveying the crowd waved me in, recognizing me, as I had been there many times recently.

Naomi spotted me from the nurse's station, where she was emailing a report. I walked over, and she pointed to room 6. Walking in, I did not know what to expect, but Axe, a.k.a. Peter Dunnigan, was the last person I had expected to see. Naomi looked on from her perch across the hallway, possibly able to hear us. Most criminals, even low-grade ones, did not call for me, especially since I specialized in gangs and homicide. The last time I'd seen Axe, he had still been with his fake gang set up by Bender to move product, the Emerald Jetters. His story had been he was distraught over Pearl, his girlfriend leaving on the train. —or so he had tried to convince us. Ethan was dead, but he'd had a solid alibi and played no part in any crime we'd been investigating.

I just stood there, watching him. The only thing I asked was, "You asked for me?"

"Tonight," he stated with much duress, all coming from his internal self, "I am not able to hold it in any longer. I feel responsible for Ethan's death. Pearl was my girlfriend, and if I had been watching her movements instead of following the load of medical supplies, Ice would not have had the chance to kill Ethan." Then he spilled the rest, looking relieved to do so—but I was quite certain he wondered if I would be taking him away for his recent crimes.

"Pearl contacted me and acted all lovey, like there was never a gap in time from Ethan's death a year ago until now. She said she had another heist of electronics to move and knew I was experienced from the last time. She said convinced me I did everything right. If I had thought any further than her lies, I would have realized she didn't know about what had happened on the heist of the medical supplies because she was on the train. I wasn't thinking right, just happy to have my Pearl back by my side—and her trust.

"We drove by the warehouse in south Seattle, and she showed me where to be. It looked closed, like it hadn't been used for some time. The doorknob had moss growing on it, and ivy was entering the building through the crack in the concrete next to the large, steel, roll-up door. I wondered what industry this building had housed until Pearl punched me, saying, 'Stay on track! Are you with me?' She assured me there would be a delivery that morning, and they would pick it up that night. I was to intercept at 4:00 p.m., loading the truck she would supply and then leaving it downtown. There would be no reason to worry since the goods couldn't be reported stolen. No one would know they were missing until long after they were gone. I was to transfer the goods into another truck, a much smaller one, in a few hours. Then I was supposed to meet Pearl, who showed up in coveralls and a yellow reflective vest, her hair all back and not flying like normal. I was shocked to see her that way. We transferred the goods to the smaller truck. Just as everyone was leaving downtown on their way home, Pearl handed me the keys to the larger truck, said she wanted me to meet her at East Terrance Street at 4:00 a.m. and said we could leave town on this kind of haul.

"I got there at 3:45 a.m. There was no parking, and I couldn't make the tight corner in that huge truck, one unlike I'd ever driven I drive a compact car. Pearl called and asked me to open the back. She thought she'd left something in there. I was unnerved at this time of the morning, making all this noise and surrounded by seven hundred windows that I could be observed from. I put down the lift gate while Pearl was on the phone instructing and cut my hand severely as the gate came down, realizing I had left the keys in the ignition, and it was running. I was hoping no one would steal it while I looked for Pearl's hoop earring. I gave up, demanded she come there to get me. She laughed, said, 'Thanks—I got you again.' The cold-hearted person that she is. I had no choice but to leave the truck running in the middle of the road since both the cab doors were locked, glad nothing of mine was inside. I walked away, knowing I had been played by Pearl for the last time. I wasn't sure how to proceed but did know I needed medical attention with my hand swollen—and I needed to get this off my chest."

I thanked him, got his current contact information for the report, and told him not to leave town. He stated he would be moving immediately after getting out of here so Pearl and her crew didn't find him; he said he would call with an address. I wished him well, calling him "Peter" to hopefully start the disassociation of his identity as Axe and with the Emerald Jetters.

As I turned to leave, I saw Naomi look up from her computer, knowing she had heard the entire story and was pleased she had called me. I was secretly happy she had my cell phone number and felt comfortable using it.

Bob Barton

December 2021

THIS TIME OF YEAR WAS EXTREMELY HARD ON PEOPLE, WITH THE FINANCIAL PART with Christmas, some unemployed due to seasonal occupations like construction and agriculture, then there was the matter of death. It was a subject many did not address, but it was there right in front of us, either by natural causes, violence, disease, happening suddenly, or a long illness dragging on over many years. I was in charge of placing the wreaths family members had ordered to be laid on the graves of their loved ones. So many people visited this time of year to make sure we had done our job by fulfilling their order and to also pay respect to their loved ones. I wasn't sure which was most important to some. As they stood in the inclement weather, their scarves flying, gloves being rubbed together they seemed to need to tell me of their family member or friend that had passed on. I heard stories of deep love, some of their faults. Others brought trinkets, flowers, food, alcohol, photos; they blew with the wind. We found them and had no idea where they belonged, feeling bad for not being able to match up the item with the intended recipient. People during the night would prowl for whatever they can find.

I started on the wreaths December 1st, beginning way in the back and working my way forward. Today was the sixth and I was on the last section. This was a task I preferred to do alone, out of respect. I had gotten to know many of the grave holders and their visitors.

Today I would place the special wreath on Ethan's grave. A senseless death at such a young age; potential killed at its peak or before it had even begun. After getting to know the Carls and Gloria, it was an honor that they allowed me to place the wreath. I headed up the hill with my last load of greenery for section C-7, knowing I would place Ethan's last to be able to spend some time there. I knew Ethan only in death but had heard so much about him. As I rounded the corner by the fir tree where the raccoon's nest was, I saw a car with two occupants. One got out; they were clearly having an altercation, as I could hear them from here, a football field away. The female was who had gotten out; she headed toward the area where Ethan was buried. She was not dressed for the cold weather. Her skirt was short, her jacket and top showed her midriff, the shoes were ballet flats, and she had on a scarf of fashion and not warmth. The wind whipped across these even fields and hit her head as her hair blew up on one side. This image made me shiver. She did not appear cold like her mind was on other things. The gentleman with her yelled for her to return to the car. He inched forward, and she yelled for him to wait. She was at Ethan's graveside, now sitting on the ground as if it were not frigid. The driver sped up and rounded the corner; the woman ran across the cemetery, hopping over headstones as if playing hopscotch, and jumped into the passenger side of the little silver car. She hit the driver in the head, and he swerved on the lawn making a tire track in the frozen grass as he started to backhand her. Then he stopped as if he knew better from tangling with her before. They exited through the large ornate gates, nearly missing the sign. On the road, I saw him driving erratically.

I called this incident in, if only to save others' lives. In the distance, before I was off the phone with 911, I heard tires squeal, a crash, and then the motor going full speed, sounding like a sewing machine. I knew they had caused an accident and were getting away. I heard a single gunshot, then all was silent. I could barely see the intersection from my vantage paint but traffic had stopped, and people were taking cover. The only noise was far in the distance, sirens heading to the scene. I was still on the phone with the dispatcher with no other information after the report of the gunshot since I could not see the intersection well where this had all occurred.

A call came across my radio; Seattle Police were here at the cemetery, asking where to find me, since I'd made the original report. Officer Metevior told me of a standard traffic accident caused by the erratic driving of a silver Honda. He wished to know what I'd seen of the occupants and what they'd been doing here. I told him of Ethan—he knew of the case—and that it had been a female dressed rather inappropriately for this weather.

He pulled up a photo of a mug shot online and asked, "Is this the lady?" Pearl Swanson. Sure enough, it was her.

He said they'd found the male occupant deceased from a single gunshot wound in the chest as well as the car still running and in gear up against a curb. He'd been the only occupant in the vehicle.

I said, "He was not alone when he left here. That girl was in the car."

I told the story of her running across the graves and jumping in the car. He asked if we had video of their entrance and departure; I assured him we had video, even of her sitting at Ethan's grave and running to the car. I asked the officer how she was connected to Ethan; he told me of the night of his ride with her to the train depot, the night of Ethan's death. Pearl had not directly killed before that the police knew of, but she had been the cause of a few people losing their lives. This latest death was of Rizzo Loman, an accomplice in a few recent heists, and they had been underground since the truck had been found in the road a couple months back, up by the hospitals, running and with the doors locked. I had never seen Pearl here prior to this day; I would have remembered her if I had. She seemed to stir up trouble upon entering anywhere, and her departure brought a tornado of destruction. Rizzo Loman looked like a young man, and his impatience had demonstrated that. I had only seen him from afar and this one time; it was obvious he had not been here to pay a visit to Ethan but was, instead, Pearl's ride. She was out there somewhere, in the common situation of lying low and being in trouble, a predicament she found herself in on quite a few occasions.

I asked Officer Metevior what her record was, and he said, "Loitering." He shook his head; under his breath, I heard him say, "Three dead."

Simone

December 2021

THE HOUSE WAS QUIET THIS TIME OF YEAR, EVERYONE INTO THE HUSTLE AND bustle of the holiday season. I loved all my Christmas decorations, going through the bin of the children's homemade ornaments bringing back memories. That was what I would decorate my house with this year. Thomas had not been over for dinner recently due to his heavier workload and child on the way. At least they had all stopped trying to convince me to move into a smaller home. I was making good use of this space with my art. Also, I had been working on getting rid of any excess so if I did at some point wish to move, my load would be lighter. But for now, I did not have plans of going anywhere. This was where I was used to living, and it made a fabulous art studio.

Next year, at Charlene's Place, I would start to teach painting to those who wished to relax and make art. The class would be offered to people once they had reached a certain point of the program. They would feel much more confident in their own home with something on the wall they had made. I was excited for this new learning platform for those who had lost all faith and hope in themselves and were trying to rebuild that inner confidence.

It was only a week before Christmas. Rain bounced in the gutters and on the street, the music played, and neighbors had their outside lights and decorations up. But I sat, remembering and missing my family, who were scattered here and there. Most of all, I waited anxiously on the phone call from Thomas. One more person added to our family. The last difference in count had been the subtraction of Luther almost three years ago. It hardly seemed possible that time had moved on that much without me feeling it as I went through the daily motions of living—not that I didn't feel the absence of Luther every day. Right around this time of year, I could still see him leaving for his walk. All that effort he put into his health to keep his blood pressure down and a truck left the roadway and killed him. I often wondered if we all had a moment, we were meant to leave this earth. Would Luther still be here with his high blood pressure if he had not started his walking routine, or would something else have taken him at that exact time?

As I was off in thought, my cell alerted me. It was Cora.

She said, "We are on our way to the hospital to bring Luther Thomas Washington into the world."

I could not sit here, but the hospital was not somewhere they let people in these days unless they were in need of medical attention ever since Covid.

I called Gloria and June, and they were both soon on their way over. June had a small jigsaw to keep us distracted, and Gloria had food.

They arrived in what felt like hours, but I knew it hadn't been that long, as I had kept checking my phone with only a minute passing between each glance. The time would go slowly as I waited for the safe delivery of my first grandson. I wished Luther was here with me but was thankful for my friends, who would be arriving any moment.

June and Gloria arrived like they were grandmas-to-be. We talked and paced, ate a nibble but were too nervous to finish, put the edge of the puzzle together and could not concentrate on the center, instead just picking up pieces and putting them back in the box. June found one piece of a whale; we slowly built the sea in the center of the puzzle.

When evening rolled around, a text came in from Thomas. There were no words—just a picture of my grandson, Luther Thomas Washington, with a perfectly round face, eyes wide open in curiosity, and his little hand holding his daddy's finger. We were all in tears and suddenly hungry. Knowing I could not go to the hospital like in pre-pandemic years, there was nothing I could do except wait for them to be released—and also wait for all the additional pictures they would send.

Detective Muncer

December 2021

THESE HORRIFIC CRIMES ALWAYS FELL ON MY CASELOAD DURING THE HOLIDAY season. This year, I planned to take Christmas and New Year's Day off. I would spend Christmas with Everett, Micky, and Daniel. That situation had been a smooth transition since it had already been in place prior to me being aware of Everett's needs. My supervision of his care and the two identical duplexes had come with ease.

Midmonth, I was asked to look at some footage of an accident that had turned crime scene. I saw the footage prior to talking to Bob Barton upon Metevior's request. It was not a surprise that Pearl had been involved in this incident, but I was still not sure how. She was nowhere to be found to question. On the footage, I saw her run into the shrub-filled field behind the cemetery, the one the deer used for crossing to the Puget Sound, following the creek. There were water ducts along the way that connected to the other side of town, but with her scanty clothing, I was not sure she would have survived long without someone to pick her up, as the temperature had been close to freezing. She ran into the field immediately after the gunshot that had killed Rizzo, but we could not see into the car to determine if she had fired the shot. If it had been her, she was on the run with the weapon—or it was somewhere in the vast field.

I looked at the three cars that had been involved in the wreck in the impound lot. They were all totaled. I was not an insurance investigator, but no one would want to drive these after what I saw inside—another memory I would try to forget. Cars and people were the same; if someone was a mess, so was their mode of transportation. To do this investigation properly, I attended to the scheduled time where everything would be removed from the vehicle, including the seats. I remembered Jin Mae's car being in this exact same spot not too long ago, thinking of Ha Yoon and wishing her well this holiday season.

The red car was twisted beyond recognition. The front seats came out first. It had trash in the rear compartment where no one had sat in ages. The floorboards were packed with food, wrappers, and various other pungent items. The carpet underneath the pile of garbage was growing its own colony of fungus. The gray seats were set aside for investigation. I saw something silver, assumed it was part of the seat lever, and turned away, but my instincts told me to return. Tipping the seat back, I saw there was a handgun stashed under the driver's seat where the spring had lost its tautness. It was tucked in just like a holster logged it in as evidence.

I took it to ballistics, asking if they had the results of the one bullet that had killed Rizzo. The results from the medical examiner's office were not in yet. That was when I left to hurry the outcome of this investigation while Gene Moore was still hospitalized from the accident. He had been alone in the red vehicle. Had he shot Pearl and Rizzo because of the accident, or had he been following them, and their getaway caused this accident? Only Gene and Pearl knew the answer to that. He would be put under police guard immediately. The search for Pearl had been ongoing off and on for years. She would be a suspect then we would be unable to file charges for one reason or another; this was nothing new with her.

After watching the footage again, I saw the bullet come from Gene's car and hit Rizzo in the back. I was not sure who his target had been. I paid him a visit at Harborview, placing guards at his doorway and him under arrest. I was grateful the other bed in his room was empty due to the nature of my questions for him. He told me someone else had been in the car with him at the time of impact. I knew this was not true from the footage; I showed him what I had seen and knew. He caved and said he had been looking for Pearl for a couple years, ever since she'd stood him up at Alki Beach when he'd been an Emerald Jetter. She had not only stolen his heart with her sweet talk but also his money with the promise of drugs and being in on her next big deal.

"Then, after all this time, I saw them," Gene said. "I didn't know who the guy was—probably another schmuck like me who believed her line of crap. I feel sorry for him being with her. After the impact, the driver turned, overcorrected, and that was when my gun went off. I was shocked at the car heading up the curb and knew my aim was perfect on Pearl. After the change in position of the vehicle they were in, I had no idea who'd been shot, if anyone. I was losing blood fast from the accident. I tucked the gun away where I always kept it and passed out. One second, I'm driving around on lunch to pay my rent, and the next thing I know, I'm here, wondering if the accident, gunshot, and vision of Pearl had even happened. As you can see, I have a head injury from my makeshift aluminum visor scalping me. I wonder if I'll ever grow hair again."

Gene was cooperative. He remembered the accident and shot clearly now, filling the room with regret, saying he had spent much time thinking of Pearl. He wished he knew how to regain his funds. Truth be told, since she had ripped him off, he hadn't been able to get more drugs and move to the next level, as he said. He'd been forced to work, since Jasper Walter's parents had asked him to leave when their son had confessed to Ethan's murder. They had given him a few days, knowing his parents had both been lost causes, living on the streets of Seattle. He had landed a job in a warehouse loading pallets; it paid the bills for a rented room downtown, one where the hallways had smells you wouldn't want to identify. I thought, *Like the back seat of your car?*

I told him how Ethan had been killed at the train depot, Pearl departing on the last outbound train of the night. We both had a knowing look that the train ticket had been bought by Pearl with the money she'd stolen from Gene. He signed his confession of firing the shot. I was sad for another life having been sidetracked when he'd been trying his best to get things together. It was always harder to get it together than to keep it together. He thanked me for treating him and his sudden dilemma with respect. He did not know before this anyone had passed on due to the accident—only that his carefully aimed bullet had gone astray. He asked for the gentleman's name that had been murdered, wondering if he had knowledge of him. Knowing he would hear soon, I told him, "Rizzo Loman is dead. One stray bullet." He hung his head; the bandage was all I saw as I left the room.

I took the elevator to street level by the ER, hearing footsteps running behind me. It put me on edge, as I never knew who might be after me as a detective—perhaps someone having a grievance from days past? The voice was soft but not so faint I couldn't hear it in the isolated hallway. I knew upon the first syllable it was Naomi.

I stopper and she stood in front of me, looking up, down, and up again, breathing hard from her run down the hallway. She blurted out, "I don't know what your life entails, but would you like to spend New Year's Eve with me at my friends' party by the Space Needle?"

I wasn't sure what to say but spilled the first thing that came to mind: "I would like nothing better than to attend. You have my number. Please call or text with a place and time, what type of attire, and if you would like to be picked up in the police cruiser, as that is the only vehicle I have."

She smiled, lightly patted my shoulder, and said, "I'll be in touch."

I was summoned to headquarters at roughly 9:00 p.m., the night shift and day shift all blending into one. A female was there to see me and was not revealing her name. She had showed up after hours and was waiting outside. I knew this had to be an informant of some sort or someone whose conscience wouldn't let them hold their secret any longer. I pulled up on Fifth Avenue. She sat on the concrete steps dressed in warm clothing for this cold night, bundled in a multicolored scarf, matching hat, puffy coat, and long pants. I almost did not recognize her, but for sure, it was Pearl Swanson.

She said she wanted to know how Rizzo was. She had no knowledge of my meeting with Gene Moore or Peter Dunnigan and that I was aware of her part in the heist and truck left running in the road. I asked her why she would summon me this late in the night. She spilled the story of her remorse over Ethan's death; that was why she'd been at the cemetery. She had not known of his death until a couple months after it had occurred.

She said, "I didn't shoot Rizzo. We had a plan to get out of here and move to Bakersfield, California."

At the mention of Bakersfield, I was all in. Thoughts of Gene, Rizzo, and Pearl were not on my plate anymore; I could only hear one word. I asked Pearl, "Why Bakersfield?"

She said, "It was Bender's idea that we lay low there for a while. His Aunt Danna—well, not really his aunt, just someone who he thinks of as family—has a place there big enough for me and him. Rizzo was never really going anyway. He just didn't know that. He thought he was in on this, but our use of him had run its course."

Now she didn't know of Rizzo's status or where Bender was; maybe he'd left for Bakersfield on his own. Pearl fidgeted with the ties on her hat, looking off like she was in a trance or dream world. "Bender and I were going to just leave town without a word to anyone. We sold all our furniture and anything else of value for the trip down. It was like a vacation to us."

I thought, *like you've ever worked a real job in your life* but kept silent as she babbled on. Then she looked up, realizing who she was talking to, hoping she had not revealed more than she should.

She went back to the intersection story suddenly, saying, "There was the accident at the corner and then the gunshot. I ran so I didn't get hit, thinking there would be more than one shot, but I never heard more. I was scared of whoever fired the shot."

Just then, ballistics called. I closed my window, motioning for Pearl to hold on. The ballistics on Gene's gun and the bullet that had killed Rizzo did not match. Gene was innocent of this crime. Firing a weapon in the city was his offense, but it wasn't murder. With Pearl pacing on the sidewalk from agitation and to stay warm and then sitting for short moments, picking her lip at a high rate of speed, I called Gene at Harborview and let him know of this new information. He could not believe it. He said he was smiling, and it hurt his scalp. He thanked me and asked if, I was sure. I informed him of the ticket he would receive and hung up.

Pearl was not here for no reason; she might know the answer to who fired the shot or have been the shooter. I questioned her about Rizzo and the bullet, then placed her under arrest for suspicion of murder, still not revealing the knowledge I'd acquired during my conversation with Gene. She'd been the only person in the vehicle with Rizzo at the time of his murder. I asked her where the weapon that had fired the fatal shot was; she stated she never saw a weapon, just heard the shot and was scared—her usual story. She was also questioned about the truck and heist, which she denied having any involvement with. She was booked into central lockup and held until the next day.

We took her to the scene of Rizzo's murder and had her show us the route she'd taken out of there. The K-9 units were brought in to track the way and to see if anything had been left behind. If she had had a murder weapon and had ditched it, there was not any evidence of it. She had returned to the place to retrieve it, or it had vanished. She claimed she had run to the bus stop, had seen the blood on her clothing, had stopped at a thrift store, had bought the outfit she was currently wearing, and had caught a bus home. She had slept on the floor since all the furniture was gone and had waited for Bender, who never returned. She also stated she had never fired a weapon. If she had shot Rizzo, it had been from the back seat, and cameras showed her only occupying the front passenger seat.

We had nothing to hold her on except suspicion of murder, breaking and entering, theft—her list of charges probably went on from what we knew, but we had no direct proof except Gene's and Peter's word. Had they told us that information to get back at Pearl? Could they have been in on this with someone else? She was released the next day but was instructed not to leave town for any reason.

I returned home more confused about this case than before finding Pearl, having no idea if she could be legally locked up or not. She stayed on the edge of the law.

I saw a text from Naomi saying she hoped it was not too late to text. She said she would love a ride to the party and that it would start at 8:00 p.m. She gave me her address on Cherry Street, close to the hospital. Then added it was a rock-and-roll themed costume party. I smiled, wondering if my leather pants still fit from when I'd been in the Green Pyramids twenty-seven years ago. This was perfect for me. I texted back, "Sure, see you then."

I was the one with secrets this time. On most days, the city hid secrets from me, but on this occasion, it was me with the plan to fit right into this party. I couldn't say I'd ever been to a New Year's Eve party. That was a night I'd always worked in the past, as the city was alive with activity and crime on such an event. So many crimes were planned when activity and noise levels were high. This year and last, the Space Needle had not had its in-person crowds due to Covid restrictions, but there would still be a fireworks show. It was exciting for me to go out on New Year's Eve and have a date. This entire year had created a major turn of events for me with Everett and Micky, and now Naomi.

Christmas Day was quiet in the city and at my house. I brought all the fixings for pies to Everett's and showed up early because I didn't want to be alone. If I was honest with myself, I could have cooked them at home but preferred company on this day after so many years of running solo. I arrived, thinking of the bounty hunters positioned all over the city watching for fugitives who would come home to visit family. This was the detective in me; I tried to turn that part of me off for the day. Everett had a whimsical sense of humor if you could follow it, very dry and under the cuff. Micky and Daniel appeared to be getting along well. I did not ask, only observed their interactions. As a detective, I always watched everyone.

We had all brought a present for one another, agreeing on a ten-dollar limit for each. It was not about the present itself but instead about the gift being from the heart. We were a strange family of sorts. All the gifts were under the tree. A dinner of cheeseburgers and fries was eaten—Everett's choice, and we did not mind. I suspected we were all just happy to have someone to be with on this Christmas Day.

Daniel started with his gifts, clearly professionally wrapped; they were all journals of a sort, each featuring a different cover to suit our personalities. I imagined song lyrics in mine. I wanted to ask what everyone else would add to their empty pages, but they might have secrets that should not be revealed either. Micky, being the open book of the group, reported that she wished to track her moments of thankfulness and quickly jotted down this day.

Everett went next; he had gift bags with a can of almonds and a bag of tangerines in each. He had even bought himself some; he pulled his hidden bag from behind the chair, laughing like he'd told the biggest joke. His laughter was nice to hear; he was generally a serious soul hidden inside himself. I was happy he was comfortable enough to laugh around us.

Micky had bought everyone different writing instruments. She had gotten Daniel a pen holder and pens to keep at the front desk of his shop. She had bought me a package of mechanical pencils, and a set of colored pencils and a sharpener for Everett.

I was not imaginative at all and had bought everyone a gift card for the sandwich shop Everett talked about all the time.

We ate our pie and relaxed to Christmas music; I left before Daniel, who I suspected would be heading upstairs with Micky after my departure. When I pulled away from the curb, I thought of my real family that had disappeared so many years ago. I could not picture their faces any longer— only those of the people I had just left. Working for the department was a daily reminder of my family; now I had new people to protect and a party to attend with a lady in exactly seven days. This would be different for me. I needed to go home and try on my leather pants; the platform boots that made me too tall; my torn, neon green shirt; and the vest with chains. I hoped my hair had grown out enough to spike for this event. Naomi would be surprised at what she had gotten herself into.

The next few days were uneventful and quiet. I worked from home during most of them, trying to connect leads I may have missed on older cases. Many officers were out on vacation for the week.

Rubio and I met for dinner on the twenty-ninth. I caught him up on Dae, who had murdered Jin Mae, as well as on my family life. He had news, too: his son, Albatar, was joining the military. I asked if he would like to talk to Hazel before he left, explaining who Hazel was. He said that would be a perfect plan. We decided to have dinner here next week, before he shipped out. I hoped Hazel would be up for this, as I had a feeling she might be retiring soon.

On the afternoon of the thirty-first, I got butterflies in my stomach. It hit me: I had not had a date, by choice, in many years. This was a big step for me. I convinced myself I was only committed to one party but knew if my outfit didn't turn Naomi away, this would turn into more than one date.

I pulled up as close to her apartment building as I could; the night was cold and my ripped shirt let the wind in, traveling around my torso and running up my spine. I was grateful it was not raining and messing up my spiked hair, which I had worked an unusual amount of time on to make perfect. I rang her buzzer at the entrance, and she let me in. I bounded up the stairs to the second floor, two at a time, wearing these ridiculous boots. My heart was light; I felt confident being out with the true me showing. For many years now, my rock-and-roll side had had to stay at home. I rented a car for the evening; she did not know that yet.

She opened the door with whipped up hair that was normally flat. She wore animal-print everything, including her nylons. Her dress was short and polyester, like my mother would have worn, right out of the seventies. Naomi was beautiful. I realized at that moment I should have brought flowers. I was really out of my league. I turned and told Naomi of my oversight; she smiled, handed me a flower from the bouquet on the table just inside her door, and asked if I was ready to go. I nodded, letting her lead the way. She was in charge of the night. I did not even know where we were going, had not thought to ask.

Naomi said she knew the way; her sister was the real-estate broker who had sold them the townhouse. She instructed me to head north on Seventh Avenue, west on Madison Street, north on First Avenue, left on Broad Street, and into the alley. This felt like the longest ride of my life. I was suddenly tongue-tied and felt strange meeting people for the first time dressed like this. I was usually in authority and wearing what the department wanted: slacks and a dress shirt. When I'd worn this clothing before, I'd been on stage, not in direct contact with people. Also, it had been expected back then that I look like this.

She told me on the ride there about the view and how it would be a dream for her to have such a place. She stayed where she was since she was on call all the time and it was close to her multiple shifts and I-5. We arrived. Food was plentiful, and the view was as spectacular as Naomi had promised. I thought of Carl and Hazel living not far from here, both in the air, and wondered what their plans were for the night.

These people were all dressed as equally as extravagant as I was. I felt comfortable and fit right in. We ate, then played some carnival and rock-and-roll trivia games. I was still not sure who owned this spectacular place or who had thought up all the timed activities, but I was truly having a good time for the first time in years. The music was right on schedule with the games, blaring through built-in speakers that we could not see, and the sound system was preprogrammed.

At about 11:45 p.m., we all stood at the window, watching the preparations at the Space Needle, which was right out the window. At that moment, my song came on. The second I heard, "Downtown, knowing the buildings and the streets belong to me," I started singing and dancing as if on stage. It was as if everyone at this party knew the song; they sang in unison, like a choir but with a bit of rap and rock mixed. I was not sure how they all knew this music, but I knew how I knew it; I'd written the lyrics and had listened to them for a few years. It was comforting to finally know that people knew my music and had fun with it. I had never been where my music was played, had just heard it around town coming out of cars, apartments, and blaring out of headphones on the streets.

There was a CD on the counter. Someone picked it up and said, "This is a few years old; do you listen to this while doing police work?"

I said, "Yes, I do," and saw on the back after they laid the CD down: #MunDetJ; #DJMuncer; #SeattleStrong.

Naomi was next to me. Suddenly, her eyes opened bigger than I could image. She knew my secret. I put my hand on her back as we headed toward the window. Just then, the fireworks started; midnight arrived. I looked at her, and she invited me with her eyes for a New Year's midnight kiss. I was sure the Space Needle took off like a rocket during that kiss, but my eyes were not on it—they were on Naomi. I knew this year, 2022, would be different. It had already started that way, as a year of excitement and betterment. We left shortly after.

Naomi said, "I know your secret."

I gave her a sly look as I drove the rental. She asked where the cruiser was.

"At my place," I said.

We had a tennis match of a conversation as we went up the hill with people traveling in every direction, heading home or to afterhours parties on foot. There was more traffic tonight than usual at this hour. I walked her to the wooden-and-glass entrance doors of her building, kissed her lightly on the lips, and asked for a second date. I promised to show up without the costume. She gave me a disappointed look but knew we couldn't go out everywhere like this. I told her happy new year and left, smiling with hope.

Randell Rinwell

January 2022

I grew up on the outskirts of Seattle. Most of the normal things for teenagers were always just out of my reach, and I was possibly a tad bit off the grid of the successful, as I deemed them. It wasn't that I didn't try or want success—it was I didn't know why I would need it.

In 1994, I accepted an internship at the University of Washington; my friend Marshall had applied for this coveted position. I never felt I had a chance against Marshall, a popular and fit-in-anywhere kind of guy. But he suddenly left town for another opportunity, and the spot was mine.

Then there was my home situation, which prevented a normal life. During high school, my mom worked nights, so I was required to watch my younger siblings. Amos and Vada were seven and eight years younger than me and not my responsibility at all, but still, Mom needed my help, and we all required a roof, so I diligently went home after school so Mom could work the swing shift. I helped with homework and made sure no one did anything crazy to harm themselves. I was just a piece of this pie—vital but not important in the teenagers' minds. After-school activities were something, I heard about in the cafeteria but did not have time or possibly the desire to join in on.

At twenty-one years of age, I still felt like an outsider. No one treated me as such—I just had that notion instilled deep inside of my being. I was a back-burner kind of guy. All my peers partied more than heavily and were into whatever sport was in season. While I continued living at home, not because I had to but out of choice, I was still responsible for my siblings; they were entering the teenage years. I didn't know how to act like a college student, as I had been in charge for so long, being the levelheaded one. I knew I truly did not belong with my peers outside of lecture, a social event, or the occasional sports game I attended at someone's dorm or apartment. I could never figure out the fascination with sports and being an avid fan of a team. My life was lived in accordance with everyone else's needs, but I lived solo at the same time. Even when I attended the parties and viewing events, I saw the unity in friendships and on television—the cohesiveness of the crowd as they cheered or were in sorrow after an unfortunate play on field by a much-loved player. It wasn't that I didn't understand the strategy since I was a business analyst; I couldn't grasp doing anything with anyone. Depending on another human to act in any predicted way was not in my realm of thinking. I acted on my own, provided for myself, and took opportunity as it was presented. I was pleased to be considered part of the crew and acted accordingly when with them. Behind closed doors was another story. Randell was Randell, and that would be how it was until the end—or so I thought.

Professor Aland was contemplating retirement due to health reasons and had created quite a successful business analysis corporation while employed as a professor. He saw talent in me, he said. It was a maturity and talent he'd once had after a few years in business. That was when he asked if I would like to look over some spreadsheets in my spare time. They were related to a new company with state-of-the-art software which I was familiar with. Professor Aland had been under the weather, thinking it was age. I was happy to take on this project and any other new ones I was sent out to investigate.

A few months into the newly appointed profession, I felt confident I belonged here and knew Aland was not returning, as he was absent from the firm more and more recently. Being too ill to teach, he left the university and turned over the office and all accounts to me, who was helping wrap up the last of the open assignments and closing the establishment that had been created by him so many years ago. Aland knew nothing of the last few accounts that were opened as new calls came in. Right or wrong, I used my own business cards that I'd designed for this time. They named a fictitious company; I called it PNW Analytical. After completing the proper closing of Professor Aland's business, I turned over the files (after making copies for future reference), checks, and any other pertinent information. When Aland asked what I would be doing, I genuinely thanked him for the opportunity and told him there was a new position at PNW Analytical that was opening for me, thanks to my experience with his company. As far as Aland knew, Randell was onto a good start in life—one that he had helped with. I never saw or heard from Aland again.

As I sorted Aland's paperwork, I found the lease information, applied for a business license, and transferred the phone to my name, keeping the same established number. It was officially mine, and I have been able to keep the business in service for twenty-five years. For some reason, I fit into this profession quite well. People were comfortable sharing with me, mostly financial information, but sometimes personal tidbits that were way out of the scheme of my contract.

One lady confided in me about going to a church other than the one her family thought she went to; at another contract, an upstanding business owner disclosed he had stolen some clients from another business. A different woman secretly told me she hated living where there were any cloudy days but was in a marriage, she could not leave due to financial burdens her husband's gambling had placed on her. Who was I to judge, when I had started my company almost the same way, on false pretense?

Most of my business came as word-of-mouth; there had never been any advertising except the sign on the mailbox out front of the three-story brick building—when the weather didn't take it away. I finally put the sign inside the aluminum locking box for mail identification purposes only, not needing an actual sign outside anyway. The noise of the mailbox was a sure sign someone was entering the building. Only residents or office-dwellers crossed the threshold; my clients never met me at this location, only at their facilities.

My goal was to not see other people except when we met at their location, where all the paperwork I needed would be anyway. I always put on one of my three suits; it had never taken more than three in-person meetings to finish any project. It was always the blue suit for the first meeting, the brown for the second, and black for the third—if my presence was required that many times. After each meeting, I felt the urge to rush back to the office, where I kept the standard uniform of a white button-down shirt; V-neck, mustard-colored sweater; brown or black polyester pants; and velour slippers. Wearing this ensemble made me feel as if I were in a 1950s sitcom. Every weekday, I was fanatical about this attire. Upon entering the office, just behind the door, Professor Aland had installed a closet where I hung a few sets of this same outfit for my strict wardrobe. No one had ever seen me in my favorite attire. Upon leaving, in the back room, there was another closet where I kept my blue jeans, t-shirts, sweatshirts, and one pair of tennis shoes. I did not like to see those while working. I always arrived home in the blue jeans and tennis shoes, just like in high school. No one knew of the polyester-and-sweater fetish; it was how I felt comfortable, smarter, like a uniform.

This small office was in the back of the building, without windows, which was preferred. At the end of the well-worn carpeted hallway, I entered under the stairs; the fourth step had a sudden creak. When leaving for the night and opening the heavy wooden exit door, which had a window so dirty I could not see out, I always played one of my favorite games: guessing what the weather was like. Some days the door would be taken by wind; others were sweltering, with the heat radiating from the sidewalk—so hot I could barely breathe.

On Tuesday nights, I had the whole evening to myself. Mom was off that night and stayed home for her children and responsibilities. I preferred to eat at UR the Guest, a small diner between my office and the northbound bus tunnel, not having any desire to be with my siblings or at home. This night to myself was my gift to me. My favorite—and what I always ordered—was a cheeseburger and fries with extra pickles on the side.

It was on one of my nights there in 1999 that I noticed Fleur for the first time. She entered as I was paying to leave. No one had caught my eye like that before. Her step was easy, and her mood seemed light as we passed through the door almost together, her entering and me exiting. I could smell her—a perfume that was possibly her own scent. Her clothing was flowing and sheer. There was a sparkle about her, as if she were there but somewhere else at the same time.

By the next week, I had forgotten I was going to arrive an hour later. As I was leaving, in she came as if we were right on schedule, me being the one ahead of a schedule she wasn't any part of. I knew the following day I must try to meet her again. She was not there on Wednesday, and I had to be home, as I was already late for my obligations. The following week would have to be when I made this plan work.

It was on my unusual journey to meet this beautiful lady with hair wrapped in a bun that I started noticing people. It was like an awakening of my senses; I noticed how individual each person was. Normally I would come in and bring my paperwork or a business magazine, not caring about the world around me or anyone else. This was my time—a time for Randell Rinwell, to be myself and unwind. The people in the diner before the Seahawks games would all be like those college friends, only grown-up versions—people who held steady jobs and were still out acting this way over sports, boisterous and energized.

The following Tuesday, an hour later than my normal schedule, with stomach growling, I slipped into my usual booth, second from the back, and patiently waited for the intriguing lady. She did not show up—not that Tuesday or the two after. On the third Tuesday, I did notice a hint of neon-green feathers poking out of the crease in the booth where the vinyl seat back met the puffed-up seat bottom, so neatly sewn with buttons and seams. While pulling gently on the feathers so as not to damage the item, I carefully slid to the other end of the bench to relieve some weight on the cushion, and the neon-green-and-navy-blue feathered scarf suddenly let loose of its unfortunate place. I had every intention of turning the scarf in while paying, but that was not what happened, not at all. Shocked by my own actions, I tucked the neon scarf down the sleeve of my coat. Just as I looked up, there was the lady, the one I had been waiting for, almost running by in a leotard and headband, her skirt flittering in the wind and sticking to her back. I thought it was a tutu if I had the terminology right. I wondered if she had seen me stealing the scarf. I exited; outside on the sidewalk, in the blustery evening, she was nowhere to be found. She had vanished after the first sighting weeks prior.

I checked my watch and realized I had the option of two more express busses thirty minutes apart before I would be forced to take the regular city bus home. My decision was to take the scarf back to my office, my private space, the one no one entered. No one would be able to see my stolen property. I would hang the brightly colored scarf up under the set of clothing I never wore—the just-in-case set. This felt silly and embarrassing—that I, Randell, had stolen the extreme-colored object and was now hiding it. I could not remember ever stealing anything prior to this; I had never wanted anything like this and surely could have afforded to buy one if I'd wanted to. There was no way this object could be brought home—no way I could be seen with it. It was stashed, and I hoped I could forget about the silly boa, as I now fondly called it, claiming it as mine.

On my way home, looking out the bus window, the only colors I could see were neon green and navy blue, in every store window and on many people, each wearing their Seahawks costumes. When had such a vast amount of people chosen different forms of costumes? Who had made them all? Shirts, hats, jackets, shoes, jewelry, and laces—I had to get this out of my mind. I started picturing all the posters and pennants, too. After all, I had worked downtown and had eaten at UR the Guest for a quite few years and had never even thought of sports or all the gear associated with them. I thought, *I will create my own costume secretly*, wondering where I would obtain the needed items.

I started noticing people in the next few weeks with wigs and face paint and knew I could create a new identity for game days. I wanted to have a connection to the people and sports. A need suddenly arose in me almost an obsession; maybe I would get a television and watch the games from my office in the new costume. My other identity would be Stu the Game Man. I would be able to paint my face; be a number-one fan; wear big, crazy, mohawk hair; and yell outside of the stadium eventually. So, unlike my true self, this would be an outlet. Stu was a good name—three letters in a row. S. T. U. No one would know it was me. The idea was coming together. This would be a way to fit in, to release my frustration of not belonging. I would become one of them, a die-hard fan right on the streets of Seattle—but first I needed a plan on how to go unnoticed in my transition, as no one could ever be aware of my identity.

The following week, I devised a plan after acquiring a few more football items online that were mailed to my office. My analytical mind went to work with location and game days. The trains came in, and people gathered as they went to and from their destinations. I could incorporate with the crowd, go totally undetected. I was not sure why this was so important to me, staying undercover or dressing up in character. I arrived on foot, shortly before a train was to approach, with my carry-on gym bag filled with the costume of the day, which had been carefully tried on in the back room of my office. I knew exactly how to transform quickly. Inside the duffel there was the white, green, and blue makeup and a mirror to hang on the back of the stall door. The rest of the costume already on under my street clothing. Then I would put gloves on so every part of myself was covered, not that my hands had any identifying marks, but I would feel more comfortable being protected from sight. I would look over the stall to see if anyone was out there. This was a thrill, entering the stall as Randell and emerging as a new person, a man named Stu—someone I had created.

I had a few of Stu's own jerseys made my own sketched signature style with "STU" imprinted on the back and "#1 Fan" on the front. The gym bag went into the locker, the same one each game day, locker number 73 (for the year I was born and so I would not forget upon returning). I was hyped up from the crowd and also paranoid someone I knew would see me. On the day of a game, I would drive my olive-green Oldsmobile Omega into the lot for passengers and park at the train station. Always having a City of Seattle parking pass from some ongoing business of various city agencies, no one ever questioned the use of it. It was official; not everyone received one of these parking passes. I hardly ever drove the car and could park anywhere with this highly-sought-after access. If anyone watched me, even though my schedule was so precise before each game that they could have figured it out, I would look like just another traveling man who blended in perfectly, as if on business. I would enter the depot as close to one hour before gametime as I could and coordinate with the train schedule.

Always leaving the station on foot with the rest of the fans who came in by rail, in the beginning, I was not exactly sure what I was supposed to do once arriving across the street. Everyone else would enter the stadium; I had no desire to see the game but couldn't help but hear it from blocks away. I observed the yelps and behaviors of the crowd, made up my own system of hollers, shouts, and maneuvers. When I heard the stadium roar, I danced and hollered, too, like I had never done before. Stu was helping me be confident, and this is harmless, right? With all my other odd behaviors, I was not hurting anyone.

I was getting to know the vendors who set up outside; they all knew my character as Stu. I never bought coffee or food even if he was hungry or cold; my greatest fear was that the white makeup would melt and show my identity, even though I never, in all my years being Stu, ran into anyone I knew in my other life. During the time being Stu, I had seen a few people I recognized from work, but from afar. Even though it didn't matter, it mattered to me to keep Randell and Stu separate entities.

Fleur and I met on the fourth Tuesday, the week after I had discovered the boa. When she walked in, my first thought was, *did she see me steal the feathers?* Then it hit me that she might think I was a weirdo or had a fetish. If she had seen, what exactly had she seen—the thieving or the hiding?

By the time she walked in and sat at the table directly across from me, I was blushing unable to control myself from anticipation. She smiled; there wasn't a need to look at the menu, as she was a regular, too.

The waitress took her order by asking, "The usual for you, Fleur?"

They talked a bit about surface things like the weather and if business was steady. I nodded and said hello to Fleur, now knowing her name, and we both knew we recognized each other from a few weeks prior. There was not a basis for conversation, especially across an aisle. With thoughts of why she hadn't been in, I didn't feel I had the right to ask her anything, still not knowing her at all. She seemed tired and amped up at the same time.

I learned she owned Toe Tip Productions by a phone call she received during her meal of grilled cheese with tomato, fries, and a cup of tea. I studied every graceful movement without being too obvious, feeling I should leave first since I had been there when she'd arrived. She was there for nourishment, and I to meet her, unbeknownst to Fleur.

The next day, I discovered Toe Tip Productions was a dance studio just around the corner from my private office, in a direction I had never traveled. I was a man of routine. Suddenly, I felt seedy, being as I had a hidden office that no one saw and two alter personalities, and Fleur was out there for the world to see at a dance studio with floor-to-ceiling windows, costumes being worn in public all the time, an assured and forceful personality teaching people how to move their bodies in all sorts of ways which she must already know. I wondered: If I took dancing lessons from a studio far from here, would she find out? Did all the dance people know each other? This was my analytical mind working overtime. Maybe Stu could take lessons and use the moves outside the stadium; then I would know some dance terms, too.

Realizing at that moment I did not have any people skills and knew nothing of how to really act around friends, I panicked at the thought of being in a group of dancers—or any other gathering, for that matter. During the ones I'd attended in college, I would talk when spoken to. At work, I was in charge and made recommendations—never anything of personal nature. My mom came and went, the siblings were almost of another generation, and they had their own lives, ignoring me as an obstacle to their lives. This was when I realized I had never had a real friendship with anyone.

I wracked my brain, trying to figure out how to spend some time with Fleur, and had no ideas. But I knew that was what I wanted to do. She knew I existed but not my name. I was not even sure she would like to know me or anything about my life. At least I had a job title that sounded important and a business card without an address on it, just a PO Box, phone number, and email address. She wouldn't know that I had rerouted my walk to go by her place of employment now instead of the previous way; she probably didn't pay attention to what went on outside. She didn't realize I knew where she worked, nor did she seem interested enough to ask anything about me. She appeared spent while eating dinner on Tuesdays. It seemed as if my world was becoming something no one could know about, with many sneaky maneuvers, all with motives to connect.

How could so many harmless secrets have been attracted to such a plain man in polyester pants? I now wore neon-green spandex in my office, exchanging them for the polyester pants more often than not. The fluorescent-green tennis shoes were a bit over the top, but they were what made the costume come together. I had an eye for this type of thing; it was a new skill for me. My mind seemed to be always on the costume and how to better it. I would come into the office, change a few times, and get to work on my current project. Making business calls dressed like Stu had allowed me to be a bit more forceful with my decisions about other people's companies. Maybe Stu was good for me—not mentally, though, as I was torn between the two most of the time. Sometimes I forgot which person I was supposed to be—Stu or the polyester-clad analyst.

It was an unspoken standing agreement that Fleur and I would have dinner together on Tuesdays, her at her table and me at mine, across the aisle. Rarely would I not show up, but she had her times when she wouldn't or couldn't be there. Sometimes weeks would pass without us seeing each other. I was sure this bothered me much more than her; she never let me know in advance or apologized later. We didn't have an unspoken or spoken obligation. After all, we were just two people in the same restaurant weekly; we had no other connection. I wanted more than this. We would only eat and leave. There was no lingering for conversation; we were both preoccupied business owners, her with dance and me with my mind on her.

One Tuesday, almost two years after meeting, I asked if Fleur would like to go for a walk on Saturday, maybe somewhere like the Botanical Gardens, Woodland Park Zoo, or Alki Beach. She said yes, to my surprise, she would love to get some lunch and go for a walk.

We continued our Tuesday routine and added Saturday most of the time. This went on for many years, occasionally adding a night out, or we would be each other's dates in the evening to social business functions. I would not say it was a love affair on Fleur's end, more a matter of convenience since I fit in and was not insistent to her about anything, but we did truly enjoy each other's company. She was extremely busy at different times of the year for recitals and at the beginning of classes. I would have gladly taken this relationship further, but Fleur seemed to be content, and I feared if pushed, she would escape from me altogether. This arrangement was working, and there were not any strenuous requirements to it. We talked business a bit, but I thought this gave me an outlet to see the city, wear my suits, meet new people, and especially spend time with Fleur, who was flightier than anyone I had ever met.

My thoughts always wandered to the reality of Fleur discovering my identity as Stu. She had never stopped by my office or asked exactly where it was. She did not even know of my sweater-and-polyester attire; I would keep it that way. This arrangement worked for us, as strange as it was.

I had been Stu for about twenty years and had enjoyed my weekend activity, as I didn't have any others except my walks with Fleur, weather permitting. If the weather was bad, we didn't even have lunch on Saturday; I was not sure why we didn't find an alternate activity.

One night, I was outside the stadium and heard a laugh. It was September 19th, the night the Seahawks played the Titans. I immediately knew it was Fleur; she did not often laugh loudly—or, at least, not with me—but this was her, no mistaking that. She was with a man, one she touched on the arm while laughing. He turned to see a street acrobat, and I saw he was much younger than me or Fleur. This threw off my routine for the whole game. I had considered myself a professional entertainer prior to this moment; everyone who attended knew Stu, but this threw it all off.

It ate at me all weekend. We met on Tuesday as usual, and she did not mention going to the game or say who the man was.

On October 7th, during a game with the LA Rams, I positioned myself in the same location. She arrived just as before, not laughing but smiling with the same young guy. On October 25th, she did not show up or I missed her; I wondered the entire game. On October 31st, the game against Jacksonville, Fleur showed up with the same man, both in costume—he as a bird resembling a seahawk and her as a cat, probably one of her costumes from work. By this time, I was upset and wondering who this man was and how she knew him. Fleur did not show up for the game with the Cardinals on November 21st nor December 5th for San Francisco.

I did not hear from Fleur the week of Christmas, nor did she show up for our usual dinner on Tuesday, December 21st, to my utter disappointment. There she was, happy as can be, on December 26th at the game with Chicago. It was not that I didn't want her to be happy—I did, fully happy in every aspect of her life. I just wished I could have made her happy. But then there was Stu. I could not spend time with her and enjoy the game on television or from inside the stadium like this young guy. Fleur had never mentioned her love of football to me. Maybe it wasn't football she liked but the gentleman she attended the games with.

On January 2nd, she showed up as usual with Mr. Season Ticket Holder, as I'd dubbed him. The longer this went on, the more sarcastic I became. The game was almost over; the Seahawks were clearly winning from the raging noise escaping out of the stadium. I was almost ready to leave to meet the next train so as not to blow my cover. This being the last home game of the season, I stayed a bit longer. Dread covered me; I knew Stu would be closeted until next year, and now wished I hadn't stayed so long.

A group of four extremely intoxicated men approached me, demanding my wig and identity. I would never reveal either; my driver's license was in locker number 73 across the street, so they would never find out. They did not know me anyway. I turned to escape their comments, and hands grabbed me. Three of them told the fourth man to leave me alone. I was almost behind the stadium now; with the crowd roaring, no one would hear me if I yelled. I did not want to bring attention to myself at all, just wanted to get back to being Randell for the duration of the off-season. I had never thought Stu would be in danger, someone who had never harmed anyone. The other three had left the scene; the fourth, intoxicated man grabbed me and knocked my head into the side of a steel girder by the base of the stadium. I didn't realize how colossal this structure was from this vantage point on the concrete looking up. I did not remember anything after that.

My last thoughts were advice from my mom. I could still hear her say, "Always carry your ID in case you pass out somewhere." Advice I had not heeded this time.

Simone

January 2022

THE GRANDBABY WAS SO PRECIOUS. IN OTHER TIMES, I WOULD HAVE BEEN allowed to see him more and bring friends by, but for now, to be safe with Covid, pictures would have to do. The first week the new family was home, Gloria, June, and I cooked a few meals, and I delivered them. Thomas had a couple Christmas projects to wrap up at work, so Cora and Luther stayed home, out of the cold.

This Christmas was bittersweet, more so than any other since Luther could not see his namesake grandson. While at home, I took out pictures of Luther, putting all the holiday ones together and looking at the dates on the back, arranging them in chronological order. When I turned the first one in the stack over, I saw it was Luther in Atlanta not long after we'd met, when I had attended Emory. He was polishing up his mama's Plymouth Savoy. Not a car he drove often, but he said it was the only part of Grandma Clara he had left. I wondered whatever happened to that car. We hadn't brought it to Seattle. I looked in amazement as I laid the photos in order on the table. No children to four children, and Luther still had that genuine ear-to-ear smile. He was always cracking up, as he called it, making fun of himself, and creating real humor. He had been goofing around and making me laugh the morning he'd left for his walk just a few minutes before he'd passed away on December 27, 2018. How had I made it into the fourth year and not checked in? I answered myself: staying busy.

I needed to set the program in motion for Charlene's Place. I found a slip of paper and took notes of what I had, what was needed, and where this program would be headed.

I napped that afternoon with my picture of Luther, the one of baby Luther, and thoughts of my other children, Clara and Drake, so far away. Lucille was here but on another schedule. They all had busy lives. I rarely sat in Luther's recliner, but today I sat, lay it back, and covered up.

I was awakened at 5:00 p.m. by the doorbell. It was Clara, Drake, Thomas, Cora, baby Luther, and Lucille. What a pleasant surprise for dinner! They had not all been able to attend for Christmas. Clara walked the halls, loving the artwork. Everyone looked like they had as children. I was Mom again if only for a moment of observation. They saw the pictures on the table, taking them all out of the order I had arranged them in, looking at the dates on the back, saying, "This was after I was born," or, "This was before you." I enjoyed their company, interactions with one another, and the family I had created. Luther was missing, but I was sure he was here in spirit.

The night drew to a close. No one assumed they could stay here and had rented hotel rooms. They all left, and the house was quiet again, like this evening had been a mirage. I went back to sleeping in the recliner, missing them all and seeing life from the perspective of my parents when I'd gone away. My children would return in the morning and cook breakfast before returning to their chosen lives. I had a few more hours with all of them. How could I miss them so much when I had no idea they'd been planning to come here?

I knew deep down each moment was a treasure. There was no room for sadness or wishing this or that. Life was what it was, and thankfulness for each moment was what was required to make it through this tough journey, some days harder than others. I had raised them all to be independent, strong leaders, and that was what they had become. Proud of them was what I'd hoped for Luther and me to be able to say about our children. They probably didn't even know how much they were loved.

Detective Muncer

January 2022

WITH THE SEATTLE PD BEING SHORT ON STAFF AND THE CITY HIGH ON CRIME, I was called out to a vast number of calls that would generally be taken over by homicide or street crimes units. This one was particularly involved. Thousands of individuals milled about. Everyone was a suspect until we knew they were not, but we couldn't hold every one of them. We started by talking to each person exiting this side of the stadium as they passed by, determining their whereabouts at approximately 3:40 p.m. There was no way for us to know the exact time of this heinous crime. Stu, a man who had been a regular at nearly every home game for almost two decades, lay in Harborview Hospital, just up the hill. I was unaware of his condition. When he'd been found, the Seattle FD had rushed him into the trauma unit. His blood still stained the asphalt where he had laid. With knowledge of this, I could not keep myself from looking that way.

People walked by, unaware that a crime had even happened just around the corner of a typical pathway out to the parking lots and mass transit. Most all of them were there to attend the game and had been inside the stadium the whole time, as it was a critical point in the last home game. People wanted to see every play and get their money's worth, treasuring the football season as it came to a close. After the crowd thinned, the remaining people were vendors set up outside who were in the process of dismantling their canopy and tables and packing up the goods that hadn't sold on this cold January day. Snow was still on the ground in many places from our unexpected Christmas snowstorm. The wind whipped through the gaps between the cars, people, and buildings bringing pieces of trash and aromas of food.

I wondered how Stu had ended up back here, in a location no one walked through frequently. Either he'd been running from someone, had been pushed here, or had been dragged. This was not somewhere he would have ventured on his own; he had always been up front, by the door, to cheer the crowd on.

I headed north on Occidental Avenue, the city being my friend. I knew it, and it knew me. I turned from King Street onto First Avenue, then up Yesler to Eighth, then Ninth Avenue. I found parking on Alder Street, which was a rarity, overlooking the downtown core of the city I had just been swallowed up in. Here I was again on the hill, at the trauma unit, always wondering when I arrived if it was for nothing. Would the patient be able to recall anything that had happened? Would they be sedated or worse? I headed in, using the emergency ambulance entrance, encountering fewer people this way. I tried to avoid crowds, when possible, with Covid in the air, a sickness without parameters, which had changed the ways of life as we knew them. I remembered who I was and what my business was this early evening.

Naomi smiled as she saw me enter, which suddenly became important—that she was happy to see me. She directed me to room 22. I entered, and Stu was alone but not there, his face covered. He had left us before I'd been able to arrive. I wished I had come here first instead of talking to the crowd. I bowed my head and thanked Stu for so many smiles given to people everywhere.

Dr. Hernandez approached. He informed me Stu had already been gone long before he'd arrived here after every effort to save him in the ambulance. There was nothing anyone could have done. They were investigating next of kin for notification and waiting on the hospital morgue to pick him up. Some of his white face paint had been smeared off during resuscitation attempts, trailing onto his number-one-fan jersey. There was not a wallet or any other form of identification on him. No one even knew if Stu was short for Stewart, Stuart or was even his name at all; in all these years, no one had ever asked or had a meaning conversation with him that we knew of. He had been a happy fixture of football. My next step would be to contact the stadium's vendor coordinator, then talk with the outside vendors for January 2nd. Not as many had been in attendance this day due to the inclement weather and it being the final home game of the year. Sales were normally down on gear as the season wound down.

On the morning of January 3rd, I made contact with the stadium staff, requesting the vendor list and feeling as if I should tell them of Stu. But the investigation continued. Not many people knew there had been a crime committed outside yesterday during the game, especially office staff. I wondered if they would even care. Did they know who Stu was? I asked the lady in charge; she said she had never attended a game but assured me she watched faithfully on television. She had not heard of Stu, which wasn't surprising since she only saw the interior of the stadium on television. She also stated she did not watch the news or read newspapers. She gave me the list I had requested, and I left, passing the scene of Stu's murder.

I headed to HQ, another early morning. They were trying to convert me into a day-timer instead of being an overnighter. I entered the building and took the stairs to my pretend office on the third floor, the one where no one knew I was. If they wanted me, there was the phone or radio. I set up shop with the list and a yellow legal pad, calling each of the seventeen vendors with an "O" next to their name for outside. I left messages for twelve of them and talked to five, three of which had not set up shop yesterday. Out of the two I spoke to; one stated Stu had seemed normal but was a bit sad about this being the last home game. He had left, as normal, about thirty minutes before the game ended. One asked if Stu was in trouble; I could only inform them that no, he was not in trouble, leaving their mind to wander to the unknown territory of who Stu actually was. After reminder phone calls and hearing from the rest of the vendors over the next couple of days, I learned that no one had seen anything unusual. All in attendance had the same story: Stu had left as if on schedule, and no one knew where he'd parked or if he even had a car. He had looked like all the other fans dotting the map of the city with their loyal neon-green-and-navy-blue attire.

It was now January 8th. There were no new leads on this case. We didn't even know who Stu was, his last name, or anything about him. He had been fingerprinted for identity purposes, but there were no prints on file in the database matching his. We now knew Stu had never been arrested, had never held a job needing a security clearance or state license, had not applied for the purchase of a weapon or concealed-carry license. We knew a lot of nots but nothing, no new leads. He had to have lived in the Puget Sound area to be at every home game all these years.

On January 31st, we got a call from King Street Station about a vehicle left in the parking lot with a City of Seattle parking pass. The vehicle had been parked in the same spot since the beginning of the month. I headed over to retrieve the city parking pass since I was close by. King Street Station was an asset to this city providing transportation and with their high security cleared out any abandoned cars from the parking lot on the last date of the month. I ran the plates on the ones getting impounded, looking for Stu as a legal owner, but had had no luck with that. One was an olive-green Oldsmobile Omega belonging to a man with a name I found familiar, Randell Rinwell. It was the car with the city parking pass. I was not sure where I knew him from—criminal or business—and was sure he would not have the pass legally if it were criminal. I retrieved the placard, took photos of the registration and vehicle, and started to leave the lot as the olive-green vehicle passed, bouncing on the back of a flatbed tow truck, the ambulance of cars. This car was not going to be repaired but to the impound lot, waiting for owner retrieval or the auction.

As I started to exit onto Second Avenue, I saw someone frantically waving in my rearview mirror. He was clad in the classic Amtrak vest. I turned around, and he said there was something inside I may want to see. This was usually not true; I did not want to see any of the unfortunate things I saw. I proceeded through the wooden doors, entering the station and admiring the architecture, clean flooring, and 1920s aura. We arrived at the rental lockers, and he opened number 73, which contained only a small duffel bag. The employee grabbed the wallet out of the bag, which contained a Washington driver's license with the name Randell Rinwell, giving an address in north Seattle off Forty-Fifth Avenue NE. This would not normally raise any alarm in me, but the car matching Randell's name and the city pass raised red flags.

Randell could have taken a train and extended his vacation. They checked all inbound and outbound tickets used from the month of January; none had been purchased in his name. They checked the camera footage from the first to the third. Randell entered the shot, and I instantly knew who he was. There was not a sign of his departure. He had done some staff reorganization recommendations at the department in the past. Randell Rinwell was an upstanding citizen and was now missing. I left with the duffel bag and checked the state website for Randell's business, PNW Analytical. I located his place of business on Second Avenue, stopping but not finding Randell at his office. I did find a letter inside the main lobby door of whom to contact in case of an emergency. I called, and they agreed to let me in at 9:00 a.m. tomorrow.

Detective Muncer

February 2022

I ARRIVED AT RANDELL RINWELL'S OFFICE AT 8:50 A.M. ON THIS COLD AND SUNNY morning. The sun and I did not get along. Shortly after my arrival, I saw a female in an expensive-looking business suit, most likely the leasing agent, waiting for me. I showed her my badge and told her the brief story. She did not want to hear it, wishing to be onto her next task. She unlocked the door. I asked if she minded if I opened it, not knowing what we would find inside with Rinwell missing. There were no signs of violence, intrusion—nothing alarming.

She waited a minute, fidgeting, then said, "Can I leave this unlocked for you and you lock up on the way out?"

I was glad to have peace and time to look for what I needed without someone else's impatience. I had fond memories of my professional dealings with Randell and wished to find him unharmed and alive. Truthfully, his suggestions had gotten some people transferred to other locations and out of my hair. I checked his computer, which was plugged in and still on. Nothing there except files with local business names, all password-protected, probably current cases for him. The browser was opened to the Seahawks schedule for the 2021 season as well as links to a couple word games. I checked the desk and found only office supplies; pens all lined up in the same direction. I saw the closet behind the door, opened it, and found white shirts, mustard-colored sweaters, and polyester pants. In the last set of clothing, I saw something shiny sticking out. It was a scarf of some sort in the Seahawks colors.

I looked around and went to the back door, picturing it opening to the alley or a back stairwell. It did not go anywhere; it was a room packed with Seahawks fan gear, shirts, spandex pants, shoes, wigs, and framed newspaper articles about Stu covering one entire wall. This room was a tribute to Stu, but how had they known each other? Had they shared the office?

Then it hit me: Randell Rinwell and Stu were one and the same. I was shocked by my discovery and that Randell had pulled this off for two decades. I was sure this would be as surprising to me as anyone. Randell had hidden Stu well.

I locked up, feeling perplexed that an outstanding citizen could be dead, someone who had only wanted to make people smile. Now to solve this crime and do right by him, I had to find out who Randell Rinwell really was and what suspects ran in his circle. I started with breakfast at UR the Guest, asking if they know Randell or if he ate there with anyone. The waitress was a wealth of information about Randell and his forever romance with Fleur, who owned Toe Tip Productions. After looking up the address on my phone, I ventured around the corner, seeing the large dance studio that was closed due to the early-morning hour. I took the number and a picture of the business hours and went back to the precinct and my pseudo-office to research Fleur Fensby. The dance studio had been established in 1994 and had been in good standing with licensing, the department of revenue, and the IRS. Taxes had been filed yearly, right on schedule. Fleur hadn't even received a speeding ticket in the thirty-two years since receiving her driver's license. There were no judgements, liens, or other court records on her; she had existed without friction or debt. Like Randell, Fleur appeared to be a model citizen.

Hazel

February 2022

On one of the windiest days of the year, with the lights flickering and the wind bringing trash and leftover skeletons of leaves in through the front door of the precinct, I thought I heard my name quietly drift down the hall. Peeking from behind the door of the office I was delivering inter-office mail to, I saw Carlton. I was surprised I remembered his name since I'd only seen him once at Atlantic City Boat Ramp during mum's celebration party. He spotted me as I left the office. I approached, having no idea why he would be there and for me. Possibly he could be in some trouble and need help or protection. His demeanor suggested he wanted something.

Shaking my hand, he was very confident. He said he was sent by the planning committee to ask my permission to build a float for Vera, since she was my mum. They felt she'd been killed at their event, and they would like to honor her. Also, they wanted me to ride on it. I was not a public person but did love the idea of a float and knew mum would love this in honor of her life and passing. She had never missed a parade, would even travel to neighboring cities to attend.

Carlton told me this had been on the agenda for a few years, then Covid hit, and the committee did not meet, and festivities were minimal.

This would be the first year going all out again. He apologized sincerely and asked if I had ideas since he had not known her at all, had attended her celebration with a mutual friend. I did have ideas; they had been forever etched in my mind after the guided tour of mum's body by Darian at the funeral home, showing all of her tattoos. How could I forget that? I asked Carlton if he had time to go to my office and get a printout of the list. He nodded and followed me. I printed the list with fourteen bullet points, one for each of Mum's tattoos.

I could tell he was not following exactly; his response was, "Not to be rude, but wasn't she elderly?"

I told him the story of my Navy career and how she had visited me in all those locations, in addition, the story of Halverson and how I had returned to Eastbourne to see him a few months back. He was in awe of the story, only expecting to come here for a yes or no, not even aware if he would find me and I would have such a detailed idea. I told him this was a shock to me, too—her death, the call to view her body, and the discovery of the tattoos. Carlton asked for my card so he could call me directly if that would be okay. I gave him my cell number and card.

He rose to leave, saying, "You never know what someone is about until you take the time to know them. I am happy to have discovered Vera today."

A week or so later, Carlton called to see if he could email me a rough sketch of the proposed float. It was a perfect replica of mum's tattoos. The right outer edge was brickwork; on the left center was a garden of daffodils. Mount Fuji was on the left outer side, and a globe twirled from the center of the float. A suitcase was featured on the front left side, a Navy ship on the front right side, a beautiful flamenco dancer was left center, a sunset on the upper rear left side, the Leaning Tower of Pisa on the upper rear right side, with waves between the tower and sunset. The Space Needle was right up the front, casting its shadow down the whole float with a special light attached for the effect. Autumn leaves were scattered around, there was a palm tree, and then the best for last: a replica of Halverson riding right in front center, concealing the float's driver. I could not have asked for a more precise model. It had been eight years since mum had been gone, and I was overwhelmed with the generosity of the parade organizers to make this float in honor of Vera. It was perfect, with some elements lying flat and others standing tall.

After my grief was under control, I emailed back that I could not have thought up a better plan and asked if we could use this float in other parades at a later time. They said the parade would be in June, but they would keep me updated on the float's progress. I suddenly had many questions: Where did they store the float bases when not in use? Was that the same place they created them? Was the same base used year after year? I also wondered if Mum knew the answers to these questions since she had always been in attendance if there was a parade. She saw them as a reason to celebrate in the streets. She had gone out celebrating, and someone else's moment of indiscretion had led to my years of grief.

I would have never thought of working for the Seattle Police if I had not met Muncer after mum's death. What a perfect path this had been for almost a decade. Many people had been helped by the clues put together in the records department, all behind the scenes. The only people who saw us were department or courthouse employees. After running the front lines being with the Auxiliary Security Forces in the Navy, this had been a pleasure—to be virtually invisible. And now, they wanted me to ride on a float.

Detective Muncer

February 2022

THE DAY AFTER STOPPING BY TO SEE FLEUR AT TOE TIP PRODUCTIONS AND finding it closed, I showed up during the posted business hours so as to not give her any hints that I was going to be there. Fleur Fensby was a small-framed, flighty woman of about forty to fifty years of age; she was in great shape due to her occupation. The open class list online had her as the instructor for most upcoming classes; this place offered a wide variety of dance styles for all ages.

I walked in, feeling awkward due to the daintiness of this establishment. There was lots of pink and bright coloring all over the sets and walls. Fleur greeted me at the front desk; it appeared there was not anyone else in the building, I wondered if she felt unsafe here alone. In my line of work, safety was a natural thought. I had waited too long to speak, and she had a questioning look about her, realizing she was basically in her underwear with a lace skirt over it and alone with a silent man. I asked if she had time to talk privately, now not actually knowing if she was alone in this large space. She nodded, and I showed my badge and identified myself as Detective Jeffrey Muncer with the Seattle Police. She was concerned with what business I would have with her; I could see her face change expression, not to one of guilt but wonder. Fleur, having never been in any trouble, might not have ever spoken to a police officer, especially one looking for her personally.

She directed me to a small table with four unmatched, antique-looking chairs in the corner by the window. I was not confident any of them were stable enough to hold me with my not-so-dainty body and movements that had felt clumsy since entering these doors. She invited me to sit, and I took a chance on the yellow brocade fabric one. It held me, so I sat still as I asked her how she knew Randell Rinwell.

She looked overly surprised at my question and said, "I just saw Randell a few says ago, am not sure exactly when."

I asked again how she knew him.

She said, "We met many years ago, possibly almost twenty, at the café around the corner. We have dinner once or twice a week and both own businesses in this neighborhood." She asked if Randell was in trouble.

I asked if she knew Stu. She did not. I asked if she had ever been to Randell's office. She stated she had not, that they had always met at the café, here, or at one of their residences. They had attended many functions together and had had a fun dating life.

I asked how well she liked football.

She responded, "Your questions are not going together. And what could you possibly want with me?"

I asked again if she liked football. She said her nephew Brian had season tickets and she had attended a few games this year. She did not know much about football but loved the unity of the crowd, the excitement, and the colors. She also said she had nothing to hide. I asked if Randell and she had ever attended a football game or any other sporting event together.

She said, "Walking has been our main activity besides dinner."

I thought, *This woman does not give answers well, and she talks of what I did not ask.*

I felt it would be a good time to tell her of Randell Rinwell's unfortunate death. I told her I had worked with Randell on a few company evaluations.

She asked, "Did I not know Randell after all these years? Did I miss some signs? Is he in trouble, or are you looking for him? He has always seemed like an upright citizen with nothing to hide. I have always been good at reading people; I can feel when they are distrustful."

I told her of Randell's death before she could interrupt me again; it was like she did not want to hear what I'd come to say. She was honestly shocked by my blunt delivery of this news. Her mouth hung open midsentence, and her face could not possibly be any redder. Tears shot out of her eyes as if a faucet had turned on.

She finally said, "I should have told him I love him. I have always acted independent, and he went along with my terms so as to not lose me. I never felt I wanted a full-time relationship with anyone, but Randell Rinwell was the closest I've ever come. He was an upstanding man." Fleur got up from the energy of sudden grief and regret; she walked in circles.

I knew she had no idea about Stu. I was not sure Randell would have approved of my next sentence, but I asked: "Can you come with me?"

She nodded, not caring where we were going.

We left her studio after she changed into something warmer. She forgot to lock the door, so I asked for her keys and secured the building for her. We turned a couple of corners and arrived at Randell Rinwell's office of PNW Analytical. I checked the mail and opened the large doors, and we walked to the end of the carpeted hallway.

Fleur frantically asked, "Where are we going?" She looked stunned to be in a building she had not been to before. Not even truly knowing if I was a policeman, she felt danger.

I told her this was where Randell had worked. She looked at me like I was not speaking her language. She said she had always imagined an office unlike this one. She regretted not knowing Randell as well as she could have.

We proceeded to the last door in this hallway, the one facing us. I gave her the key to open it so it would be her decision to enter. She walked in, and I stayed in the hallway a moment, allowing her to take in her surroundings. She looked behind the door, saw the mustard-colored sweaters and polyester pants, saw Randell's computer, everything as he'd left it. She opened each drawer, as if wishing for more information but only finding meticulously filed cases, pens, stapler, and paperclips, all in perfect order. Closed cases were all in cardboard file boxes labeled with the name and year.

I told her there was one more room if she wished to see it; it would explain why I had asked about football. She slowly stepped toward the door containing Stu's persona and opened it. She walked into the room of his memories. She laughed, saying she had seen this person at the games and asked if Randell was a fan of his or if they had shared this office. I told her they were one person; she might have been more shocked by this news than the news of Randell's death. I ran to get the wheeled office chair before she could fall right there in Stu's hidden lair.

She laughed again, saying, "This is too much. I always knew Randell hid a wild side."

We looked at the photo from the front page of the newspaper I'd brought in, lying open on the desk, and there was the story of Stu, his murder, and Fleur entering the game with her nephew Brian in the background. She asked what would happen to this office and its contents. I did not know but needed to coordinate with the investigation team, next of kin, and give the key back to the property management company. I was happy I had the key in my possession today to help Fleur through this shocking news. I simply said, "I do not know."

I walked Fleur back to her studio, asking if she would be okay alone. She nodded, saying a class was starting soon. I handed her my card in case she thought of anything. She was sad and needed to burn energy but seemed frozen in time. The line between before and after had been drawn for her. I seemed to make that happen for many people. That was probably the deepest part of my job for me: notifying the families and other loved ones. There were too many emotions to list, but they were all normal in the loss of a loved one—or even an enemy. There was no certain way to act after the delivery of news like this.

Today was just another day for Fleur, with classes coming in. Who knew when she had planned to see Randell next, maybe they hadn't had a plan; it seemed as if he was available for her when she needed him.

She hollered up the street, "Will there be a funeral?" She looked ashamed of her actions, standing on the sidewalk in front of her business and hanging her head from grief. Feelings overtook her as this all set into place in her head and heart.

I walked back to spare her dignity and let her know I would call her with the news of arrangements. I had to talk with Vada and Amos to find that out; I assumed she knew them, but she had a look of "what are you talking about" on her face. Too many shocks in one day for this graceful lady. I told her they were next of kin, Randell's younger brother and sister. She had no idea of his siblings and now knew how selfish she had been to have never asked about Randell and his life outside of their superficial dates, which had been so meaningful to her—except he would never know how deeply she felt for him now. She would attend the funeral and visit his grave.

I called Vada and asked for a meeting with her and Amos. She said this evening would work, that they still both lived in the family residence in north Seattle, the one Randell used to reside at many years ago. I rolled up about 6:00 p.m., wondering how close they had been to Randell and who had notified them of his death. They must not have been in contact frequently since no one had filed a missing person's report on him. He hadn't been close to anyone, it appeared, nor had he maintained a predictable schedule on any given day since he'd been self-employed with no one to answer to. Each assignment he'd been contracted to complete took different skills and distinct timetables due to the type of business and what it needed to be accomplished. I walked up on the porch of the Craftsman-style house, painted ironically a mustard color with green and maroon accents. The screen door was made of the original wood with peeling paint, and the screen sagged, puffing out as if it were trying to escape. The doorbell made a squawking sound like there were a short.

Vada opened the door and said, "You look like police. Come in."

I thought she must be rebellious and hard to deal with. Her hair had clearly been chopped with scissors by her own hand at random angles. Her makeup looked as if it had been thrown on in blotches, and her clothing looked like she had just stepped out of an upscale office. The odor of weed permeated her perimeter.

She turned and said, "Yep, I manage a pot shop. Amos is into cyber security."

We sat at the kitchen table, which I was sure had been purchased in the fifties, like the ones I'd seen in the movies. Amos entered the room from upstairs; he shook my hand and thanked me for coming. They explained they had not seen Randell for quite a while. He mostly called or emailed; they said he had probably tired of them twenty years ago.

"Vada says we never fought—just didn't have common ground, being as he was our authority figure. There were many meetings with the three of us when Mom went into memory care. We were all put in charge of making her medical decisions and had to agree. She's still there, out by the airport. Doesn't know any of us anymore and has no idea about Randell's death.

They pulled out an OD green box like the ones that held military ammunition. It had all of Randell's important paperwork: his will; life insurance policy; and keys to his office, condo, and vehicle on an Oldsmobile key ring with an extra unlabeled key. They did not know what to do and asked for my help. I told them I knew the extra key went to a safety deposit box. A piece of knowledge I had just gained with Mrs. Johnson's passing. We sorted through it all, made a list, and talked of plans for a funeral. Randell had been very specific about his wishes and wanted to be buried as Stu. Neither one of them had read this paperwork prior to my arrival.

They both looked at me and asked in unison, "Who is Stu?"

I pulled out my phone and typed "Stu Seattle" into the search engine; multiple images came up in the search results. I handed my phone over to Amos, who shared the view with Vada.

Again, in unison, they replied, "No, that's Randell." They were clearly shocked and wanted to know why he had done this and for how long?

I told them of the office downtown that either needed to be cleared out or rented for another month, giving them the key and property management information. On the list we'd created, I wrote Darian's name and phone number at City Square Cemetery where Randell had specified he wished to be buried. I requested to be updated on the funeral arrangement, as Fleur wanted to attend. I also let them know where his body was to be transported, which Darian would take care of once paperwork had been signed. They both seemed overwhelmed by the legalities and also the fact that I had an answer for all the new tasks at hand. Vada asked who Fleur was. I left to go home, knowing I would hear from these two again. Even though they were adults, they were like children, still living in the home they'd grown up in and with each other. They had probably asked Randell for advice frequently.

Traffic was just starting to die down; the southbound express lanes were clearing out. People were home, out eating, or trying to settle in for the night. I got off 99 at Raye Street, which became Queen Anne Drive, turning right as if on autopilot to Warren Avenue, then turning right again on Etruria Street. I was finally home; the day had been long, and I felt as if I had been a help to a few people today while also collecting people who needed my services outside of police work.

After collapsing Fleur's world, I had gone back to Randell's office and had notified those on his current case load of his death, then taken all his other files with a plan to return them to the companies they contained crucial information about. The research and travels had taken most of my day, last the visit with Vada and Amos, who had needed my help. This evening, I would relax and hope to take a few days off.

Fleur

February 2022

After spending days in shock and not believing Randell was gone I pulled up to the funeral, celebration of life, get-together, whatever you wished to call it. The cemetery was not somewhere I went at all, ever. My parents had been killed in a car accident when I was a small child, and my aunt, a ballet instructor, had raised me after that. She would take me along to work; I danced during every class. I could credit my profession and the good fortune of my successful studio to her. She had saved all the life insurance money from my parents and had given it to me when she thought I was ready to settle into a profession that I'd known I'd wanted even as a small child. Dancing and grace were talents of mine; I found it so natural to flow and wear clothing which was barely there. I was avoiding the other part of this story. Aunt Bess would take me to the cemetery in our hometown of Blaine, Washington. We would place flowers on my parents' graves, rain or shine, on the first day of each month. As a child, I had felt closer to my parents there, but I'd known they were not truly there and would not be returning to me.

I'd been asked by the detective to arrive early to meet Vada and Amos and to assure a seat. I drove through the beautiful grounds, thinking I was glad the weather would not be cold. I pulled into the chapel's circular drive, seeing the detective entering and not remembering his name.

My heart was heavy today. The acceptance that Randell was gone was setting in today. The past few weeks, I had kept busy at work with new classes and anything else that would occupy me except eating at our cafe. I had an overwhelming sense of guilt that could not be shaken. For over twenty years, Randell had waited patiently for me, and I had given him only small pieces of myself.

Inside the door was Detective Muncer—now I remembered—and two people who were introduced as Amos and Vada. They each bore a slight resemblance to Randell. My mind kept thinking, *Amos Rinwell, Vada Rinwell.* It was a loop I could not stop, probably due to where we had met. I thought I should have known these people before now. Detective Muncer guided us in, as the service would start in about half an hour. The casket was up front, a dark wood one with mustard-yellow trim patterned after his sweater and polyester pants collection. I wondered what he was wearing inside the closed lid. Was he Stu or Randell? The flowers on top and the wreath next to the casket were neon green, blue, and white.

Suddenly it became loud inside the small chapel. I thought the entire city had arrived since I had sat down, but I was scared to look behind me. All I knew was I was between Vada and Amos, one holding each of my hands.

Vada, smelling of marijuana, said to me, "Stu was a surprise to us."

All the fans and vendors from the Seahawks games who knew of Stu had arrived in unison. Randell's clients from PNW Analytical were trying to get in. Detective Muncer introduced me to Bob Barton, who worked at City Square Cemetery. Bob would get some speakers on stands and broadcast the service outside. Stu's cheering crowd had agreed to be out there and share their stories at the graveside service after the planned one.

The service went on as planned, I guessed; I had never attended another funeral after my parents had been buried. This one had some laughter with stories of Randell, the discovery of his wardrobe and the connection to the casket, his precision of business, and the help he had provided to the city of Seattle. Then it went on to a slideshow of his life. There I was, up on the screen, a couple of times at the company functions we had attended together. Suddenly, I wished we had some photos of us just having fun, like maybe a vacation or camping trip. It was too late for that now. The mood got lighter as the pictures turned to Stu and his life in motion, dancing, jumping, cheering, the elaborate costumes, his large smile.

We exited the building, being instructed by Bob where to go to the graveside. Vada and Amos already knew from their planning of the service, even though Randell had had everything in place once it was figured out that Randell Rinwell had been Stu.

We sat in the front row again, much closer to the casket and Randell's body. This would be the last time he would be on the same side of the soil as me. I made a vow to return here to bring flowers and say what was in my heart without all these people around. They said many more words, and the crowd got louder. I could not turn around and look. If I moved, it felt as if my body would break.

Suddenly, Vada was lying across my chest, sobbing, as if I were her mother and should hold her when I felt I needed to be held. I put my arm around Vada as she lay across me. Amos held my hand again as if he knew me. We had a common bond to a very special man: Randell Rinwell.

The casket lowered into the ground. The crowd in back suddenly surrounded the emerald-green tent we sat under; they chanted football cheers for Stu. We did not know how to react but sat still as they proceeded. Detective Muncer asked if we wished to leave, but I felt as if I could not walk, and Vada was possibly asleep on me. The crowd dispersed around the tent. I heard snippets of stories: Randell this, Stu that. Everyone had known him differently, and I suddenly saw each person having many facets to their lives except me. I danced, my only platform. I thought I was happy.

Bob interrupted my thought with a picture of Randell's headstone, saying, "I thought you would like to see it since you were not present for the decision-making process."

Vada and Amos had made some tough decisions by themselves. I wondered, *What is still in the office?*

We all went to a local restaurant that I had not ever been to prior to this event. I did not catch the name on the way in. I just drove, parked, and entered. I was not sure how I could eat with these heavy thoughts but would try and get to know Vada and Amos a bit if they wished. I ordered a cheeseburger and fries in memory of Randell, something I would never eat. I looked to see Vada had done the same. We ate when our order came with strength from one another, agreeing to meet at the office tomorrow morning to clear it out and unravel Randell's life. When we left, after hearing cheers and stories, seeing tears and laughter, I was proud of myself to have made it through this difficult service and headed home with the anticipation of seeing Vada and Amos tomorrow.

Maybe I would figure out why she smelled so strongly of marijuana.

Detective Muncer

March 2022

ANOTHER WINTER WAS ALMOST OVER. THIS HAD BEEN A LONG YEAR; PEARL HAD been on my mind most days. Dinner with Rubio was in order to lay all the different cases out that involved Pearl without proof of her actual involvement. We had the word of Axe, a.k.a. Peter Dunnigan, on the heist with the truck left in the road; all the sightings at First and Marion, where Rizzo and Bender also resided with stolen goods; the scene where Rizzo lost his life—but never anything substantial to file charges against her.

Rubio and I met the first Thursday of March at a diner on East Marginal Way. It was a place we were familiar with from working on other cases. Bender and Pearl were the topic of discussion tonight. Bender had not surfaced since Rizzo had been murdered. We still did not have a lead on the weapon used; our inside source at Ohm It Up Electronics in Tempe, Arizona, had disappeared; Pearl was nowhere to be found. It was as if the remains of this multifaceted, multi-jurisdictional case had been swept off the earth. I had some vacation time, and so did Rubio. We had agreed to do some off-duty surveillance in Bakersfield, California, starting at Danna Martin's house.

I booked the flight and made reservations for our stay and car rental; a week should tell us if Bender or Pearl were there. We would fly out next week. I was anxious to see what was happening there.

After we arrived and checked in, we stopped for food at a roadside stand and headed over to Danna's house. In front was a large, white, box truck with an orange cab. The logo had faded off one side, and the other had been painted over with mismatched white paint. A man about Danna's age hopped out of the back with a small box and briefcase as if he had just arrived. We watched as she greeted him at the door. He entered but came back out almost immediately for more identical boxes stored behind the fold-down seat in the cab. From this distance, we could not read the writing on the side, but I recognized the logo as Ohm It Up Electronics'.

I saw the shadow of someone in the backyard, but they were not coming this way. Our guess was he or she had entered the house. We only knew it was not Danna or Michael Martin since they were both visible from this vantage point. There was not an alley at this property, and we were not on official police business so could not access the neighbors' yards for a better view. We also should not stay here for any length of time lest the neighbors bring attention to us. We didn't know who might be connected, if anyone, or it could be someone just being neighborly and alerting the block with a phone tree. We left and agreed to come back after dark. Maybe the curtains would be open, and we'd be able to see who the other occupants were.

It felt strange for it to be winter and seventy-five degrees at 7:00 p.m. The sun had set, and we were back in position. Just as we pulled up and barely got the car turned off, the front door opened and out came Danna, Michael, Bender, and Pearl. They hopped into a red SUV and left without any recognition of us. Three of the four knew me, but no one knew Rubio. After they left, we looked for cameras, a high-tech doorbell, anything that would give our presence away. I stayed in the car, and Rubio rang the bell. No one answered, it appeared only the four of them were staying here. We put a tracker on the truck and left.

The following morning, the truck was on the move and so were we, positioned in the neighborhood since early this morning for their potential movement. Bender and Michael took State Highway 18. We followed, glad that we had a full tank, knowing we might be on our way to Tempe, Arizona.

A few hours into the trip, they got off the highway and acquired fuel. We expected them to keep heading east, but that was not what happened. They headed down the driest road I had ever seen to a freshly painted barn posing as a storage area. Bender opened the large sliding double doors; the box truck barely cleared the entrance. Bender closed the doors, and they disappeared as if they had never been in Lucerne Valley at all.

Out here on this dry land, there was nowhere to hide, so we headed back to town and the general store, happy to have A/C and a tree for shade. We got out, stretched, and bought some drinks from the store. The cashier asked if there was trouble. We assured her we were just passing through on the way to a wedding. She nodded, knowing that was not the case. We wondered if she was in on the story with the box truck. There wasn't anywhere to hide here.

Looking at the map, we saw this was about the halfway point from Tempe and an unlikely place for any crime to happen. Just as we were back in the car and discussing the odds of this, here came the truck, pulling in next to us. Bender for sure knew who I was. I was thankful the car was already running. I put it in gear and left just as they parked. Wondering if the cashier would mention anything to them, I headed west on 18, knowing they would catch up to us shortly. We pulled into a roadside stand in Littlerock, waiting for the truck to pass so we could follow them to their drop-off point.

They passed us and kept going right past Bakersfield to Buttonwillow. It was almost the same story here, just a drop-off or pick up point. This only took a few minutes, and they were headed back to Bakersfield and Danna.

Knowing there was nothing else for us to see today, we contacted Detective Allen from Tempe to see what he had on his end. He had witnessed a truck picking up merchandise or something else in the middle of the night from Ohm It Up Electronics, then heading out on Highway 10. He had not tailed the truck, nor had he recognized the driver. Rubio and I suddenly realized this was how they got the loads to Seattle.

We headed back to the hotel, packed up, and checked out. We got back to Buttonwillow and waited—for what, we did not know, but this appeared to be a slow process. The loads had to be added and subtracted from along the way, like mail order. We knew there were more than electronics in those boxloads.

Rubio dropped me off since I might be recognized by someone along the way. He approached the truck that pulled in and asked for Ray Martin, said they had been friends for many years. This would either raise red flags, or possibly the lower-level electronics transport people did not know the drug carriers. The driver said he didn't know Ray but heard he had moved up north. They did not open the barn door as we had hoped, but at least Rubio had gotten a good look at the driver. Just as he left to pick me up, in came Bender and Pearl, without Michael. I was positive at this point that they were trying to overtake this load from its intended destination. I saw Pearl talking to the two in charge; she handed them money. We were too far away to know what had transpired, but the driver and helper left in the car Pearl and Bender had showed up in. The helper kept looking back, like he knew something was not right with this plan.

Pearl and Bender took the truck, headed north on I-5, and got off in a couple exits. They had a truck waiting to transfer the load and then headed north again. No one was even looking for this smaller version of a box truck. They had heisted the heist, but we did not know if this had been planned by Michael or Bender and Pearl. If they had taken the load from Michael, they had lost their safe house or what they had thought was safe. Now I wondered if Danna had told anyone about my visit—or did she have her own side jobs going on? No one could be trusted in this mess.

It looked like we were driving to Seattle or wherever they planned to ditch this load. After they stopped, we would need to put a GPS on the truck to be alerted upon movement. They slept in the truck at a rest stop near Mount Shasta. We had been on this unexpected road trip for over seven hours now; luckily, there had been a good amount of traffic so we could blend in. The tracking device was installed. We called the rental car company and arranged for a 7:00 a.m. exchange of cars, had some breakfast, and were alerted that they were on their way north.

They appeared to have an end stop for this load. They exited a few times through Oregon for fuel and sightseeing, then suddenly, in Portland, they stopped by the Amtrak station and got out of the truck. There were the two gentlemen who had been driving the last load. Bender and Pearl got out, handed over the truck, and got in a yellow hatchback. We were unsure of who to follow, but the odds were Bender and Pearl would take over this load again somewhere along the way. They entered Washington, crossing the Columbia River, and headed north toward Seattle. This had been no vacation at all for us, but it might be the biggest case we had ever solved. Bender and Pearl, who were sticking close to the truck exit in Tacoma, met someone on Fifty-Sixth Street, handing over keys and a piece of paper—presumably, instructions. They returned to I-5, heading north.

We were home, back to familiar territory, still not knowing what Danna and Michael had to do with this web of crime. But we did know they were in on it somehow. I wanted nothing more than my duplex, suddenly wondering if I'd watered Margo, my houseplant, my only responsibility. Then it hit me that I had Everett, Vada, Amos, Daniel, Micky, bank accounts, and two identical duplexes. The list had kept compiling with obligations since Esmerelda and Rayner Martin's murders and Randell Rinwell's tragic death. My priority tasks of the week would be to contact Fleur since the funeral is over and see where Dae was on the court docket. Immediately, my mind snapped back to my current location and situation, much of it tied to the past year or more. It was my place to unravel the tragedy and misfortune. I thought of Ice, a.k.a. Jasper Walters, who had killed Ethan and knew the lives of those around them had changed forever. Even though I'd done what I'd been hired to do as a detective, the story still ended with families torn apart, sons gone forever or in prison. One second and a moment's decision could change life as it was for everyone.

Rubio asked, "Are you tired, or is something on your mind?"

I responded with, "Do you think we're even making a dent in this tangled-up mess of crime?"

He just looked at me. We both knew from our long conversations that we were making a drop in the bucket but with the outcome different than we wished. We never wanted to notify a family of the death of a loved one, no matter what they had been up to. We wished our cases were closed and there wouldn't be any new ones. Maybe it was the time away or the long road trip, but I was tired, wishing Pearl and Bender would finish this transaction so I could go home.

The small box truck exited I-5 in Federal Way, stopping at the truck stop right off the interstate. They met someone who looked familiar from a distance. As we got closer, we saw it was Michael with an ill-fitting red headed wig who got out of a green eighteen-wheeler that had a shipping container on the trailer. They backed up and unloaded into the container, acting as old friends did. Michael had been in on the theft since the start. He stepped out and came back in again after Bender and Pearl stole the merchandise, then sent it on to where? Michael got back in the cab. Pearl and Bender left with an empty truck and ditched it for a white sedan across the parking lot before Michael had even pulled out, leaving the box truck. Michael headed south on I-5 to the port of Olympia and dropped the trailer with many others.

We called, asking for a warrant. The local PD assisted with a suggestion to Harbor Patrol of suspicion of contraband. The container Michael had delivered was opened along with six others. Officers found stolen electronics, weapons, and a large variety of pills with a street value of over one million dollars. Only knowing Michael was in the semi and Pearl and Bender were in the white sedan, we had no immediate suspects to apprehend. I called Detective Allen in Tempe to have him contact Ohm It Up Electronics to verify this load had been stolen. I also contacted Federal Way Police to have them intercept Michael Martin if he returned to the truck stop for an exchange of the box truck. Michael showed up almost immediately and switched vehicles, now both empty, so he thought he was free and clear of everything, not knowing we had the load he'd delivered, a load we had followed for many miles. Michael was pulled over and brought into the station in Federal Way but needed a transfer to Olympia since that was where the load of contraband was located. We could not transport him since we were in the rental car and waited in town to question him.

We ate at a café on the waterfront. There were historical signs about cheetwoot, meaning "land of the bear." For the first time this week, I finally felt I was on vacation, walking by the water, eating fish and chips, and just observing life without a focus on criminals. I knew this was something my mind needed more of. I was thinking of retiring, but not yet. My plans were set in place for the near future. Rubio was about the same age as me and was probably having the same thoughts. We had served our cities and people well, to the best of our ability and with whatever facts we'd been given or had dug up. Just as the sun was setting and we finished dinner, I received a call and instructions of where to meet Michael Martin.

We headed back to the Port of Olympia, and there sat Michael, with his wig in a plastic bag along with his wallet, keys, and other personal effects. We knew who he was, but he had no idea of our involvement all the way up the West Coast. We were all ushered into a room probably not used for this on most days, as there was not a table, only four chairs. Their officer sat in and took notes of the conversation. We might not know where Pearl and Bender were, but we did know we had them on something: the transport of narcotics, weapons, and stolen goods across state lines.

Michael sat holding his bag once the cuffs were removed. Someone brought us a six pack of generic lemon lime soda. Michael sipped one while nodding to our questions: Do you know why you are here? What is your involvement in this racket of goods? Who is your contact in Tempe? How is Danna involved? At the mention of his wife's name, he looked up with fear in his eyes, realizing we knew more than he'd suspected. So far, he only knew we had evidence here in Olympia and possibly Federal Way, but now he knew we knew the route of stolen goods. He told of his connection, Albert, in Tempe at Ohm It Up Electronics. He spilled the information on Rayner Martin and how he had used Esmerelda. He stated he wished he did not know any of this and he should have never been a driver for these people. The semitruck he owned had not passed the new stipulations and his career had been over just when he had two years left to retire. Ray had come to him with the idea of transporting some merchandise. It had all fit in for nearly two years; in one more month, he would have been able to retire with Danna. She was not in on this at all; she was just a host of drinks and a comfortable accommodation as they filtered through town.

Michael did not even know as much as we did; he had no knowledge of the stops in Lucerne Valley or anywhere else. He just knew where to show up and had enough connections to borrow a truck for short transport like this load. Bender and Pearl could not have gotten this product into the port or the container on the dock alone. Michael's connections were his specialty. He swore he had no idea what was in the loads, but deep down, he'd known all along it wasn't good since Ray was behind the deals.

Just then, my phone rang. I stepped out, recognizing the number as Peter Dunnigan's. He talked so fast I could barely understand him. He said he was sorry he hadn't called with his new address, but Pearl and Bender knew where he was and would be showing up soon, as they needed a safe place to stay. I got the address from him by text and had him delete it on his end, along with his call to me. I instructed him to make them at home until we arrived.

I opened the door with more force than needed and told Rubio we needed to go now. The people who held Michael would continue to contain him until charges were filed. We immediately left. For not being on duty, we sure were working a lot. We headed north on I-5 to Peter Dunnigan's house on Lake City Way NE. Really, it was a shed behind a house. We located the white sedan that had left the truck stop as soon as we pulled in the driveway. Almost forgetting, we requested backup, who arrived immediately with the monstrosity of this case. We finally had Pearl and Bender on something. We had had them in custody many times but never on any charges that would stick. I wished to rush in immediately and not wait on anyone. The time was drawing near to find out who had murdered Esmeralda, Rayner, and Rizzo. I had a thought that ballistics had not compared the casings in the murders of Rizzo and Esmerelda. We knocked and entered, throwing Axe, a.k.a. Peter Dunnigan, to the ground. We saw Pearl just sitting there in her usual stance and Bender attempting to bolt out the back door, which was nonexistent. We took them into custody, bringing all three for questioning to headquarters downtown in separate patrol cars.

On the way from Axe's shed house to headquarters, Rubio and I kept saying, "This is it, the day we've been waiting for." It was hard to believe, even though we knew it was happening.

Each person in custody knew a piece to this story. We stood outside at a distance from the side door as Bender, Axe, and Pearl were escorted in separately. Pearl, in her usual behavioral mode, acted innocent, and Bender undoubtedly hoped to not serve any more time, being as he'd gotten out of the last arrest with some information we had not yet figured out. And we thought Axe knew more than he was saying.

Pearl started in by saying she hadn't done anything, obviously unaware of our road trip together. Bender said he had information on who had shot Rizzo, and Axe was silent. This all happened prior to us asking any questions. We read Bender his rights and started with him.

He said, "There is a programmer, Nathan Timberland, who lives in Central City, outside of Phoenix. We met at a local frisbee tournament a few years back. He saw my tattoos and asked if they'd been done in prison, said he recently became down on his luck with work and had a business idea, wondered if I was interested. I agreed to meet and hear about it since I had recently been released and, with my record, was having trouble finding employment.

"Nathan had mistakenly accessed Ohm It Up Electronics' website and was able to lower the prices when he put in large orders and then put them back to regular price after. That was the start of this. I called Rizzo to help with distribution, and then, while visiting Michael in Bakersfield, we met Ray Martin, who added the other bits to the load. Ray was the brains of the operation, or so we thought. We didn't know he worked for a larger syndicate. He always acted like he was in charge and took over where we left off. We would meet in different places along the way, trade vehicles, add and subtract merchandise and goods. We usually didn't know the exact load we were carrying, just had the receipt for the load from pickup, which was always shrink-wrapped on a pallet or two. Nathan never met Ray, Michael, or the rest of the crew; he was out of the picture once we paid him for the electronics at a lower-than-wholesale cost—but not so low it would be discovered. The loads were shipped out of different ports since

Michael had access to them with his semitruck, until the new regulations went into effect on emissions. Michael didn't know what he was carrying, either. Ray did—until his mistake, which led to his death."

Bender said he did not know of Esmerelda and how she fit in, nor who Ray was connected to. He recalled our last meeting with their accident in the desert with the safe and said, "I still don't know what was in there."

Bender seemed to be at the end of his story, his hanging, long hair covering his face. We told him of escorting him up the coast with his last load.

He said, "I'm usually onto stuff like that, but being with Pearl and Rizzo's murder had me off my game. I don't have any idea who shot Rizzo but surely miss him. He always knew when to keep his mouth shut."

We left Bender in the interrogation room and went on to Pearl, who had had time to concoct her alibi.

Pearl was using her arms as a pillow and was not responsive as we entered. We read her rights to her, and she did not move. We could see she was alive and breathing; she was sniffling under her arms.

She looked up and said, "No one else really knew the whole program. It was all on my shoulders. Five Pin in Ohio is dead; Esmerelda was not supposed to be dead on her Christmas vacation; Ethan, my friend and helper, is gone forever; Rizzo, the one I sat up nights laughing with, my true love, is gone. I had no idea how far I'd gotten into this until now.

"In high school, after my father passed away, my Uncle Spear said I would be good for the family business, like my dad. Spear told me what to do, where to be, and who to meet. I just followed orders. That's why I was always on the outside, looking innocent—because I was. I only put the deals together; I wasn't the person who executed the orders. I knew people who trusted me and would help, people who needed cash. I was paid well to set everything up. Sometimes, like on the corner of First and Marion, I was loitering as a lookout. I didn't know what was in each load and generally didn't transport, either; I just intercepted loads, at which time other items were added to them by Uncle Spear's group, who were the ringleaders Ray Martin worked for.

"Uncle Spear lives in Kentucky, where I went for a short while before going to see Five Pin in Ohio at Uncle Spear's instruction. This explains all the coincidences of my locations at the time of the crimes. Sure, I stole a bit from Uncle Spear, but never anything more than electronics. I don't do drugs, use weapons, or even drink many beers. I have discovered in the past few months that I have a conscience. I am remorseful and miss my friends. I am willing to answer any questions in exchange for my freedom, a bus ticket to anywhere except here. You will never see me again."

We told Pearl of our northbound West Coast ride following them with their load of stolen merchandise and other illegal goods. She had no idea she'd been tailed due to being overwhelmed by grief for Rizzo and trying to figure his murder out.

We booked Bender and Pearl for the night and questioned Axe, releasing him with instructions not to leave town, although he had not been upfront with the department in the past in giving his whereabouts. We dropped him off at his shed house and left a plain-clothes officer for surveillance until this was solved. Sure enough, less than two hours later, Axe was on the move. His car was loaded with all his earthly possessions, and he headed south on I-5. He was followed until he stopped in Oregon just south of Wilsonville at a nice hotel, where a tracking device was installed under his rear bumper. He exited the hotel a few minutes later with a Styrofoam to-go container. As he stood by the hood of his car, eating a burger and dipping his fries, Axe had no idea he was being tailed or that anyone had a clue he was no longer in Seattle on Lake City Way. We would not send a crew to wherever he was going unless we found specific evidence that he was further involved in this ring. My intuition told me he needed space between himself, Pearl, and Bender, as he might be in danger like Ray and Esmeralda if he were involved.

Everywhere was short-staffed; so many people wished not to work this far into the pandemic. Our department was short on officers; we detectives were out on the street, not focusing on our caseloads but on immediate crime. There was no way to know if this multi-faceted case would have been solved by now if there had been more officers. It was a well-planned syndicate; many people had come together to make it happen, each person not knowing the next step or the ones prior. We would like to get Michael Martin booked up here from Olympia, but that was for another day.

My vacation time was over. Rubio wanted to go home, and I needed to call Naomi.

Carl III

March 2022

THE INITIAL SET OF TEENS WERE READY TO COMPLETE THE FIRST REQUIREMENTS OF Ethan's Edge. This time, we did many projects downtown, cleaning up from the riots last year, disposing of abandoned campsites, covering graffiti, and taking care of a few projects for the elderly and disabled. It had been a learning curve for them, and there had been many difficult days for me, interacting with teens so close to Ethan's age and him not being here.

We had located an apartment building in south Seattle not far from Charlene's Place to take over so we could provide more support to graduates from our programs who wished to be on their own but could not afford regular housing. There were one hundred apartments in this complex, and we needed twenty-five to start our program. The previous management company had agreed to stay on and find alternate housing for a few residents who wished to move on so we could remodel our units and move people in on a sliding-fee scale.

Ha Yoon had solely made this purchase and was on board to help our vision, making it her own. She did not work for us but was a vital asset to the Women's Shelter and Charlene's Place. She had moved into the unit of her choice as a paying resident; no one had knowledge of her ownership, not even the management company. She received the check for the rents through direct deposit; paid the taxes, insurance, and utilities; and donated twenty-five units to us for the experimental program. We were forever grateful to Ha Yoon and her generosity. The financing may have been impossible without her stepping in. Her attorney, Mr. Clark, handled the sale for her; he had advised her to purchase something, but he'd had no idea she would do this. Remembering Kimber and her hard times, Mr. Clark was happy there was somewhere for people who needed a place to be to set down roots and reconstruct their lives, like his daughter had done with her catering company.

It had been four months since Carl Sr. had passed, a long winter. I just noticed I had not heard from Garry. Not that I'd ever heard from him prior to the meeting at Carl Sr's apartment or the funeral, but I felt it would be comforting for me to talk to him. I called and invited him to dinner at an Italian place close to their home. He agreed to meet on Tuesday evening.

I arrived before him, wondering if he would show up, but I didn't see a reason for him to not be there. He walked in on this chilly night just before the start of spring with his blue-and-green plaid scarf tucked into his winter coat. He looked up at the decorations, then over at me.

He said, "Your grandpa loved this place much more than me, but we came here all the time for him."

I asked if he was okay to stay or if he wished to eat somewhere else.

He said he wanted to order exactly what Carl would eat since he had never tried it: cheese and spinach ravioli. "Maybe I was too picky or just stubborn, but that is what I'll have tonight."

It was a bit awkward at first since we did not know each other. We were seated, and both of us ordered the same thing in honor of Carl. We spoke of our city, and I told him of how Ethan's Edge was coming along and the apartment building. Garry said he was good with paperwork and would love to help with filing and such if there were any assistance needed. He inquired of Gloria and thanked me for inviting him out this evening. He needed to get out and had thought of calling, but since he had never been part of the family or even been known to us, he felt out of place, even after being welcomed at the funeral dinner.

We parted ways out on the sidewalk in the blustery evening, full of ravioli. I turned to ask, "Garry, what did you eat here?"

He said he would just have spaghetti. We agreed to meet next month and talk in between about the paperwork. He said he would bring a few items of my grandfather's that I might want. We both left smiling and with lighter hearts, two strangers who met during a horrible experience that now had a bond. I was happy I had called. We would probably meet again, but I had left that phone call up to Garry. Now, home to call Gloria and tell her of the evening; she would like to know Garry was doing okay.

My news of Garry surprised Gloria; she said she had been thinking of Garry. When I told her of the Italian restaurant, she said, "Oh, yes, the spinach ravioli. We went to that place when we were first married. I haven't been there in years."

Well, Carl Sr. had eaten there until he'd become too ill, and now Garry and I had.

Gloria said, "I wish to go there. How about Friday for lunch?"

Twice in one week, I ate spinach ravioli and honored my namesake, Carl Sr. Something told me this was somewhere I could be at peace with all that had happened. It was a place of comfort and good food.

Naomi

March 2022

THE JOLT OF THE PHONE RINGING PULLED ME FROM A DEAD SLEEP AFTER A THIRTY-six-hour shift. Being awake so long, I hadn't been able to sleep after returning home. The things we saw in the emergency room were haunting sometimes. Some days, some people stayed in a room meant to treat a broken bone, with only curtains, and now entire areas were quarantined, containing Covid patients since there was a shortage of beds upstairs. Patients without Covid were being treated in the waiting room and hallways, lined up as if to get in somewhere they would enjoy but only trying to get relief from a gallbladder, injury, or auto accident. The EMTs asked where to put the incoming patients who arrived by ambulance, but there was nowhere. They didn't know this had become the normal answer. All this ran through my mind on autopilot as I remembered the phone ringing.

Before I opened my eyes, I prayed it was not the hospital needing me to come back. My legs had almost been unable to carry me home that morning as the sun had risen over Seattle to awaken the people ready for the start of a new day. I craved sleep. I looked at the missed call and smiled bigger than I had in days; it was Muncer. We still had not connected since

New Year's Eve with our ridiculous schedules. I was not awake but called him back, and he answered on the first ring as if his phone were a tool.

"Muncer," he said.

I could see him driving and not looking at the phone to see who needed him. He was always on the front line, willing to help. People knew his name when he rolled up, no matter where.

I said, "Hi, stranger."

He laughed, knowing this might be the only call he would receive today that was not to discuss business or bad news.

We set a date for Friday, three days from now, to have breakfast. I knew no matter what, I would be there. The life I had been living as a nurse was rewarding, but, in these times, it was not living. My social life, my DJ gigs, and my time to relax had all disappeared. Muncer would pick me up at my apartment, and we would see where this next date went. Dating quarterly was an experience.

Friday, March 18th, the day after St. Patrick's, which was a long one in the ER with all the green-beer parties, I showered after a sixteen-hour shift and walked home with the cool morning dew still present. Another hour and Muncer would pick me up. I could not sit or sleep would come. I knew he must be exhausted, too, after all the street parties and a night up rolling through the city. I wondered if we would talk of leprechauns.

At 8:00 a.m., I headed down to sit on the front stoop of my building. Before I could sit, Muncer pulled up, smiling. No words were said between us. We had seen each other since New Year's Eve, but only twice in the ER. It was almost like that date or kiss had never happened.

He had said in his text that he knew the perfect spot for breakfast and to bring a coat. We headed north toward the zoo and Green Lake. I rarely got out of my neighborhood; it was refreshing to see new sights and the construction happening downtown, the various shapes and materials of the new buildings. We pulled into a parking area by Green Lake. Muncer pulled a couple of thermoses and a small cooler out of the trunk, we found a bench close to the water and jogging trail. He took my hand as we walked over like two people who had known each other a long time. He said he had croissants, butter, jelly, orange juice, and coffee, unsure of what

I preferred. We both poured orange juice and rested, truly rested, being away from all work-related images.

I awakened; it was after 11:00 a.m. We had been sleeping, leaning on each other, perfectly balanced. We woke up, laughing at our date and the night turning into day, breakfast becoming lunch. We knew life would be this way until one of us didn't work like we currently did. I thought if I quit, he would still be out there; he voiced something similar to my thoughts. We were happy for the moment, took the cooler and thermoses to the car, walked partway around the lake and back again. He drove me by his other duplex, as he called it, and told me the story behind it. Then we drove by his duplex, going into neither one.

He said, "It's only fair you know where I live."

I nodded, happy he had shared this much of himself with me, knowing there probably weren't many people who knew anything about him.

He said, "Next time, I can cook dinner for you if you would like."

I nodded, smiling at this invitation, and said, "Let me know when and what to bring."

He added, thinking of me not having transportation, "I can pick you up."

It was nice to be around someone who thought things through. So many people I saw lived in the moment. My occupation was that way—fix what was in front of you. He drove me home on the slow route. I pictured him coming back here and sleeping. It was comforting to know where he would be.

On the ride home he had not asked about my family. I did not have any except for my sister, whom I had met while in foster care. I didn't believe I had any relatives and had never looked for them if I did. School, college, and now the hospital were my family and life. There were people whom I had worked with for over ten years. We pulled forty-eight-hour shifts sometimes, worked all the holidays since we didn't have family. We each brought in food to share and ate when time permitted. Most everyone here didn't know much about one another, just that we united on hospital grounds.

Detective Muncer

March 2022

PEARL AND BENDER HAD SAID ALL THEY WERE GOING TO SAY. PEARL HAD BET HER freedom on Uncle Spear's antics. Pearl was guilty. The case was so twisted; it needed to be sorted out. For sure, we could charge them both with bringing narcotics, weapons, and stolen property across state lines. The property charges would most likely be dropped since the goods were technically not stolen but had been purchased with an underhanded discount by Nathan, whom we hadn't talked to yet. He was the low man on this investigation— but not so low we would let him slide.

Ballistics had the results of the bullet that had killed Esmerelda; it matched the bullet that had killed Rizzo. If it was not Axe who had fired the shot that had killed Rizzo, someone should have seen something in an intersection as busy as that one, with eight lanes of traffic plus four turn lanes and cameras facing all directions.

Axe, with the tracker on his car, one I highly doubted would get very far, had almost made it to southern California. He had been acting innocent and feeding information but at the same time knew Danna and Michael Martin well enough to visit their house. Michael was still here with us, but Danna was not. She had probably received a call from Michael and Axe by now. We should request a tap for their phones and surveillance of the house. A background check on Danna Martin would be in order, also.

Pearl Swanson and Bender George both pled not guilty at their arraignment with public defenders. We had requested they be held without bail, and they were transferred to the Federal Detention Center south of here in SeaTac, along with Michael Martin, all receiving charges on the federal crimes. I thought of all the crimes Pearl had been involved in, and this was where she'd been caught, not before others died but when no one had been murdered.

Sure enough, Axe had gone to see Danna Martin, formerly Danna Dunnigan. Danna was Axe's mother. When we'd met him, he'd still been in high school and had lived with his father. A mother had not been present nor investigated in any dealings with him. We'd had no idea that a mother still existed, thinking his father had left town and he was on his own.

Danna must have been filtering him information to feed to Pearl in exchange for money. Pearl had double backed on him many times, but he kept jumping into her lies, wanting to believe she loved him as much as he loved her. Axe had gone to great lengths to get Pearl information, and to be betrayed this many times, he had already admitted he wanted revenge. Could it have been him that had shot Rizzo with another weapon we had not found? He had already admitted to shooting at Pearl, but could he actually want to save her and be rid of Rizzo Loman? If Axe had murdered Rizzo, he had also murdered Esmerelda or at the very least, had access to the weapon that had. Then who had killed Rayner Martin?

The case was technically out of our hands, and I was on to other open files, new and old. This one had grown on me, lasting over a year, with all the travel, players, and multi-jurisdictional departments. In all my years working for Seattle PD, I had never left town on any case, but this one had used up my vacation time to finish it off. That had been a smart move; otherwise, we would have never been able to follow the trail on anyone's time. All the specially designed stops at barns and loading zones looked normal; they would have never been observed. I had to admit they had the right people in place to pull this off without suspicion. I wondered if someone at each stop along the way would be charged. If I hadn't known

Pearl and Bender, made a visit with Danna, and spent time in Tempe earlier with Detective Allen, this never would have been discovered. What a long, drawn-out, tiring case.

It had been almost a year that I had been jotting down lyrics; the notebook I'd received for Christmas had many starts of songs. My world had become too chaotic to put it all together. The lyrics were always in my head and would roll out as I headed to a call, another tragedy, someone's life changed forever, and another day I could not write. I had decided this summer I would take a couple of weeks, maybe a month, off with my notebook and pound out some words. That would be good for my spirit and the release of my old life.

I liked having new people to be with. Having some that depended on me was new, and I was working through it, but it made me happy. I loved seeing Everett Sunshine smile when I saw him; he didn't show his emotions for anyone else, just voiced his opinions, mainly about leaving home and food. But he talked to me about everything on his mind. Daniel, a suspect-turned-friend; Micky, who relied on me for help with Everett (I never asked about her and Daniel's relationship); Amos and Vada, who had been thrown into the mix quite by chance; and Fleur. Then there was Naomi, with our two dates months apart, one kiss, and one nap. I needed to make more effort to continue this with her. I thought we could be something special.

Detective Rubio

April 2022

THE CALL CAME IN ON MY CELL AT APPROXIMATELY 3:00 A.M. I WAS SO TIRED AND not sure if I was on the phone or dreaming. I had been working extra hours to deal with my empty house since Albatar had left for the Navy. My emotions were a mixture of sadness and pride; my video-game-playing son was using his technical skills to save the world.

I kept saying, "Speak up," until I sat up and recognized the voice, a tone I would never forget, one who had pulled me out of a risky situation many years back and had endangered his life in doing so. It was Lyle Preston.

I couldn't make out what he was saying except, "Come get me, now."

There was no telling where he was with the double lifestyle he lived, floating from drug house to trap house or anything in between. He played both sides of the game, even if he would not admit it to himself. We had let him drive without a license for his words, information we would not have had if it hadn't been for his addicted ways. When he tried to get clean, we saw him with people who were not involved in drugs at all; then he would return to his ways rather quickly.

I kept repeating, "Where are you?" I knew he was in trouble and could not speak up, but I was in no position to help if I didn't know his location. He was my prime, most-trusted CI, the one I could send in anywhere. He knew everyone, and now I couldn't help him. He always had a burner phone so there wouldn't be tracking on it. The line went silent, Lyle no longer begging for my help.

Then I heard a male yelling, "I think he has a phone!"

I heard them shuffle around as if looking for it, but no one could locate it. I heard from their conversation that they made Lyle stand and took him away. The room was silent on my end and his. *I must help my friend*, I thought. It was strange to call him that, with me being a detective and him with his drug occupation. He was not on any cases for me at the moment. I thought back; I had not seen him around the area for a few months. Either he was working for someone else or was deeper into the drugs. Each time I saw him, I wondered if his brain would be too scrambled from drug use the next time he came around. He had done side jobs for the department for close to twenty years now; that was many years of heavy drug use.

There was no going back to sleep that night. I thought of all the places Lyle had popped up at during my calls as a patrol officer and, later, investigations as a detective. King County covered a vast area. I was often surprised to roll up to a dispute off the beaten path of the well-traveled roads and there was Lyle, walking around the side of the building, not wishing to be seen by the police. Even though we knew him, his acquaintances did not know of our agreements.

One time we pulled up at a two-story apartment building at the end of a dead road with a warrant for Bart Fields, a gentleman we all knew had violated his probation again. It was his mom and brother's place, but when it was called in, Bart had been there. His brother, Jake, not being quiet right, came out when we knocked with his hands up, yelling for his mom, who was still inside. I could still hear him: "Diane, Diane, Diane." We had thought Jake and Bart had been the only two in the residence, so we tried to breach the door that was barricaded. Bart came to the window with his arm around Lyle's neck, holding him hostage. Bart let Lyle go and came out with his hands up shortly after the escapade. This was just another example of how Lyle would pop up and how inefficient it would be for me to just go looking anywhere for him now as he was everywhere.

I figured this time Lyle might have played too many sides of a card and gotten himself wrapped up in a mess even I could not bring him out of, as had happened so many times in the past. I couldn't count the number of times I had arrested him only to stash him at a safe house right inside the county or close by a day or so later, dropping him at the door with the promised cash for his information and his time spent in lockup with his friends and free meals. A few days later, he would call me or another detective, wanting another assignment. I suspected he was not just working for King County; he often made trips via bus and would be gone a few days at a time.

I lay back down with too many memories of Lyle Preston in my mind. He could be anywhere or nearby, but I could not help him this time. He might have gotten himself in too far by the sound of the man on the phone. If it was not a burner, I could have traced it—maybe the line was still open—but I had hung up already. With the lack of sleep, surprising wake-up, and my need to help overshadowing my thinking, I did not know if we could trace the call. Metevior would know, but he was on vacation, Lyle was on his own this time.

I rolled over and must have fallen asleep immediately. Upon waking, I thought it was all a dream, but looking at my call log, I saw that was not the case. I called in an APB for Lyle with no reason and no backstory, simply stating that I needed contact with him.

Bob

May 2022

IT WAS MEMORIAL DAY WEEKEND AGAIN. WITH SO MANY PEOPLE OUT OF TOWN, it was a great weekend for maintenance. At the end of last week, we had placed flags on the veterans' graves and had made lists of which graves needed attention. Darian always came outside for this event; he was usually indoors, helping people, but being raised in a military family, he liked to honor the veterans. I always saw him in his dress shirt and trousers, but not this weekend he always wore the same flag T-shirt, jeans and a sweat jacket for this event. He organized the garden party, as he called it, compiling buckets of yard tools and making phone calls to see who would be attending the event. He was very passionate about this; so many graves were connected to people who didn't visit due to distance—or possibly there wasn't any family left. The cemetery mowed the lawn and did some trimming, but there were still many graves that something had grown over during the year or something had spilled on, like sap or flower-petal staining.

This year, there were just over two hundred graves that needed to be trimmed around, to have moss scrubbed off, or needed other minor repairs. I came in early; Simone showed up shortly after with boxes of donuts and coffee. Then June showed up and next Gloria, who had a couple of places to visit this year. Daniel and Micky attended this event together. Muncer, who knew firsthand how quickly life could be taken, was also present. Rubio was a new volunteer this year. Carl usually attended this event, but Gloria said he was visiting his dad in Florida for the holiday and that she would make sure Ethan's and Carl Sr.'s graves were fine. Ha Yoon was here with her new gardening gloves, saying she had never done yardwork before. Hazel was missing from the crowd, off promoting her children's book, *Halverson.* Kimber and her dad, Mr. Clark, would be here right before lunch since she was catering the event. I made a mental note to find out Mr. Clark's first name.

We started at the bottom back, in the corner, all of us staying together in one area to get each section done. The small tractor followed us so we could dump our yard waste. We were fortunate to have perfect weather today. The bottom tier was completed by lunchtime. We ate in the tent set up behind the funeral home so as not to be a distraction to others who had come to mourn, pay respect, or put flowers on the grave of a loved one. I looked around at this close-knit group of people who had all lost someone, either recently or long ago, and was grateful for our friendship and generosity of time, skills, talent, and willingness to give.

Thinking of last year, I remembered June with her red, white, and blue lawn chair; she had wandered off to see the ceremony. Many things had transpired since that day. All these people had come together to start Ethan's Edge and The Pathway Apartment program. Many lives had changed in the last twelve months. It had been just over ten years, a whole decade, that Charlene had been gone. My life had changed tremendously since working here. It hardly seemed possible that time moved that quickly as we went through out living days. I smiled at peace, knowing we were on the right track.

I thought about the preparation for the service coming up on Monday. I could still see the flag being raised by the fire department ladder, as it was done every year, waving to express the freedom we had because of individuals from our past, present, and future giving us liberty to be as we were and change what we could for the better. Knowing each day is a gift to use wisely.

www.ingramcontent.com/pod-product-compliance
Lightning Source LLC
Chambersburg PA
CBHW060622260626
47161CB00008B/2772